The Five Stages of Courting Dalisay Ramos

The Five Stages of Courting Dalisay Ramos

MELISSA DE LA CRUZ

U

UNION
SQUARE
& CO.

NEW YORK

UNION
SQUARE
& CO.

NEW YORK

UNION SQUARE & CO. and the distinctive Union Square & Co. logo
are trademarks of Sterling Publishing Co., Inc.

Union Square & Co., LLC, is a subsidiary of Sterling Publishing Co., Inc.

ISBN 978-1-4549-4767-7 (paperback)
ISBN 978-1-4549-4768-4 (e-book)

For information about custom editions, special sales, and premium
purchases, please contact specialsales@unionsquareandco.com.

Printed in Canada

2 4 6 8 10 9 7 5 3 1

unionsquareandco.com

Cover design by Erik Jacobsen
Interior design by Kevin Ullrich
Image credits: PeterPencil/DigitalVision Vectors/Getty Images: 80, 81, 99

For Mommy and Papa
Still the best love story I've ever heard

CHAPTER ONE

The airport is like Evan Saatchi's second home. He's used to the routine of waiting to check in, zipping through security checkpoints due to his Global Entry status, calculating how long it will take to walk from one end of the terminal to the other to plan the perfect route down to the second. Airports, no matter where you go, are mostly the same. The same kinds of food options, mostly sandwiches that are quick to make and easy to carry or eat while standing in lines; the same coffee chains, with the paper to-go cups and wooden stirrers and packets of sugar; the same bookstores, with the best sellers and magazines and gadgets for reading on long flights. He has the flight attendants' entire safety speech memorized, knows all the sounds airplanes make, what actual bad turbulence feels like, the best angle to sleep at so as not to get a leg cramp, and the quickest route from the airport to the office that avoids Bay Area traffic. Efficiency at its finest.

This kind of efficiency has helped him chart his career, land his dream job writing and traveling for a living, and buy his own condo. It hasn't let him down so far. And today is the day he'll know if he'll become a senior editor, his ultimate dream job.

The moment he pushes through the revolving doors to his office building, Evan spots a shock of red hair through the crowded lobby. Riggs is waiting for him, as usual, so they can go up to the office together—a perk of working at the same company as one of his best friends.

Carrying a tray of coffee in one hand and rolling his suitcase in the other, Evan asks, "Did Tallulah give you any grief?"

William Riggins—Riggs—looks up from his phone and grins. He always reminds Evan of a ginger cat, same coloring and temperament. "Tallulah? Total nightmare. Demanding as ever, running around in circles looking for you, bit me in the ass."

"You probably deserved it."

Riggs accepts a coffee from Evan's tray and laughs. "Okay, I made that last one up. But she missed you."

Tallulah, Evan's elderly dachshund, prefers to lounge on the couch all day, lying on her own pillow like a proper hot dog, and falling asleep to eight-hour-long videos on You-Tube called "TV for Dogs." She's everything Evan could have hoped for when he rescued her. Somehow sleeping in a four-star hotel without her curled at his feet makes him homesick.

"Thanks for looking after her," says Evan. "I owe you." His usual dog-sitter hadn't been available.

For the past three days, he's been in Paris, hardly his longest business trip for boots-on-the-ground research for Overnight, but it feels longer, especially after traveling for the past fourteen hours. While it's the fastest-growing travel app according to *Forbes*, Overnight doesn't have the budget to send editors like Evan, junior ones at that, abroad any longer than necessary. Sure, being so tall Evan has a hard time sitting comfortably in such small spaces for prolonged periods and resents dealing with people hogging all of the overhead bins, and before he finally got pre-check, he's had his fair share of annoyances from the TSA, what with having a Persian last name, but he can't complain about the perks of the job. Getting paid to travel makes it all worth it, even if getting to and from the airport is an odyssey all on its own.

Riggs checks the time on his phone. "You just barely made it. Bettie break down again?"

"As a matter of fact, yes, but I managed to push her into a parking spot, so it doesn't count." Bettie is Evan's car—a Honda Civic that's old enough to buy beer without getting carded by the bartender. Some might call her a piece of shit, others might call her a road hazard, even more might call her a piece-of-shit-road-hazard. Her red paint flakes off like rose petals in the wind, she's constantly coughing like she's got black lung, and she still smells like cigarettes from the previous owner no matter how many times Evan cleans the upholstery. Everyone told him not to buy her, but he didn't listen. She's his first car paid for with his first paycheck from Overnight, and that matters to him.

"Can't believe you came in to work today," Riggs says as they file into the elevator with the other nine-to-fivers. "If I were you, I'd be home right now."

"And miss the all-hands-on-deck meeting? Not a chance. I have to know if I got the job or not," Evan says as he takes a sip of his Americano and winces. Paris has ruined American coffee for him. Not to mention wine.

"Naomi wouldn't tell you in private first?" Riggs asks.

"She said she'd make the announcement at the end of the week." Evan gestures around them, as if proving a point. "It's the end of the week."

He's been eyeing the senior editor position ever since Naomi, their boss, talked about starting an Urban Asia division to reach a larger audience. As soon as the listing was posted, he applied. Becoming a senior editor would be a big promotion, with all the perks of his current job, including an all-expenses, multicountry tour through Asia, a part of the world he's always wanted to visit.

Currently, Evan and Riggs make up half of the European editorial team for Overnight, writing guides about hidden gems and the best deals for tourists in all the perennially popular and coolest up-and-coming cities across the continent. They spend hours compiling data and working with locals to determine the best experience for users. Some of the most beautiful cities in the world now feel like a part of him. He practically has a map of the best coffee shops in Europe imprinted in his soul. But he's ready to see more.

Objectively, he knows the new job would be a reach. He's never even been to Asia. But he's always dreamed of going, and Naomi knows he's a fast learner. Plus, visiting Tokyo on Overnight's dime? He'd be crazy not to apply, at least to see what happens.

As the elevator rises, Evan slides his travel bag between his legs and unzips his bomber jacket with one hand while checking his reflection in the shiny walls of the elevator, making sure his dark curls aren't sticking up every which way from the blustery San Francisco winds and staticky airplane pillows. He can't come in looking like he rolled off the tarmac, even if that's exactly what he did.

When the elevator doors *ding* open, the two of them make their way into the bullpen, finding the office mostly empty, with everyone already gathered in the conference room. "The meeting could be about layoffs," Riggs says, scanning the empty desks.

"It's not layoffs." Evan taps Riggs on the chest with the back of his hand. "That doesn't make sense. We're expanding." While Evan is generally the more cynical of the two, he's not the type to catastrophize. "I think you've had too much caffeine this morning."

Riggs inspects his coffee cup and twists his jaw in consideration. "Yeah. Probably."

The conference room is already packed by the time Riggs and Evan slip through the door. The chatter is light and conversational, not the type you'd expect ahead of an announcement that a quarter of the company had been "impacted." Evan and Riggs stand together at the back of the room, finishing their coffee, as some of the higher-ups chat with one another in front of a large projector screen with Overnight's logo as the screen saver.

Riggs leans in and murmurs. "Fine. If it's not layoffs, wanna bet we've been bought out?"

Evan quirks an eyebrow. "Doubt it."

"Twenty bucks." He flashes Evan a bill folded between his fingers.

"If it is layoffs—which it's not—you're gonna need those twenty bucks."

"Being proven right will make it all worth it."

With a breathy laugh, Evan nods. If he has one weakness, this is it. "Okay, I'll take that bet."

Evan's still smiling even as he takes a cursory glance around the room when he notices an unfamiliar face. Overnight is a relatively small company, with fifty developers and even fewer editors, so seeing a stranger in a meeting of this scale piques his interest.

Like Evan, she seems to be in her mid-twenties. Her skin is light brown, and her long black hair falls below her shoulders. When she smiles with full red lips, her dark eyes brighten. She wears an oversized white button-up, with one corner tucked into tight black jeans, and ankle boots. The woman's eyes flick toward him, catching him staring, and he tears his gaze away.

"All right, folks!" Overnight's CEO, Naomi Ito, a smartly dressed Japanese American woman in her forties, claps her hands at the front of the conference room. "It's the top of the hour. Let's get this meeting started, shall we? Thank you all for coming, *yadda yadda yadda*. I know we're updating the app today and we're on a tight schedule, so without further ado . . ." She extends her hand to the new woman, who strides up to stand beside Naomi at the front of the room. Smiling, Naomi says, "Everyone, I'm very excited to introduce the new senior editor of the Urban Asia division, Dalisay Ramos."

The office claps for her politely while Evan's stomach plummets like he's hit turbulence at cruising altitude and his whole body goes cold. This wasn't how he expected to find out he didn't get the job. Naomi gives Evan a slight nod when he catches her eye, a subtle acknowledgment, while Dalisay steps up to the front of the room as the applause dies down.

Dalisay doesn't appear flustered talking in front of a room full of strangers. Confidently, she stands tall, smiling. "Good morning, everyone. I'm Dalisay. I moved here from the Philippines a few months ago, I'm a graduate of Ateneo de Manila University. Before this, I worked for Weisure, another travel app and . . . You're bored already!" The room comes to life with polite laughter.

Makes sense. Overnight would want someone who is familiar with the region to be the senior editor. If Evan had known what he was up against, he wouldn't have applied for the job. He never stood a chance. She seems like the perfect fit.

Watching her, Evan can't look away. Heat rises from the back of his neck, and when he looks at Dalisay, his heart pumps like it's trying to get his attention.

"Honestly," she says, "I'm thrilled to join the Overnight team and can't wait to work with all of you."

Dalisay's eyes catch Evan's, and she smiles wider.

And Evan can't help but smile in return.

By the time Evan finishes hitting send on his final email of the morning, he's fully back in work mode. Being jet-lagged hardly slows him down. He's already planned his next trip, a few days in an igloo hotel in Finland, for an article about unconventional honeymoon destinations.

Movement across the floor snares his attention. Dalisay. The new editor.

She walks along the outer wall across the floor, holding a mug and heading to the office kitchen. She's smiling to herself, eyes down, and he wonders what she's thinking about.

A voice in the back of his head tells him he should go talk to her, introduce himself, but another, louder, and more annoying voice tells him to ask her out for coffee.

Evan's heart has made a home in his throat and he swallows it back down. Ask her out? That'd be ridiculous. They've never spoken to each other. But he can't ignore the way his heart nearly jackhammered out of his chest when they locked eyes. He's never had a heart attack, but he bets it was close enough. Her smile might crack his rib cage in two. He's never believed in love at first sight; that's the stuff of poetry. (Plus, he's always been more of a high-fantasy guy anyway.) He does, however, believe in attraction at first sight, the feeling as solid as a roundhouse kick to the sternum. With her dark hair, and that smart gleam in her eye, and damn, her *smile* . . . It's a megawatt smile that makes everything brighter. What he wouldn't give to see more of it.

Before he realizes it, he's standing and following Dalisay to the kitchen. When he passes Riggs's desk, Riggs gives him a curious glance, but Evan doesn't turn back. He has to introduce himself at least.

When he enters the kitchen, he finds Dalisay alone. She's organizing the sugar packets, putting everything into neat stacks. Kitchen upkeep is a job for one of the interns, but Dalisay hums happily to herself while she does it, waiting for the stainless-steel kettle to boil. When she taps all the packets into a straight row, Evan can't help but notice a flash of silver on her hand, but on a second glance, it's a dainty silver band with an infinity loop around her middle finger. Not an engagement ring.

But what if she has a boyfriend? Or a girlfriend? Someone that gorgeous has to be in a relationship. He's not a homewrecker. Suddenly, his nerve starts to dwindle. *Come on, get a grip*, he tells himself. *You're saying hello to a new colleague, not proposing. Be normal, idiot.*

But Dalisay glances up when she hears him enter and smiles. When she does, he knows how the water in that kettle feels, full of potential energy waiting to bubble over. With a deep breath, he walks toward her, but navigates to the cupboards instead. Being this close to her, he can smell her perfume, and it makes the world spin. Orange blossoms, like a summer in Capri.

"Hi," he says, giving her what he hopes is an easy smile.

Her eyes dart to him, and she tucks a ribbon of black hair behind her ear. "Hey."

She goes back to sorting the sugar and sweeteners, and Evan tries not to stare. He grabs a mug from the cupboard and dollops some honey into the bottom. He silently offers her some, and she nods, giving another smile.

"Dalisay, right?" he asks.

"Yes, I think I saw you at the meeting."

"I'm Evan."

"Oh! Of course! Evan Saatchi. You must be the one I've heard so much about. European team, yes?"

"Yeah, I just got back from Paris. Seriously, only a couple hours ago."

She juts out her lower lip, impressed. "You're holding up well," she says, stowing away the rest of the packets, neat and tidy, and color-coordinated.

"Barely."

She laughs and tucks more of her hair behind her ear. "When I flew here from Manila, I could hardly function. My jet lag was awful! I didn't feel like a person for ages."

"Been there, for sure," Evan says, grinning. "This is your first time here?"

"Yes! I traveled all over Asia for Weisure, but everything's been so busy since we moved, I haven't had a chance to really check out San Francisco yet. I'd love to visit the Asian Art Museum soon, see how it compares."

"The museum is awesome. They have this mochi pounding demonstration—the way those guys hammer at the dough at lightning speed, it's amazing. That, and mochi in general."

"Well then, I have to go now!" She shifts a little so she's facing him, her back flat against the edge of the counter. "You like it here? At Overnight?"

"Yeah. I do. Been a junior editor just over a year now. It's a good gig. Is Naomi helping you get settled?"

"Yeah, it's been great so far. But heading a brand-new department is huge. And adjusting to a new job is always nerve-racking."

"For sure." Evan sucks in a breath. He should tell her that he applied for the position. He'd hate it if she found out secondhand and risk her thinking he resented her. Better she hear it from him directly. "I actually applied for your job, so I know it's a lot."

Dalisay's eyebrows rise. "Really?"

"Yeah, but I think they picked the better candidate to be honest. No hard feelings whatsoever." Making her smile is like serotonin injected directly into his brain. It's stupid-good.

"Well, thank you for the vote of confidence."

"No problem. I'm sure you'll figure everything out, but if you ever need anything, I'm happy to help."

"I may take you up on that."

Dalisay's eyes sparkle. When she smiles with her lips closed like that, the dimples in her cheeks come out, but she seems to catch herself doing it. Her face turns more serious, and she takes a deep breath as she drags her fingers through her hair.

She turns away from him and opens a cupboard only to find a wall of mugs. She opens another one—mugs. Another—mugs all the way down.

Every corporate event, every team building getaway, every convention, commemorative mugs come back to the office. There are more mugs here than there are people in the building.

Dalisay looks baffled.

"Here," Evan says. He holds out his hand and Dalisay steps back. He pulls a handle below the counter and reveals a drawer full of tea bags, coffees, and terrible instant espresso. *"Voilà."*

"My caffeine hero."

"Not all of us wear capes."

Dalisay tips her head to the side playfully, grinning, but she catches herself again, clears her throat, and starts flipping through tea bags with dexterous fingers.

The water bubbles in the kettle, making it rock slightly in its dock, and clicks off. Steam rises from the lid when Dalisay opens it to cool off a little and chooses a mango green tea. She offers him one too without realizing that it's his favorite, second only to his morning espresso.

"Thanks," he says, as she pours them both a mug.

Evan chews on his bottom lip and shifts his weight from one hip to the other. He should ask her out, he'd be crazy not to. There's a spark between them that's hard to ignore. He's used to asking women out, but this time, something feels different. He can't quite place it, but whatever it is, it's making his mouth dry.

Before he can chicken out, he says, "Look, I don't normally do this, but I was wondering if you'd want to grab a drink with me sometime."

Dalisay pauses, then slowly puts the kettle back in its dock. She turns, squares her shoulders to him, and looks him up and down, taking in his navy-blue sweatshirt, jeans, and blunnies—his go-to travel wear. Something flashes in her eye, a brightness he doesn't expect, and one corner of her mouth lifts.

"You travel a lot, don't you," she says. Not a question.

He looks down at his outfit and decides to play along. "Comes with the job. I like to think I know my way around an airport at least." He gives her another smile, but Dalisay hums and curls her lips. "I'm free tomorrow, if you are," he says.

When Dalisay laughs, it rings. "Wow." She shakes her head in disbelief and dissolves the honey in her tea with a wooden stirrer. "Tomorrow. So soon . . . Really?"

"You have plans?"

Dalisay flips her hair over her shoulder and squints one eye at him, like she's looking through a microscope. "Let me guess—correct me if I'm wrong but let me try. Europe is like your playground. You've been there so often, you probably think you know how the rest of the world works."

He's not sure what she's getting at. "Travel enough, you start to realize people are the same everywhere. I'm not quick to judge."

"You may be right. But the thing is, though, I'm from the Philippines. It's a long way from Paris."

"I didn't know I was getting a geography lesson today," he says. He likes the way her eyes crinkle at the corners when she smiles.

"Perhaps you should study some more then."

There's a distinct shift in the tone of the conversation, and Evan's charm starts to wear from his smile. Is that a hardness in her eyes now, or is he reading her all wrong? He starts to scramble for some sort of excuse. Is this about his sweatshirt? His Blundstone boots? He always dresses comfortably for long flights, but he wouldn't call his style sloppy. "Is it something I said?"

"No, not the particular words themselves."

"Mind filling me in?"

Dalisay sighs and tosses the wooden stirrer in the trash. When she looks back at him, he's captured in her gaze. "Let me be clear then. I'm not interested in American hookup culture. No drinks, no dinner, no coffee. That might work with someone else, not me."

Evan balks. She doesn't have to sound so haughty. "A simple no would have been fine."

"Then the answer is no." Her dark eyes sparkle, shining like the night sky, and she looks down her nose at him. "You're going to have to try a lot harder than that."

Evan raises a curious eyebrow as Dalisay turns and leaves. But before she disappears from the kitchen, she looks back at him.

"You may know Milan, Evan Saatchi, but you don't know Manila."

CHAPTER TWO

After kick-starting Bettie with luck and a prayer after work, Evan parks her in front of The Basement, a board game store in the Mission District. Riggs gets out first, balancing the pizza boxes with one hand and a grocery bag in the other. "That is *brutal*," he crows, head thrown back in laughter. Evan told Riggs all about what happened with Dalisay while they were grabbing food for their gaming sessions. "'You're going to have to try a lot harder than that'?! Sounds like a threat."

"I think it was," Evan says, juggling two four-packs of tall boys under one arm and carrying the rest of the snacks while closing Bettie's trunk with his elbow. He's more amused than chagrined. The epic rejection was almost worth it to get Riggs's reaction.

Riggs knocks twice on the window of The Basement. The lights are on deeper inside, but at this hour the door is locked, the store closed. "You should have known. That woman is out of your league. Besides, you work together. That's ripe for drama."

"We're in different departments! I didn't think it'd be weird."

"Well, now it is!"

"I know, but it was worth a shot."

"Never mix business and pleasure. Amateur move, dude."

A hulking shadow moves at the front door and unlocks it. The six-four, totally ripped, Filipino Captain America, John-Mark—JM to his friends—smiles at them. "I smell barbecue. You better have normal pizzas in there."

Riggs and Evan step into the store. "Only one barbecue, and that's for me," Evan says. "The rest are boring like you like, don't worry."

JM locks the door after them. "Good. If I'm going to kill you guys, you'll want all the comfort food you can get."

Every Friday, they gather here after the store closes to drink beer, hang out, and play *Dungeons & Dragons*. It started when they all met at Berkeley as freshmen. They would play for hours at Evan and Riggs's two-bedroom apartment in Westbrae above a hardware store, powered by pizza, beer, and garlic knots from the place around the corner. For a trio of guys who look like they belonged in a frat, they all preferred role play, killing goblins and fighting evil wizards over partying. JM is their dungeon master, the one who designs all the campaigns they play.

"Gonna TPK today?" Riggs asks. "TPK" means a "total party kill." They all have backup characters for such an occasion. While JM is the kindest, gentlest person Evan's ever known in real life, as a dungeon master, he's as brutal as he is a good storyteller.

"Only if you make dumb decisions again," says JM.

Unlike Evan and Riggs and their liberal arts paths, John-Mark Aquino focused on the sciences. They became friends when they joined the Magic the Gathering club as freshmen. JM is still at Berkeley, going for his master's now in public health. He's also one of the fittest people Evan has ever met. When he's not studying for school or working for his girlfriend Pinky at The Basement, he's lifting weights. He can squat two Evans's worth of weight and barely break a sweat. He and Evan work out together, but Evan can't bulk up like JM can.

In the backroom, Pinky is already sitting at a small table set up with their battle map and figurines. She makes grabby hands at the pizzas and Riggs hands them over.

"Careful over there," she says, tipping her head toward the bathroom while she takes a slice of pepperoni. "The floor might still be wet. A kid didn't make it, puked all over."

Everyone cringes. Running a small business is no easy feat. Pinky Valenzuela, JM's girlfriend, owns and manages The Basement. On top of selling games, she also oversees community programs for kids, teaching them how to play board games, and giving them a safe place to stay after school. She's used to the mess, but even Evan's stomach churns thinking about cleaning up after twenty kids every day. On top of that, Pinky somehow manages to find the time to be one of the most popular cosplayers in San Francisco. Every year, the four of them fly down to San Diego to Comic-Con where Pinky wins serious money with her costumes onstage. Last year, she made a Sailor Moon quick-change costume, and the video went viral. The money she makes from Instagram alone keeps the lights on, but The Basement doesn't need it. Every weekend, the store is packed with people playing, and sometimes they host Magic tournaments. Even if it wasn't operated by some of his best friends, The Basement is one of Evan's favorite places to be. He's not ashamed of calling himself a nerd.

"What's this about making dumb decisions?" Pinky asks.

"You mean in the fae forest"—Riggs points to the battle map—"or in Evan's real life?"

Rolling his eyes, Evan plops the spoils from their Safeway run—Funyuns, tortilla chips, salsa, beer, the works—on the floor. He knows where this is going.

"There's a difference?" Pinky asks. Evan lets out a *ha-ha*.

"Evan asked a woman out and got shot down big-time," Riggs says, getting down to brass tacks.

Shrugging off his bomber jacket, Evan takes a seat next to JM as Riggs recounts what Evan told him while JM sets up his notes. "What exactly did Dalisay say again, before she left?" Riggs asks Evan, as if saving the icing on the cake for last.

"'You may know Milan, but you don't know Manila.'"

Everyone bursts into a chorus of laughter at Evan's expense, and Evan ducks his head, kowtowing with a smile.

"So, she's Filipina?" Pinky asks brightly as she twirls her pencil around her thumb.

Both JM and Pinky are Filipino. Pinky grew up in the States, while JM grew up in Cebu City, moving to California when he got accepted to Berkeley, but he goes back every summer to spend time with his extended family.

"Dalisay moved from Manila a few months ago," Evan tells them.

"Surname?"

"Ramos."

Pinky repeats the surname over and over. "I think my mom mentioned meeting a new family named Ramos at church. I'll have to check if it's the same one."

"I'm not sure how that will help," Evan says. "Dalisay seems pretty uninterested. Flat-out *N-O*."

"You do have a certain"—JM waves his hand in Evan's direction—"quality."

"What's that supposed to mean?" he asks, laughing.

"You can just be oblivious, that's all."

"What do you mean?"

JM and Pinky share glances.

"He has no idea," JM says to her. "*No* idea."

"Yeah, but it's not like it'll change anything," she says.

"At least he'll know there was no chance in the first place."

"And maybe he can know the next time."

Evan interrupts. "What are you talking about?"

Pinky and JM break out of their side conversation, as if remembering there are other people in the room. "Dalisay is from the Philippines," Pinky says, "so she probably wants a guy who goes through the Five Stages."

"What's that?" Evan asks.

"It's a tried-and-true courtship ritual in the Philippines going back generations."

"It's like the twelve steps, but way harder," jokes JM.

Evan lets out a dubious guffaw. "'Courtship.' I only asked her out for a drink. Courtship makes me think of"—he gestures to the battle map in front of him—"this! Medieval times and knights and all that."

Pinky rests her chin over her interlocked fingers, peering at Evan with her doe-brown eyes. "Whatever you call it, you're clearly into her! Sure, it's kinda old-fashioned, but it's not so strange. It's just a way a person can prove they're worthy. The first stage is called the Teasing of Friends."

"Teasing of Friends . . . ," repeats Evan. "So it's like the friends playing matchmaker?"

Pinky waves her hand. "Kinda. It's hinting at a relationship without saying it outright. The Five Stages are all about being modest and formal, about taking your time, showing interest in ways that don't come off as presumptuous. Asking to take her out for drinks was a big faux pas."

"*Big* faux pas," echoes JM. "You have to earn it."

"So it's a game," Evan says.

Pinky shakes her head. "No, it's not a game. It's about respect. Tradition is important, especially to Filipinos. Just because you move halfway across the world doesn't mean it's so easy to let that part of yourself go."

JM nods, adding, "When you're an immigrant, you're bringing everything with you—that includes your heritage. When you're starting over somewhere new, sometimes that's all you have left."

Evan's great-grandparents on both sides came to America from Iran—Persia at the time—but he never met them. He doesn't have any clue what moving to another country is like. It's one thing to travel and visit another place, it's an entirely different thing to decide to stay.

"My parents did the Five Stages; so did JM's parents," Pinky says. "I think it's been around since the Spanish ruled the country or something."

Evan's never heard of such a thing before. But maybe Dalisay was right. He doesn't know anything about her country or their traditions. His knowledge about that side of the world is particularly lacking, and it shows.

JM says, "My parents spent *years* doing the Five Stages. They talk about it every anniversary, and how my dad took forever to get enough nerve to do stage three."

"What's stage three?" Evan asks.

Pinky doesn't let JM answer. "Forget it. She already shot you down! Best to just move on and take the loss."

"Unless you want to come home scowling and soaking wet like last time you went on a date," Riggs teases.

Evan frowns. Becca. He suppresses a shiver, remembering the way the ice cubes slipped down the back of his shirt as the champagne bucket emptied over his head. Evan swallows the memory down with a swig of beer.

"Evan's not looking for another serious girlfriend," Riggs says. "Are you?"

Evan shakes his head swiftly. "Not a chance." He's barely home enough as it is. "Besides, I have Tallulah. I'm not lonely. I'm just here to have fun."

Right after his last relationship ended, he went to the pound and rescued Tallulah. Taking care of something other than himself helped occupy his heart. Before he became a dog-dad, he used to laugh when people would question whether they rescued their dog, or the dog rescued them. Now Evan knows firsthand that the latter is true.

Riggs gestures to the group, palms up, as if saying *See?* "Being single is actually fun. You two wouldn't know that." He points to JM and Pinky.

Pinky holds up her hands. "All I'm doing is telling you how it is in the Philippines."

"People actually go through the Stages? Even today?" Evan asks.

"Yeah, dude," says JM. "Though maybe not like they used to. But sort of."

The only one who doesn't seem convinced is Riggs, who sighs and bites down on a Funyun. "Well, the Five Stages sounds like a pain in the ass to me. Why do you have to jump through a ton of hoops just to tell someone you're into them?"

"It's only one of the most romantic things a person can do," Pinky says.

"I never took you for the romantic type," says Evan.

Daintily, Pinky shrugs a shoulder. "Every girl wants to feel special. I bet you would have done really well with the Stages . . . Too bad. Now let's kill some orcs." She snatches up her dice and rattles them in her hand, grinning.

JM hums and leans in to kiss her on the forehead and Pinky's smile is radiant.

She may be right about one thing. Evan isn't the type to make grand, sweeping, romantic gestures. Besides, Dalisay isn't interested in him at all. "Even if I went through these Five Stages, Dalisay still could've said no."

JM says, "The Five Stages isn't a guarantee, but you would have stood out among the crowd."

Evan grunts at that but Riggs still isn't convinced. "Dalisay seems to know what she wants," he says, "and it ain't Evan."

"It doesn't matter anyway," Evan says. "I'm not broken up over it." He's not one to get hung up on a woman, even if her eyes did sparkle like the night sky.

"At least you know," says JM. "Now, roll for initiative."

* * *

The second Evan turns the keys, he hears the familiar clip of Tallulah's nails on the floor as she comes to greet him when he opens the front door.

She's not as fast as she used to be, and she's a lot grayer in the snout, but her tail wags high when she sees him, bringing an automatic smile to his face.

"There's my Ta-lulu!" Evan says, kneeling to pet her. He scrubs his hands on both sides of her long body, and she whines, spinning in circles. At least she never asked him to complete five stages to show his affection for her. "Wanna go potty?"

Tallulah immediately walks over to the coat rack where her leash hangs and Evan snaps it onto her collar. He leads her out to the shared courtyard where she can sniff around and do her business in the dark, guided by solar-powered garden lights in the pathway.

Growing up, he never had pets. His mom was allergic, and his dad didn't want to deal with the mess. Getting a dog for himself, like buying his own condo with his own money, was the next natural step for independence. His dad tried to tell him getting a dog was a big mistake, especially with his work, and traveling, but Evan didn't listen. Tallulah has been one of the most stabilizing factors in his life.

"Go poo!" Evan says to Tallulah, unashamed of using the same voice he uses when talking to babies. He's still jet-lagged, and practically dead on his feet. All he wants to do is throw himself into bed, but Tallulah is on her own timeline, enjoying her stroll in the courtyard garden.

His complex in a quiet part of Noe Valley has four units, all of them two-story condos with their own small but fenced-in backyard and a courtyard connecting all the condos together.

Evan's unit is closest to the alley, quiet and secluded. He often spends time on his patio among the tomato plants and sunflowers to write, read, or eat breakfast in the morning before heading to work. He's never thought about it until now, but Evan's is the only condo with one occupant living in it.

All the neighboring units are lit from within, warm and comforting against the night: Ramon and Stephen cuddle on the couch together, drinking glasses of wine and watching TV; the elderly Mr. and Mrs. Kang sit at the coffee table to do a puzzle together; Alexandra pauses her knitting to lean into a kiss from her husband, Andrew, as he bounces their new baby on his hip.

Evan is used to being alone. He's used to traveling for hours, occupying himself with books, or music, eating solo at a cafe, looking out the window as the world passes below him from forty-thousand feet up. The way he sees it, every single person he encounters in airports, or in hotels, or in restaurants, is living a full life around him—the main character in their own story—and he is just a background figure, a movie extra. He's not meant for love stories. He's better off being alone.

"You're the only girl for me, aren't you, Tallulah?" he says to her with a smile.

She answers by pooping in the tulips.

CHAPTER THREE

Dalisay Ramos is a hopeless romantic. When it comes to matters of the heart, she trusts hers with everything she has. Twenty-six years on this earth has taught her that love is the most important thing in the universe. It binds everything together, keeps the world spinning. Without love of family, friends, and neighbors, what else is there? Dalisay is sure that true love is real, and it's what makes the world worth living in.

The only problem is, she hasn't had much luck in the love department. Her love life, much like IKEA's winding showrooms, is a labyrinth—full of twisting turns and distractions along the way.

"How about this one?" Dalisay's twin Nicole asks, standing in front of yet another bookcase. This one is made of wood—or the fiberboard that passes for wood in this part of the world—but would the black paint match? Dalisay tries to picture it, carefully taking in the furniture with a critical eye.

When they were moving abroad, Dalisay packed up her whole life into a shipping container. In transit, one of her two bookcases had snapped in half, and finding a replacement that matched her old one now feels almost impossible. The styles offered in America are totally different than the ones in the Philippines. Even though she's the only one who will see it, she cares a lot about the aesthetics of the things around her. She likes organizing her jewelry in neat boxes on her vanity, arranging the books on her shelves by authors' last names, and sorting her writing into rainbow-colored folders on her computer. Form meets function. Dalisay's thoughts aren't so loud when things are aesthetically pleasing. Nicole might call her anal retentive, a neat freak, but what's so wrong with wanting things to look nice? It makes her happy.

"Hmm," she says, drumming her fingers on her chin in thought. "Maybe."

Nicole looks at the name tag and laughs. "I swear, IKEA just smashes keys at this point when naming things." She looks at Dalisay again, sees the indecision written all over her face, and slaps her hands to her sides and groans. "Oh, come on, Dalisay! It's just a bookcase! Pick one!"

"I can't just 'pick one.' It has to feel right."

"I'm going to strangle you."

Dalisay could remind her that it was her choice to tag along to Emeryville, but Dalisay is more grateful for the company than annoyed, though she wouldn't share that with Nicole. It comes with the territory of being sisters.

But Nicole doesn't understand. Nicole's bookshelf is a rickety one they found in someone's garbage, Dalisay noted at the time, for a reason. It's barely holding together. One stiff breeze could knock it over. Dalisay wishes she could be as chill about anything as Nicole is.

"It's not like you're making a life-or-death decision," Nicole says.

"I don't want to regret it later."

"It's. A. Book. Case." Nicole claps with every syllable. It's always been this way between the two of them, Dalisay the one to take her time making decisions while Nicole tries to shake some sense into her. Growing up, Nicole was the one to fling herself headfirst into the metaphorical pool that is life, while Dalisay dipped her toe into the shallow end to see if the water was too warm or too cold and then decided to read under a tree if it wasn't just right.

She's careful and considerate, personality traits that seem to be a never-ending topic weaponized against her. She's the good girl, the one who never steps out of line, who does as she's told. Which is why it was satisfying as hell to reject that American guy on her first day at the new job. She'd meant to tell Nicole earlier, to see if the doctors and nurses at her hospital were as forward as apparently travel writers are.

"So yesterday at work, this hot American dude asked me out," Dalisay says, as she slides her hand across the smooth wood. "We had literally just met."

Nicole's eyes go wide, desperate for a change in subject from IKEA furniture. "And?"

"I told him no."

Nicole squeezes her eyes closed, making a disappointed sound. "I knew you'd say that."

"What! I was flattered, sure, but it's so bold! He put me on the spot."

"That's just how Americans are. They see what they want, and they go for it. Did you tell him about the Five Stages?"

"No," she says, running her hand along the edge of another bookcase. "I didn't see the need."

"You should have said something. You can't keep expecting people to be mind-readers." Nicole sighs and throws herself onto a nearby couch, with one leg thrown over the back, and the other draped over the armrest, getting a little too comfortable on the model furniture. Dalisay half-expects Nicole to take off her scrubs and sprawl out like it's movie night, just as she does at home. There's no way anyone, even a stranger, could confuse the two of them despite being identical.

"What's this guy's name?" Nicole asks.

"Why, so you can hunt him down?"

"Maybe."

Dalisay would pay money to see that happen, even though Nicole is all bark. "Evan Saatchi," she says, then adds, shrugging, "Besides, I was thinking about the list . . ."

Nicole bursts into laughter and opens her mouth to start singing.

"Don't you dare!" Dalisay exclaims, but she's laughing too.

"Handsome and sweet," Nicole chants, pumping her hands like a cheerleader with pom-poms. "And he likes to read—"

"Stop!" Dalisay cries, trying and failing to plaster her hand over Nicole's mouth.

"Modest, respectful, can't be neglectful—"

Dalisay successfully clamps her hand over Nicole's lips, silencing her. "I know! I know! Shut up!"

When she was in middle school, Dalisay crafted a list in her journal meticulously detailing the perfect guy she would marry. She hasn't seen the journal in years; it probably got lost somewhere in the chaos of going to university, then her father's death, then moving to San Francisco, but Dalisay still knows the first few entries by heart.

The heading on the lined page, detailed in bubbly flowers, read: *Dalisay's True Love List*

1. *Handsome*
2. *Sweet*
3. *Likes to read*
4. *Modest*
5. *Respects his family*

When she caught her working on it one day, Nicole teased Dalisay relentlessly for it. She even made up that annoyingly catchy song that the whole family ended up singing for years. As they grew older, and Dalisay's list grew longer, Nicole said that no guy would be able to meet all her criteria, but maybe, Dalisay thought, that was the point. She knew what she wanted, and she wasn't going to settle for less. That was the hopeless part of being a hopeless romantic. Besides, the one time she didn't follow her list, she'd had her heart broken. His name was Luke, and they were nineteen and dumb and she thought she was in love. If it hadn't been for her older brother Daniel, it could have ended a lot worse than it did.

To be fair, though, based on first impressions, Evan didn't seem at all like the mistake that was Luke. Unlike Luke, Evan has a certain steadiness about him, a kind of gentleness that makes her feel comfortable and quick to laugh, which makes her feel steady too. Luke barely made her laugh, which should have been a red flag from the start.

Just thinking about Evan still makes her heart race. The way he smiled at her, the sound of his voice, the way he simply looked at her . . . If she were more like Nicole, maybe she wouldn't have shot him down so quickly, but a little voice in the back of her head—one that sounded a lot like her father's—reminded her: *remember where you come from.*

Tradition, for someone like Dalisay, is in her blood. Literally. It's as important to her as it is to the air she breathes. And the Five Stages is the kind of tradition that Dalisay has always wanted to experience. It reminds her that even though she is separated by time from her ancestors, they took the same journey she will in finding true love. It's like something out of the epic romances or a fairy tale from her grandmother's books. All that, plus it's downright romantic.

That's how her parents met. Dalisay loved listening to her father tell the story about how he had to win her mother's heart. It seemed like something out of a fairy tale, straight from the pages Dalisay devoured throughout her childhood. Even when the cancer progressed, and he couldn't sit up in bed, her father would recount how much he loved her mother. Dalisay wanted that too. She wanted the kind of love that lasted. Even after you were gone.

And when her dad died, it was important for her not to be a burden on her mother. She had to be the older daughter, the example, the responsible and mature one who would be helpful to her family. She's set in her ways, sometimes to her own detriment, for the sake of everyone else. Her love life had to take a back seat.

Perhaps she is a little picky, but then again, she wants to be sure she won't make a mistake. Not again.

But now that she's thinking about it, Evan exceeded that first criteria in her list. He wasn't just handsome, he was downright hot. But a proper, respectable Filipino girl such as Dalisay should stamp down that warmth in her belly and distract herself by any means necessary.

She lifts her hand from Nicole's mouth, certain she won't be singing any more about that dumb list, and says, "I want to look at the *flurbagerb* again."

Defeated, Nicole groans in her patented *Nicole-is-exhausted-and-done-with-today* way as they navigate to another showroom.

"Daisy, Americans don't know about the Five Stages," Nicole says, posting up on yet another couch and pulling blankets and pillows around herself to get cozy. People stare at her because she looks like she might just take a nap. Dalisay knows she really might.

"Unless you're looking to date a Filipino guy, which Mom would be over the moon about, you're sort of setting everyone up for failure."

"I don't want a Filipino guy. I just want . . . someone who gets it. I want someone who's serious, who doesn't want to hook up and leave." But saying it out loud feels like an excuse.

"You won't know unless you give them a chance," Nicole says. "The only way to find out for sure if he's that kind of guy is to actually, you know, go on a date. Throw that list away and live a little."

"Is that an American thing?"

"It's a *dating* thing. Period."

"How do you know so much about dating?" Dalisay asks her perpetually single sister, raising a teasing eyebrow.

Nicole slumps back into the couch. Of course Nicole shuts her down, putting on her haughty, know-it-all face. "It's common sense."

Dalisay laughs and scrunches up her nose. "You're right. Enlighten me, dating guru."

Nicole moves to kick her thigh but misses as Dalisay swings her hips, making her swipe at nothing but air. "Rude! You have a pattern. The moment anyone remotely interesting comes into your life, you find every reason not to go for it."

"That's not true!"

"Oh yeah?" Nicole says it like a challenge. "Tell me you don't always take the safe road, play disinterested because you've set your expectations so high that they're impossible for anyone to achieve, and therefore you prove yourself right by default."

"I don't!" It doesn't even sound convincing to Dalisay's own ear, but she tries to smile anyway.

"What about that guy at church? The one with the tattoos."

"He kept calling me sweetheart."

"Fine, but what about the other one who asked to buy you a chai latte last month?"

"He snapped his fingers at the barista to get her attention. Big turnoff."

"Okay, yeah, fuck that guy. But you hardly give anyone a chance!"

Nicole's only half-right. It's not just that. She's terrified that if anything goes right in her life, something equally terrible will come soon after. The same week she got the job at Weisure, her dad was diagnosed with cancer. It's a flawed way of thinking, Dalisay knows, but she can't help it. Everything comes in pairs: one good thing happens, and a bad thing is just waiting around the corner. When her father died, it was a stark reminder that good things were temporary. There are a lot of reasons why she's been single all these years.

Their parents were adamant that none of them were to start dating unless they had gotten a college degree. Even though all three Ramos children—Dalisay, Nicole, and their older brother Daniel—have long since received their diplomas, none of them has dated much. But this lecture is rich coming from Nicole. She never showed any interest in anyone in Manila. She comes off as a little intense, perhaps too intense, for prospective suitors. Her wicked sense of humor and cleverness sometimes turn people off. Dalisay and Nicole are total opposites when it comes to personality, but they talk about *everything*. Maybe it's a twin thing, maybe just a sister thing, maybe both, but Nicole always calls her out on her bullshit, whether Dalisay is ready to hear it or not.

"Who knows, if I keep my list, maybe I could find the perfect guy," Dalisay says.

Nicole snorts in doubt. "Perfect guy. Yeah, right. No one is perfect."

Dalisay doubts that. There must be someone in this world who is perfect, at least perfect for her. She just has to find him.

When she first laid eyes on Evan, she felt something shift, thrum, vibrate inside herself, like someone had rung a bell behind her chest. Those dark curls, the line of his nose, the way shadows played on the grooves of his pale neck . . . She digs her fingernails into the crook of her elbow and takes a shuddering breath to ground herself. While, yes, she can admit she finds Evan attractive, she has to keep it together. She's worked too hard for this new job to throw it all away for some guy. They *work together* for crying out loud.

"I'm in no rush to date," Dalisay says. "When I find the one, I'll know."

But Nicole isn't listening. She's staring up at the ceiling, one hand tucked behind her head, her gaze distant.

Dalisay nudges her, snapping Nicole out of her daze. "What?"

"I'm serious," Dalisay says. "I don't want to get hurt."

Falling in love with the wrong person hurts, but falling in love with the right person and then losing them will hurt more. She wants to be careful because it's the only thing she can control. A heart is a fragile thing to play with, so why is being careful with it such a bad thing?

"Right. I know," says Nicole. "But that's part of life." That's as good as Dalisay's going to get.

But Dalisay squints at her. Something's off. It's not simply exhaustion from a long day at the hospital—there's something else dragging the corners of her sister's lips down, making her eyelids heavy, slumping her shoulders. Nicole is staring at the ceiling again.

"What's wrong?" Dalisay asks.

Nicole sits up and says, "Nothing," before abruptly getting up. "I'm going to get some Swedish meatballs. Come get me when you finally make up your mind!"

Nicole disappears, leaving Dalisay standing alone in a mock living room.

Dalisay keeps looking at the *flurba*-whatever bookcase, and the longer she looks at it, the more she realizes that maybe yes, it could work, that even if the shade of stain on the wood is a skosh too light and the height is too tall, it would suit the rest of the decor in her bedroom nicely.

Okay, maybe Nicole has an iota of a point. Dalisay is her own worst enemy. She really does play it safe with life in general. It's called a comfort zone for a reason! It's safe, secure, home. No one actually wants to be in a *dis*comfort zone. But she has to admit, she might be playing it *too* safe.

Honestly, what's the worst that could have happened if she'd let Evan take her out for coffee? A lot, actually, now that she thinks about it—

She rolls her eyes at herself and has to physically shake the thought out of her head. This is what she always does: catastrophizes, makes mountains out of mole hills, finds every excuse not to do something. And all this time, according to Nicole, it's been holding her back. She's never put herself out there for fear of disappointing her family, or making them ashamed of her, or calling forth the wrath of the universe. And maybe that's her problem.

Maybe it's not too late to change all that. She could prove to Nicole—no, prove to *herself*—that she's not stuck in her comfort zone, that she's not afraid of life.

It's not too late for second chances.

The next day, as thanks for dragging Nicole through IKEA, the kindest, most sisterly thing Dalisay can think to do is surprise her with some comforts of home that she got at Unimart: a couple sticks of *karioka*, sea salt and vinegar Pik-Niks, and a ride home after her shift.

With the bribes ready, Dalisay sits in her car across the street from the main entrance to Kaiser Permanente, her hands tight on the steering wheel. After all this time, being near hospitals still sets her muscles on edge, like she needs to run somewhere far away from here.

A pit hollows out in her stomach. It's times like these, when she's by herself with only her spiraling thoughts for company, that she starts to feel like she's really, truly alone. She starts sorting the loose change in the cup holder to distract herself, but it only marginally helps.

She misses Manila. Mostly for what was left behind. Or rather, who. Life wasn't the same after her dad died. But she was born and raised in Manila. It's her home. She grew up writing her first stories in artista notebooks with her celebrity crushes' faces on the covers, playing patintero in the street with her neighbors until the streetlights flickered on and they were all called home for dinner, or walking with Nicole to get ice cream with sprinkles after school. The food, the TV, the smells, the clothes—all of it they left behind.

Dalisay was the one person in the family who didn't want to move in the first place.

When her older brother Daniel secured a spot at Stanford for his doctorate, her mom said it would be a wise move for everyone to go too, that it was a good opportunity for change. Everyone would stick together, including their grandmother on their father's side. Lola is almost ninety and leaving her alone in the Philippines was out of the question. Despite not being blood related, their mom insisted. "Family stays together," she said. They would all take care of her, just like she cared for her son. No one disagreed.

Her father had only been dead for three months but packing up the house and moving to America without him felt wrong, like they were abandoning him somehow. He used to tell them America was a land of opportunity, that it was a place they could thrive. But how could any of them thrive without him?

Dalisay had been terrified. She would have to start her whole life over. What if she didn't make any friends? What if she couldn't find a job? What if she hated it? But she never told her mom about her anxiety. It took them a whole year to organize, and in all that time, she never spoke up about it once. It's Dalisay's weakness; she would rather die than be a burden to someone else.

The only person she told was Nicole, who of course kept it a secret, but assured her that so long as they were together, they could get through anything.

Six months on and that promise still holds up. Dalisay knows she's scared of change, but she couldn't have gotten through it if it wasn't for Nicole. While Dalisay may be choosy with who she loves romantically, she's not choosy when it comes to family. She would do anything for them.

Across the street, the sliding glass doors of the hospital open and Dalisay spots Nicole. She's about to honk the horn to get her attention when she notices Nicole is holding hands with someone. Not just someone—a woman.

Dalisay doesn't recognize her. She's tall, with curls of auburn hair, and she wears scrubs just like Nicole. They look like they're taking a stroll through the park, laughing and smiling, and it takes Dalisay a second to realize that Nicole hasn't looked this happy in years. She's practically glowing.

Like dancers at a ball, Nicole pulls the woman toward her, smiling slyly, and swoops her in for a kiss.

It's like something out of a movie, and all Dalisay can do is watch, shocked.

They pull apart, smiling and looking deeply into each other's eyes before going their separate ways, glancing back at each other one last time.

It appears that love has found one of the perpetually single sisters after all.

CHAPTER FOUR

By nine that Monday morning, Evan is already at his desk eating a ham and cheese croissant, looking over an article before he has to turn it in, when he hears the elevator doors open.

Evan's eyes flick toward the lobby to see Dalisay walking toward her section of the office. Her hair is braided today, a plait lying delicately over one of her shoulders, and she's wearing a knitted gray sweater and gold bangles on her wrists. In one hand, she carries a packed lunch from home. He doesn't mean to stare, so he snaps his attention back to his work; this article about Pompeii isn't going to finish itself. But out of the corner of his eye, he sees her coming his way. The closer she gets, the faster his heart races. Is she coming to chew him out for staring? She must think he doesn't know that "no" is a complete sentence.

Evan frantically brushes away any lingering croissant crumbs that might be on his chin right before she gets to his desk. When she arrives, she pauses for a moment, like she's trying to think of something she's forgotten, but she doesn't look angry.

There's a beat while they both stare at each other.

"Hi?" he says, filling in the silence.

At his desk nearby, Riggs hears Evan's voice and swivels around in his chair to see Dalisay standing there. She looks at Riggs briefly before turning her attention back to Evan. "Do you have a moment?"

Evan juts out his lower lip, confused but intrigued. "Sure."

Riggs makes an open-palmed gesture and mouths: *What's up?* But Evan only shrugs as he gets up from his desk and follows her into the kitchen. She puts her packed lunch in the fridge, then turns around to face him, the color high on her cheeks. Is she blushing?

"I wasn't fair to you the other day," she says, jumping right to it.

Evan's eyebrows shoot up. "Is this an apology or something? Because I really don't need one. Message received."

Dalisay shakes her head and folds her arms over her chest, making her bracelets chime when they clink together. "It's not that. Listen, where I come from, when people ask each other out, there's this courtship ritual—"

"The Five Stages, I know." This time Dalisay's eyebrows shoot up, so Evan explains, "My friends told me. And believe it or not, yes, I *have* friends."

She almost laughs but catches herself and tongues the inside of her cheek. A thrill rushes through him at almost making her break. But she made her views quite clear last week.

Dalisay twists the ring on her finger. "Well, I thought about it some more, so I'm giving you a chance to try again," she says.

"To ask you out?"

She nods, and Evan lets out a laugh. Now it's time for some payback. "Ah, I see. Well, five seems like a lot of steps just for one date."

Dalisay's eyes flash but a smile curls her lips, making dimples appear on her cheeks.

"Are the Five Stages really that intimidating?"

"No, I just know when to cut my losses."

Dalisay narrows her eyes slightly, like she's X-raying him. "And here I figured since you were so bold as to ask me out on my first day, nothing could scare you."

"I'm not scared."

She tilts her head. "No?"

"No. I'm not really into pursuing women who aren't interested in me."

Dalisay inspects him for a long second. "Well good, because you're right, I'm still not interested."

There's no way Evan is looking away first. He lets his eyes bore into her. "So then why were you giving me another chance?"

Dalisay shifts her weight from one hip to the other, looking right back at him. "I wanted to see if you would try it, maybe to prove that you're not like other American guys." Then a spark of something ignites in her eyes that makes Evan's heart squeeze painfully in his chest. "You know what, I *bet* that you can't do all Five Stages."

A buzz of interest hums through his brain. Is that a hint of playfulness in her smile? He can't help but smile back. "A bet, huh?"

Those are fighting words. Once, in college, his friend Yoon-gi bet him a hundred bucks that he couldn't eat ten ghost peppers in one sitting. Granted, they'd had too much tequila and not enough sense to realize how dumb of a bet that was, but Evan agreed anyway, and used those hundred dollars on a plumber to fix his toilet. It was one of the worst experiences of his life. One may have expected that he'd learned his lesson, but he just smiles and licks his lips. "You don't think I can do it?"

"Hmmm, yeah."

"Is this some reverse way of getting me to ask you out?"

Dalisay shakes her head. "No. At the end, you don't even have to follow through. I just want to see if you can do the Five Stages. Call it an experiment."

"No strings attached?"

"None."

Well, this would at least take the pressure off.

She starts to say, "The first stage—" but Evan finishes for her.

"Teasing of friends. Like I said, I know."

"So you know what the others are too?"

"Nah, didn't ask."

Her smile curls higher. "Good. Knowing more would make things too easy, Mr. Saatchi."

"And we can't have that."

Dalisay steps closer to him and he catches a whiff of lavender. "Once I feel you've adequately completed each stage, I'll give you further instructions."

It sounds like something out of a spy movie, and excitement begins to course through Evan's veins. This is starting to feel fun. "So, what's in it for me?"

"Besides learning what it feels like to lose?"

Evan can't help but feel turned on by Dalisay's smirk.

"Do all Five Stages—just like it's supposed to play out, fair and square—and you win . . ." She thinks about it a moment, humming, then says, "The tour. The all-expenses-paid cross-country tour from Kyoto to Bangkok that Overnight's sending me on. I know you wanted to go. So do all Five Stages and you get to go in my place. I've already been to most of the cities anyway." She crosses her arms over her chest and juts out her chin, as if daring him to take the bet.

There has to be a catch, Evan can feel it. "What's in it for you? What do you get if I fail?"

"The satisfaction of proving you wrong."

He scoffs. "Come on, there has to be something you want. Make it an even trade."

Dalisay considers him for a moment, looking him up and down. "I don't know. What do you have?"

"Honestly?" He holds out his hands, gesturing to his reasonably priced clothing. "Not much. I'm not exactly in the lap of luxury."

"Then how about something you care about? Your car or—"

With a laugh, he says, "You don't want my car. Trust me." He wouldn't thrust Bettie upon anyone, even his worst enemy.

She seems to believe him, and rightly so. "Fine. How about if you lose, I get to go on one of your trips, since you seem to love Europe so much. *Ooh*, Vatican City! You go to Italy all the time, right? I can check that off the bucket list. Finally see what all the fuss is about."

"Deal." Evan's smile widens. "What about the rules? It sounds too easy."

"Easy?" Dalisay laughs. "The only rule is you have to play fair. Really convince me. Go through all the stages like you're supposed to, no cheating or half-assing it."

"Oh, don't worry, I will full-ass it. Whole-ass."

"'Whole-ass'?" Dalisay almost laughs again, and Evan feels a touch of accomplishment.

"So when do we start?"

"Right now. The second we're done here, it's no contact."

"No contact?"

"In the Philippines it's all about modesty. You can't show your affection outright. Doing so would be disrespectful."

"But what about work?"

Dalisay considers it for a moment. "Fine. We can talk at work. Overnight is a neutral zone. Sound good? You still have a chance to back out."

Evan lets out a huff of a laugh. "You underestimate me, Ms. Ramos. You really think the Five Stages are that hard?"

"Don't get cocky. Not everyone has what it takes." She looks him over, as if gauging whether he's worthy or not, and meets him in the eye again, smirking as if she's seen everything she needs to.

"Believe it or not, I'm no quitter," he says. "When I commit to something, I go all-in."

"I'd like to see that for myself."

Evan's heart jackhammers in his rib cage. Seeing this competitive glint in her eye is making him feel like he's touching a live wire. It's no secret he's been eyeing that trip. It would be a dream come true, and here she is, offering it up on a silver platter. How can he turn it down? He'll take whatever she throws his way. How hard can it be? JM said it was like the twelve steps but way harder, but Evan highly doubts that. It's a courtship ritual, not the *Hunger Games*.

"Okay, I'll do it," he says, and holds out his hand. She shakes it, her grip firm and sure. "I'll send you tons of photos from *my* trip."

Dalisay's smile is sweet, but her eyes are sharp. She doesn't let go of his hand. "Whole-ass, Mr. Saatchi." His words tossed back at him bring a slight blush to his cheeks.

When he leaves, he can feel her eyes on him as goes back to his desk. And when he sits down, the ghost of their first touch still lingers on his skin.

Evan's at the dog park with Tallulah after work when his phone buzzes in his pocket. It's Pinky.

The second he hits the green button to answer, he has to hold the phone at arm's length, Pinky's scream is so loud. "EVAAAAN! You're doing the Five Stages!"

Some of the other dog-parents glance his way, no doubt hearing Pinky's voice carrying from the phone. Once Pinky's done screaming, he puts the phone back to his ear. "Let me guess . . . Riggs."

"He told me everything!"

After Evan shook hands with Dalisay, of course he told Riggs, who of course told JM and Pinky. Nothing stays secret for long in their friendship circle. "Yeah, well, don't get your hopes up. It's to prove a point. Dalisay and I have an agreement."

"It doesn't matter! I can't believe she's giving you another chance! This is going to be so much fun."

Evan smiles. He's not sure this counts as a second chance, especially when that's not what this is about at all, but Pinky's excitement is a little infectious. "Sure, fun. So, what, are you calling just to scream in my ear just because or—?"

"I'm going to help you, dummy. Teasing of Friends, remember?"

"Right," he says. "Figures that 'friends' would be involved in the 'teasing' part." While he's on the phone, Tallulah comes over, tail wagging, to check on him and he bends down to give her a scratch on the head before she bounds off again to chase a chihuahua, yapping happily. Easily, he has the cutest dog in the park. He'll be taking no questions. "What's the plan then?"

"Turns out my mom does know Dalisay's family, which is great, because she's going to invite them to my cousin's birthday party this weekend. It'll be the perfect chance for all of us to hang out and talk you two up."

"When? Where?"

"Saturday, Fil-Am Community Center, two o'clock."

"Okay, I'll be there." Pinky cheers, making him hold the phone away from his ear again. "Just remember," he adds, "it's not real. Don't get your hopes up about this turning into anything."

"I don't care! I love doing the first stage! It's one of my favorite things."

Pinky has several favorite things: cosplay, board games, donuts with jelly on the inside, and—of course—JM, but Evan has no doubt that setting her friends up on dates is high up on that list too. He can't help but smile.

* * *

"When you said it was a birthday, I assumed there would be . . . ," Evan says, trailing off.

"Fewer clowns?" JM offers.

Pinky and JM stand on either side of Evan like bodyguards, as chaos reigns around them.

Pinky's nephew, Angel, just turned five. It's an educated guess, what with all the number fives decorating the room in sparkly banners and shaped balloons and the tiered cake with a number five–shaped candle. But for a kid named Angel, perhaps he really is the devil. What child actually wants to be around a bunch of Bozos of their own free will?

"If I'd warned you, I worried you might not come," says Pinky.

"And lose this bet?" Evan tries to sound casual, but he knows it's a weak front.

Angel, the birthday boy wearing a golden paper crown and a Teenage Mutant Ninja Turtles T-shirt, runs screaming through the hall, leading a pack of equally hyper children as they careen around the open community center space.

Five clowns are scattered throughout the hall, entertaining groups of children with magic tricks and balloon animals and something Evan can only describe as "kazoo comedy." Evan can't look at any of the clowns. Perhaps if he doesn't make eye contact, they will find easy prey somewhere else.

"Relax," JM says. "We'll talk you up to Dalisay, easy as pie, and be out of here in no time."

Evan's trying his best to act cool, but at what cost? His back is already running with sweat, and the close clown proximity is making him want to turn tail and run. He was way too young when he saw the miniseries *IT* starring Tim Curry. At the time, his babysitter—a sweet elderly woman who was partially blind and mostly deaf—thought the clown on the cover was kid-appropriate. He carries those mental scars with him forever.

Sure, he's used to being around people in costume at conventions, but clowns are apex predators. An entirely different species. They can smell fear.

Before he can set a foot further into the room, JM and Pinky both grab Evan around the biceps and spin him around.

"You are not allowed to talk to Dalisay," Pinky says.

"Don't even look at her," adds JM.

"I know!" says Evan, throwing up his hands in surrender. "I get it! Stage one, let you do all the talking. I'll try not to get murdered by a person wearing a big red nose."

"You're learning fast," says JM, and catches him by the elbow. "Come on, I'll protect you."

Evan keeps his eyes down as JM guides him to the back of the room toward a table stacked with presents. Before he came, Evan stuffed an envelope with twenty dollars, and he sets it among the towers of boxes and bows near another table packed to the brim with food.

He's had Filipino food before made by JM's mom when she's had them over for dinner, so he recognizes some dishes, but others not so much. There's some kind of white paste in banana leaves, what *looks* like purple mashed potatoes, and a table with food spread across the entire surface on a large banana leaf. Several people stand around it, eating pickled eggs, sausages, roast pork, pineapples, and cucumbers with their hands. JM offhandedly tells him it's called *kamayan*, a kind of meal everyone enjoys without utensils. All the food looks incredible.

Standing around the table laughing and eating are a dozen or so Filipino adults, no doubt some of the parents of the children running the gauntlet around the room. The conversation is bright, the laughter rising through the hall, and Evan's shoulders relax a little. For a moment he can forget about the looming threat of a wig-wearing nightmare lurking behind him. Still no sign of Dalisay.

JM and Pinky encourage Evan to try some food, and he gets a few cursory glances from the other adults as he grabs one of the wrapped banana leaves. He's an unfamiliar face in what must be a close-knit community, but Pinky's mom, a Filipino American woman in her sixties, calls up from the other end of the table surrounded by older aunties and uncles, smiling brightly.

"Evan!" she says. "Welcome, welcome! Everyone, this is Evan Saatchi. Pinky's friend."

He waves, smiling at the group, and does a double take when he sees a familiar face. At first, he thinks it's Dalisay wearing a black T-shirt and jeans, but unless she just cut her hair into a straight bob with bangs, it's not her. She has a rounder face than Dalisay, and sharp, angular eyebrows that give Evan the impression that he's being judged. She stands with a man, a little older, wearing a graphic tee, who also watches him carefully through round, gold-rimmed glasses. Evan knows he is the only non-Filipino person in the building, but the way they're staring at him seems to have nothing to do with that. He still smiles, unperturbed. He's used to smoothing over uncomfortable situations.

A bright voice calls out behind him. *"Kain na!"*

It's Dalisay, for real this time. She emerges from the kitchen, carrying a large stockpot with oven mitts. She passes right by Evan, doesn't even look in his direction, and sets the pot down on the table. "Who wants more rice?" she asks as she scoops steaming mountains of fluffy white rice into a few bowls and hands them around the table.

It takes everything in his power not to be hypnotized by the sundress she's wearing and how it curves around her hips.

"You really don't have to do that, Dalisay," Pinky's mom says, taking a bowl. "You're a guest here!"

"It's no trouble at all," says Dalisay. "I like to help." She smiles and then notices Evan and her smile widens and starts to curl.

"What kind of name is Saatchi, anyway?" asks one of the older ladies. It's not accusatory, simply curious.

"Persian," he says.

"Oh, Persian!" the woman says, excitedly. The table explodes into a frenzy of questions about his family, and where they're from, and how many live in America now. Immigrants of every kind seem to find kindred spirits with those who have come before them, a sort of camaraderie that comes from shared experiences. While conversation breaks out, Dalisay spins on her flats and leaves, and Evan can't help the smile that lifts the corners of his mouth. He already feels accomplished just by being here.

Eventually, the conversation morphs away from the topic of Evan and transitions into talk about other families, and school, and how big the kids at the party are getting, and Evan helps himself to more food. There's so much, he's not sure where to start. JM has him try *tocino*, a kind of crispy bacon; *tapa*, salted and cured beef; and pickled vegetables called *atchara*. It's all delicious.

Upbeat pop music plays on the karaoke machine and a handful of little girls sing a Miley Cyrus song while a clown inflates some skinny balloons to twist into crowns and flowers for eagerly waiting children.

This kind of party is way different than what he grew up with. Evan doesn't have any cousins or siblings, and this type of get-together would be seen as over the top and ostentatious for his dad's liking.

When he was seven, his parents divorced. His mom moved to India for work, and Evan stayed in California with his dad. His dad is far more subdued when it comes to celebration. Growing up, Evan's birthday parties usually consisted of a handful of friends over for pizza and cake and then they all went home by five so the house could return to stasis, peace, and quiet. He's pretty sure his dad would have a nosebleed at the idea of a karaoke machine.

Evan's in the middle of chewing a bite of *puto*, one of the rice cakes wrapped in banana leaves, when the man with the glasses approaches.

"Evan Saatchi," the man says. His voice is low, level but friendly. He holds out his hand and Evan shakes it. "Nice to meet you. I'm Daniel Ramos."

"Nice to meet you too, Daniel." *Ramos, as in related to Dalisay? Is this her brother?*

Evan's eyes are drawn toward Dalisay, who he notices is now deep in conversation with Pinky. She smiles and laughs, and Evan drags his gaze away from her to look at Daniel. He can see the family resemblance in his face.

As if reading his mind, Daniel says, "I'm Dalisay and Nicole's older brother." So Nicole must be Dalisay's twin.

"No kidding!" Evan jokes.

Daniel has an easygoing air about him when he smiles and folds his arms over his chest. "Yup, it's not an easy job but someone has to do it. Do you have siblings?"

"Nope, just me."

Daniel clicks his tongue. "Lucky man. Bet your house was always quiet growing up."

"Maybe a little too quiet! You're not a fan of chaos?"

"Not when I've got a thesis due, and the family decides it's time for a spontaneous dance party in the living room. I'm getting my doctorate at Stanford."

"Oh, whoa. That's awesome," Evan says, genuinely impressed.

Daniel shrugs again, like it's no big deal. "What about you? You in school?"

Evan's eyes flick toward Dalisay again and he can't help but smile. He wonders if the "teasing of friends" stage that JM and Pinky talked about goes both ways. Are JM and Pinky scoping out Dalisay like Daniel seems to be scoping out Evan?

"I actually work with Dalisay," Evan says, testing to see how much Daniel knows.

"No way! At Overnight? Small world." The way Daniel says it, with a small twinkle in his eye and a knowing smile, gives it all away.

"Yeah," Evan says, amused. "Crazy running into her here."

"Not exactly ideal, having a meet-cute at a clown birthday party, right?" Evan genuinely laughs at that. "I'm really proud of her, though. She's worked hard for that spot at Overnight. She's always been the word nerd."

"Yeah? Me too."

During the twenty minutes or so that they chat, Daniel drops information about Dalisay, telling Evan that her favorite novel is *Pride and Prejudice* by Jane Austen and that her favorite adaptation is the one with Kiera Knightley and Matthew Macfadyen; that she loves going to bookstores and has been known to spend hours perusing the aisles; and that she always orders a chai latte from any bookstore cafe. She's got a big sweet tooth, and she loves anything with chocolate. They have a lot more in common than Evan thought. He feels like he should be taking notes for some reason.

"Daniel!" Nicole, Dalisay's twin, calls over to him from the front door. "You need to move the car."

"That's what I get for double parking. It was good talking to you, Evan," he says, shaking Evan's hand again.

"Yeah, same. See you around."

Daniel gives him a final, encouraging smile and while Evan eats some more *puto*, Nicole takes his place at Evan's side.

"Liking everything?" she asks with a smile, eyebrows lifted high enough to disappear behind her bangs.

"Yeah," Evan says through a mouthful. The *puto* is sticky, practically gluing his jaw shut, and he covers his mouth so as not to be rude. "Really good."

"Hi," she says, extending her hand. "I'm Nicole. That one's twin." She tips her chin toward Dalisay.

"Which one of you is the evil one?" It's a bad joke, and Nicole definitely isn't laughing but she does grin a little wickedly. He has a habit of making jokes in awkward situations. "Sorry. I'm Evan," he says, holding out his hand.

"Yeah, yeah, I know who you are, Evan Saatchi," she says. "I know *all* about you." Her voice is husky, casual, but betrays the sharpness in her eyes.

Evan swallows the rice cake with some difficulty. "So, uh, what do you do?"

"Ha, typical American. First question is always what I do for a living."

Evan isn't sure how to respond to that. It *is* a stereotypical American thing, one Evan learned while traveling. Most people in other countries don't ask what a stranger does for work. Americans have a habit of making a job an identity, a habit Evan tries to break. Now he's being called out on it.

"Since you care so much," Nicole says, glancing at him sideways, "I'm in med school. Following in my family's footsteps, as it were."

"Oh, wow." So not only is Dalisay supersmart, she also comes from a family of brainiacs. "That's cool."

She doesn't ask him what he does for work in return. Instead, she says, "Are you single, Evan?"

The *puto* nearly comes back up. "Uh, yeah," he chokes. "Yeah."

Nicole laughs. "Don't worry. I'm not interested, if that's what you're thinking."

"No, I wasn't—"

"Glad we cleared that up." She slaps him on the back, and it helps dislodge the *puto*.

"You have nothing to worry about," she says. "I'm glad she's giving you another chance." Nicole's gaze blazes like a fire, and she leans in, making her voice barely above a whisper. "But I love my sister more than anything in this world. She deserves nothing but the best. And I'll protect her, no matter what."

Now she's speaking Evan's language, saying exactly what's on her mind. He smiles, matching her tone. "Then *you* have nothing to worry about, because she made her intentions quite clear."

"I know she did."

"Then you'll remember I'm here because my friends Pinky and JM"—he gestures to the two of them in conversation with Dalisay—"invited me."

Nicole looks at him, a sharp smile of her own spreading across her face, and she tips her head. "I like you, Evan."

Evan grins back, coy, and eats another *puto* as innocent as can be. While he knows this isn't a game, it is becoming kind of fun. And because his guard is down, he doesn't hear the clown coming up behind him.

Evan actually showed up. She can't believe it. And yet here he is, eating *puto* and chatting with her siblings.

She had her suspicions after her mom had mentioned the family had been invited to Angel's party, but she didn't actually think Evan would follow through with the first step. He's lucky her mom couldn't make it today or else she would have been hounding him for hours. Dalisay can't stop herself from glancing his way, and every time she does, she scolds herself for checking him out. These Five Stages aren't real, she has to remember that.

His friends, meanwhile, have taken it upon themselves to see the first stage through to completion. Pinky wasted almost no time introducing herself. Even though this is the first time they've met, Dalisay feels like she's known the short, chatty Filipina American girl for years. Pinky has that kind of extroverted energy that wraps introverts like Dalisay into a spiderweb of friendship so quickly that the introvert doesn't know it's happening until it's too late.

Pinky's shorter than Dalisay, with a round face and her hair in a high ponytail that bounces when she talks, she's so animated. "I was telling your sister earlier, too. You should come to my store," Pinky says. "We have tons of board games, and anyone can play for free. I have a feeling you're into games."

"What makes you say that?" Dalisay asks, amused. She likes Pinky already.

"You're smart, you like strategy, and you have a competitive glint in your eye."

That makes Dalisay grin. "Am I that obvious?"

"It's only a theory."

Pinky's not wrong. Dalisay is a big fan of games, especially anything that has a booklet of rules and takes hours to learn. She used to play a game called Ticket to Ride with her father when he was in the hospital. She'd sit, pretzeled at his feet, and they'd play well past visiting hours. It didn't matter if it was cards, or a board game, or chess, she and he were always the ones who enjoyed some friendly competition. They'd sit and talk for hours while playing. Papa was the one she went to first when she needed advice; he was a good listener.

Maybe it was naive of her, but she thought he would get better, and they could play together for years to come, but it was only after he died that she realized she always won against him, because maybe for him it was never losing. The memory pricks deep in Dalisay's nose and she rubs it to clear the feeling away.

"I *have* been looking for something to do after work," she says. "I need someplace to decompress after dealing with my American coworkers all day."

Pinky's lips curl knowingly as Dalisay's eyes flick toward Evan.

Idly, she knows that Daniel is taking shots at Evan, probing him for information, and she's surprised how well he seems to be holding his own, though she can tell Evan's a bit on edge. He's jumpy and keeps glancing over his shoulder for some reason.

"Speaking of, you two have so much in common," Pinky says. "Evan and you."

Of course. The oh-so-natural segue. "Really?"

"Really! He's not at all what he seems. And I'm not saying this because of the first stage."

Dalisay raises a dubious eyebrow. "His first impression was not ideal. Are all American men so bold?"

"Evan was just having an off day. Wasn't he, JM?"

JM appears, handing Pinky a red Solo cup to drink. "Wasn't he what?"

"I was just telling Dalisay about how good of a guy Evan is even though he was so bold as to ask her out on a date?" she says, prompting him with an elbow nudge. "How he's not a slob, and dresses well, and showers daily. And that he loves games."

"Oh!" JM jumps. "Yeah! Definitely. He's one of my best friends. You two would be a good match."

That makes Dalisay laugh. Her gaze goes back to Evan as Nicole trades places with Daniel after her brother leaves.

Nicole's whole face brightens when she laughs with Evan. They seem to be getting along.

It's been days since Dalisay saw Nicole at the hospital. Who was that woman she was with? Dalisay can't stop thinking about it. All this time, she thought her sister just didn't like anyone . . . She'd hoped that Nicole would tell her in her own time, but so far Nicole has been silent on the matter.

It is satisfying to see Evan squirm a little while Nicole talks with him, Dalisay has to admit. Perhaps Nicole's powers of intimidation can knock some sense into him. She takes a deep, steadying breath. "You really think Evan can do all five stages?"

"When he wants something, he'll go for it."

Dalisay laughs, doubtful. "I have high expectations."

Pinky touches Dalisay lightly on the arm and leans in, talking low. "From what I heard, you can really hold your own against him. You threw him for a loop with that Manila line. You're both quick-witted, I'll give you that."

"He's definitely something! I didn't know what to make of him. Like, when he first agreed to do the stages, he said he would 'whole-ass' it."

Pinky laughs, eyes crinkling. "He said that? 'Whole-ass'?"

"Yes! I didn't know what he was talking about at first! I thought that he meant 'asshole'!" Dalisay snorts, covering her hand with her mouth as she laughs.

Pinky bends over laughing too. "Oh my God, what a dweeb. That's so Evan. I love the shit out of him." She looks at him across the hall wistfully, and Dalisay can tell she means it. Pinky reaches out and touches a hand to Dalisay's shoulder. "No, but for real, Evan's probably the furthest thing from an asshole, trust me. But he does have a tendency to be stupid when he sees pretty things. Now that I've met you, I can see why he'd get all dumb, so don't hold that against him."

Dalisay wants to ask more, but just before she can— *HONK!*—a party horn goes off.

And Evan screams: "FUCK!"

Dalisay looks toward the sound. From the looks of things, a clown sneaked up behind him and blasted a party horn near his ear.

The whole room drops into a shocked silence, staring at Evan. The clown mimes laughter, throwing his hands up in celebration, and skips away on squeaky shoes, off to find his next victim.

JM gapes, Dalisay slaps her hand over her mouth, and Pinky nearly spits out her drink, also struggling to contain an outburst of giggles.

While Evan apologizes profusely, Dalisay spins around so no one can see her smile. He's afraid of clowns! Somehow learning that about him is akin to picking up a rock and discovering it's a geode—there's more to Evan Saatchi beneath the surface than she thought.

While it's admirable he's made it through the first stage— she's getting teased by his friends, isn't she?—he's got a lot of work ahead of him. She's not sure he's ready for what comes next, and no matter what Pinky or JM says, she's determined not to let him win. She *is* competitive, and two can play at this game.

As if on cue, one of the children asks their parents, "What does 'fuck' mean?"

CHAPTER FIVE

"I gotta say," says JM, looking up at Evan while he's prone on the bench press, "you really know how to make an impression."

At the gym the following morning, Evan and JM meet up for their usual workout. At this hour, the place is packed, full of sounds of clanging iron plates and up-tempo pop music and the whine of the blender making protein smoothies.

Standing behind JM, Evan spots him as he starts his reps, breathing in and out with each press on the bar, but Evan's thoughts are still at the recreation center yesterday. "I'm such an ass."

JM laughs but it comes out like a hiss as the veins in his neck start popping out. "You aren't—ugh—an ass." His words are strained. Comic-Con is months away, but it's never too early to start beefing up for the right look. "You just—*hff*—messed—*hng*—up."

"That's ten," Evan says, and JM heaves the bar back into place, and they switch. Evan plops down on the bench. "Dalisay probably already thinks I'm an ass, though. Good thing I'm not actually trying to date her. That ship has sailed."

"You seem to really care a lot about her opinion of you." JM pauses for a moment, then asks, "You sure this is about a bet?"

"What are you talking about?"

"Never mind. Don't overthink it." He slaps the bar. "Quit slacking. Ten reps, go."

Dalisay is the first thing Evan sees when he walks into the kitchen at Overnight. She's got her back turned to him, but she looks over her shoulder when she hears him come in. A flush threatens to creep its way up his neck, but he tamps it back down as he walks toward her.

She's making herself a cup of mango green tea and offers Evan a tea bag, which he accepts gladly. She doesn't seem mad about what happened at the birthday party at least.

"So, did I pass the first stage?" he asks as he pours some still-hot kettle water into his mug.

Dalisay brings her own mug to her lips without taking a sip and instead gently blows on her tea. "Technically yes, the teasing of friends did occur."

Evan smiles. "And you thought I'd back down."

"That remains to be seen. You've barely even started."

"Whatever you've got, bring it."

Dalisay's eyes sparkle and her lips part into a wider smile. She sets the mug down and levels her shoulders. "Stage Two is the Presentation of Gifts."

Evan lets out a laugh. "For real?"

"Flowers, notes, little things. Think Valentine's Day but all week, starting next Monday."

"What, you think I'm made of money?"

"I'm giving you five chances to impress me." She tips her head back to look down her nose at him. "Or are you giving up?"

Evan drags his teeth over his bottom lip and grins. "Joke's on you. I'm an *unbelievable* gift giver," he says.

"We'll see."

Evan shakes his head and laughs. This was starting to sound like bribery. "Okay, Ramos. You better be prepared to have your socks knocked off."

"Socks better not be one of the gifts."

"They aren't now."

"Impress me," she says again. Her nose wrinkles when she smiles wider and Evan's heart thumps. She moves to leave but pauses. "Oh, and I looked over your article for the holiday rollout. I sent you some notes on it. You might want to review before you send it to print."

"You edited my article?"

"I saw it in the shared submission folder and noticed there were some errors, so I made the appropriate changes, and gave you some suggestions on your next pass. You can thank me later."

A pang of annoyance shoots through him. "I didn't ask you to do that."

"Is it a problem?"

Heat rises on Evan's cheeks as he lies. "No."

Dalisay turns and dips her chin into her shoulder as she shrugs. It would be adorable if Evan wasn't so flustered.

Before work the following Monday morning, Evan makes a quick stop at a boutique near the office called Gifts & Such. He chooses a huge, white teddy bear, a bundle of shiny red balloons, and a fancy, embossed card. Sure, it's cliché, but isn't that kind of the point? To be ostentatious? Or is it *too* cliché? It takes him a second to remind himself that the gift itself doesn't really matter. This is simply about getting through Stage Two. And one stage closer to the tour. He's not going to let Dalisay win that easily.

The fact that Dalisay critiqued his work is still a sore spot whenever he remembers it. Sure, he types fast and auto-correct is his worst enemy, but he doesn't need her to be his editor. They don't work in the same department, why should she care? But if it had been anyone else, would he have gotten that flustered about it? There were some embarrassing mistakes in there. He might have even been grateful. Maybe it's because of the bet that he feels like he's in constant competition with her. He needs to really wow her with Stage Two if he wants to win. He grabs another balloon.

By the time he gets Bettie to the parking garage it's still early and Overnight's office is quiet and unpopulated, but Evan makes quick work of dropping off the gifts on Dalisay's desk without being seen. Who knows how HR would react if they saw him giving gifts to a coworker, even if she does work in a different department?

Despite the fact she's only just started working at Overnight, she's already made the space her own. A soft, gray sweater drapes across the back of her office chair, and a few framed photos of her family smile back at him from around her computer. In one photo, he recognizes her, Daniel, and Nicole smiling at a Mexican restaurant called Otra. He loves that place; he'd recognize the blue papers hanging on the ceiling anywhere.

Lavender hand lotion and a cute ceramic tissue box shaped like a pineapple and a small, mason jar terrarium make the space downright homey. All her paperwork and notes are meticulously organized, not even a pencil out of alignment.

So this is where she corrects his articles, cutting through his ego with a simple click of Track Changes. The more he gets to know her, the more it feels like they're on opposite teams, vying to score the first point. Evan is determined not to let her get under his skin so easily.

He sets the stuffed bear down on her chair, situating it so it looks like it's typing on her keyboard, and ties the balloons to the armrest so they don't float away. Propped up on her keyboard, he places the card.

On it, he'd written:

I hope we're not polar opposites! —Evan

He didn't need to write a note, but he'd wanted to. From across the floor, he hears the elevator doors open and glances at his watch. She'll be here any minute.

Evan crosses the floor, returning to his section, and shrugs off his jacket just as Riggs gets to his desk, the coffee Evan bought already waiting for him. "For me? You shouldn't have!"

"Yeah, yeah," Evan says, distractedly, unable to stop himself from glancing back at Dalisay's desk.

"What are you doing here so early anyway?" Riggs asks.

Evan explains the parameters of Stage Two and Riggs spots the gifts at Dalisay's desk. "Balloons? Really?"

"I wanted to go all out." He keeps glancing toward Dalisay's cubicle, wondering when she'll arrive. He can't wait to see what her reaction will be.

Riggs huffs a laugh into his coffee. "You have no imagination."

Evan spreads his palms, baffled. "Yeah, okay, like you know anything about romance."

"I know enough to know *that* won't get you in her good graces."

"I'm not trying to change her mind about me. If anything, I'm proving that this is a lot of work for one date." Riggs laughs at that.

"And this is why you're single. Which reminds me, I've got a new neighbor. Get this—she's recently divorced, a Pilates instructor, *and* she has the cutest golden retriever puppy. Want me to set you up?"

"No thanks."

"You sure?"

"I'm sure."

"You're taking this bet really seriously."

Evan screws up his face, about to ask him what's wrong with that, but just then, he hears Dalisay's ringing voice say good morning to the receptionist.

Here she comes.

Evan can't help but watch as Dalisay navigates her way to her desk, smiling and greeting people as she goes.

When Dalisay reaches her desk, she pauses there, with a small, amused smile dimpling her cheeks. She looks around, and sees Evan standing there, still looking her way. What's the point in hiding?

She raises a delicate eyebrow, and her smile grows wider.

Hiding his own smile, he raises his coffee to her as if to say *Cheers.*

Dalisay takes the balloons in one hand and the teddy bear in the other, his card pinched delicately between her index and middle finger like a cigarette, and starts walking toward the far wall.

She stops at a tall trash can next to the kitchen. With little ceremony, she shoves the bear into the trash, punching its large head through the opening, then uses her teeth to let the air out of the balloons one by one. Finally, she reads the card, lingers on it for a moment, then throws it in the trash with the rest.

She looks back at Evan and cocks her head, as if to say, *Your move.*

Naomi appears near the conference room and calls out to the floor. "Editorial meeting! Five minutes, people!"

The editors, including Dalisay, Riggs, and Evan, join her in the conference room but even after the meeting starts and Naomi has written ideas on the whiteboard for new articles, the only thing Evan can think about is Dalisay.

She sits across the conference table from him, listening dutifully as the senior members discuss assignments, but their voices become a monotonous drone in Evan's ears.

She didn't like his gifts. No, that's not right. She *hated* them. He's going to have to try a lot harder if he's going to win the bet. Daniel and Nicole gave him some hints about what Dalisay likes, but those things now seem too predictable. She asked him to impress, so he needs to think bigger.

While the meeting goes on, he spends most of the hour googling different gift ideas, even going so far as to calculate shipping costs and delivery times. Only when the room goes oddly quiet does Evan snap back into his body. All eyes are on him. Oh God, someone said his name.

"What? Huh?"

Across the conference table, Dalisay rests her chin on her hand, watching him with wide, innocent eyes. She's enjoying this.

He turns to look at Naomi at the front of the room, who holds her hands out expectantly. She is not a patient woman. Heat rushes to Evan's face as he shifts in his seat and clears his throat. "Sorry, can you repeat that?" It's like high school when he'd been caught reading a novel during math class.

"I *said*," repeats Naomi, slowly, "I want you to take the lead on this next project."

What this next project is, Evan doesn't have a clue. His face burns but Riggs gives him a wink, signaling that he's got him. Dalisay looks infuriatingly pleased with herself. Is she some kind of witch? Did she cast a spell on him? He loves this job more than anything in the world, but all he can think about is her.

Evan recovers and gives Naomi an easy smile. "Not a problem."

Naomi snaps her fingers. "On second thought, I think you need some help." Before he can assure Naomi he doesn't, she says, "Dalisay, how about you two team up on this one."

At the mention of her name, Dalisay's smile drops. She sits up straighter in her chair, tearing her eyes away from Naomi to look at Evan. The way she's acting, it's as if Naomi asked her to leap off the roof.

"Sure," Dalisay says, her cheeks turning a dark shade of pink. "Evan needs all the help he can get."

* * *

Every day of the week, Evan tries again, and each time, he means to impress Dalisay. For real this time.

On Tuesday, he brings her truffles from Kokak Chocolates because Daniel said she has a sweet tooth.

On Wednesday, it's a bouquet of lavender flowers from Rozgol's, because of the lavender-scented lotion she uses.

On Thursday, he gives her a gourmet gift basket full of top-shelf tequila from Tahona Mercado because of the picture of her and her siblings at Otra on her desk.

And every single one of those days, he watches as she throws them all away, announcing her opinions to the office:

"Truffles are too rich," she says.

"A bouquet of lavenders are a symbol of distrust," she says.

"Tequila, before noon? No thanks," she says. Riggs fishes it out of the trash can so he can have it for himself.

At this point, it's starting to feel personal. Nothing's stopping Dalisay from intentionally disapproving of his gifts. For all he knows, she's doing it on purpose just so he'll lose. And here he trusted she'd play fair too, but she has all the power.

Evan's about ready to pull his hair out. It's not about the bet at this point, it's his pride. He always thought he was a good gift giver. He always pays attention to what his friends want or need. When his friends mention something, he actually remembers because he genuinely wants to make them happy. When he was dating Becca, he'd plan gifts months in advance, like tickets to a Broadway show on tour that she kept talking about. He isn't the type to run to the corner store on an anniversary because he forgot.

But now, it's as if Dalisay is proving how much she hates his guts. And she's almost flaunting it.

There has to be something he remembers that she likes. There has to be.

But luck is still on his side, because Thursday night, he catches a break. Dalisay's brother Daniel mentioned that she likes bookstores, and it just so happens that Heliotrope has a limited-edition scented candle that smells exactly like old books, with chai and a hint of citrus. Triple whammy. Evan saw it in a window display when he was leaving the gym with JM, and he practically burst through the glass like the Kool-Aid man to get the last one. The last time they'd had it in stock, he bought one for himself because it smells exactly like his favorite bookstore, Hooked On Books. If she hates this, there's no hope. At least he'll get to keep it when she throws it in the trash.

He leaves the final gift on her desk Friday morning, exactly as he's been doing for the past week.

The note he wrote for her this time says:

Here's to stories worth telling. —Evan

It feels appropriate. This is definitely a story he'll be telling at dinner parties in the future.

This time when Dalisay sees his gift, she reads the note, taking a beat longer than usual, and Evan's chest swells with hope.

She lifts the scented candle to her nose and takes a sniff. Her eyelids flutter and her shoulders drop. She sets the candle back down on her desk.

Evan grins. *Finally.*

* * *

When five o'clock rolls around that Friday, Evan is wiped from having written three articles this week, and his brain feels like mush. He's just about ready to text JM asking what they want to eat during D&D tonight, when Maggie the intern appears, balancing several trays of coffee in her outstretched arms that teeter dangerously as she delivers to-go cups down the row of desks. She'd gone on an early-afternoon Starbucks run for the whole office.

Maggie is barely out of high school, a college freshman with mousy brown hair, big glasses, and a soft voice. She's big into crochet, and she makes most of her clothes, including the messenger bag she wears at her side to keep all her notebooks and pens for work. All week, Maggie's been helping Evan and Dalisay with their big project from Naomi. It's a full analysis comparing cities in Europe and Asia with a *if you like this, then you'll like that* angle that Naomi hopes can spin out lots of content, and it requires a ton of cross-references and contact information for hotels and tour guides. And caffeine. Lots of caffeine.

He can see the looming disaster playing out in slow motion.

Before Evan can jump up to help her, Maggie lets out a squeak as the trays get unbalanced and topple sideways. A dozen to-go cups spill over, emptying their contents down the front of Evan's shirt.

He stands frozen, arms up, coffee plastering his button-down to his chest and dripping down his elbows. The coffee's so hot but he doesn't notice.

"Ah! Sorry, Evan!" Maggie cries.

Evan blinks coffee out of his eyes, still frozen in place. "It's okay! I'm okay!" Evan says, assuring her. She looks like she's on the verge of tears and the whole office is staring at them, but he addresses everyone with a smile. "Can't get enough of the stuff."

His lame joke brings everyone's attention away from Maggie. He's been an intern before, he knows how it goes; she's doing her best. Riggs offers to call the custodian and Evan picks up the coffee cups while Maggie rushes to the kitchen for paper towels. When she comes back, she's red-cheeked and on the verge of a panic attack.

"You don't have to help!" she says to Evan, her voice thick. "It's my mess."

"Please, let me. It's the least I can do." He takes one of the paper towels and wipes his face before using it on the floor. "You didn't have to carry all this. You could have made a few trips."

"I'm so sorry!" she says again. Maggie's blush is bright.

"It's okay, really. Next time you can take it slower. I promise, coffee isn't that important." He smiles at her, and she blushes even more furiously. Something in her purse on the floor catches his attention. It's a Heliotrope candle.

A lump forms in Evan's throat. "Um, Maggie. Where did you get that candle?"

Maggie looks at him, wide-eyed, then looks in her crocheted bag. "Oh! I didn't steal it, I swear!"

Evan lets out a breathy laugh. "I didn't think you did. I was just wondering."

"I-I-It's from Dalisay," she stammers. "She wanted to thank me for all my hard work this week. I don't think she knows how much I love these candles."

"Yeah, me too," he says, a little crestfallen. He had really hoped this gift would be the one she loved.

Once they've cleaned up what they could, and Maggie thanks him again profusely, he grabs his travel bag, the one he usually keeps under his desk for short-notice trips, and takes out a fresh shirt.

Before he goes to the bathroom to change, he makes a stop in the kitchen for some table salt, a hack he picked up when he spilled coffee all over his pants in the middle of a transatlantic flight, so he knows what to do before the stain sets.

But, as luck would have it, Dalisay is tidying up in the kitchen, reorganizing the tea bags. Of course, this day is getting better and better. He bites back a curse, but she hears him come in, and her eyes nearly bug out of her head when she looks at him. That's when he realizes how transparent his thin, white button-down is when it's wet. He might as well be shirtless. Her mouth drops open, gaze flicking to his torso briefly before returning to his face with a stupefied expression.

Exposed, Evan shields himself with his arms, but it's not hiding a lot. Something about being perceived by her is doing something to him he can't quite articulate.

Heat burns through him, almost as hot as the coffee did. "Salt," he says, as if that would make sense to her.

But without question, she opens the cupboard and holds out the salt canister. Evan has to shuffle over to take it, because she's averting her gaze, her jaw muscles clenched tight.

"Thanks," he says.

She nods stiffly. "Baking soda."

"What?"

"Baking soda works too, if the salt doesn't."

"Right, uh, yeah. Thanks," he says again, walking backward. Still using his arms to hide, Evan rushes to the bathroom.

At the sink, he douses his shirt in table salt and lets it soak up the coffee for a few minutes while he changes, trying to rid himself of the memory of Dalisay's face when she looked at him. In cosplay, he's used to being stared at, but this was different. This was Dalisay.

Half an hour later, with his wet but stain-free shirt in hand, he leaves the bathroom, fully clothed once more. This week couldn't have been any more of a disaster. He's pretty sure he's still blushing from the way Dalisay stared at him, and it doesn't go away, especially not when he spots her leaving for the day, her bag thrown over her shoulder.

He must catch her eye too, because she looks his way, and her mouth presses into a thin line. Wordlessly, she stretches her hand overhead and waves goodbye. Pinched between her fingers is the card he'd given her with the candle.

Something between them just happened, and he isn't sure what to make of it. One thing is for sure, he's met his match. This really wasn't as easy as he thought.

CHAPTER SIX

In the middle of the pantry aisle at Cal-Mart, Dalisay stares at the canister of table salt in her hand, her mind firmly back in that kitchen at Overnight. She can't stop thinking about seeing Evan in that soaked shirt.

She knew something had happened from the way Maggie hurried into the kitchen in a panic, grabbing all the paper towels before leaving again, but Dalisay didn't quite know the . . . extent of it, not until Evan walked in looking like Mr. Darcy climbing out of that lake. A coffee-filled lake, for the purposes of this scenario. The way Evan's wet button-down clung to his body was hardly better than if he were naked. She could see *everything.* How solid his pecs are, how narrow his waist is compared to his shoulders; she could even count his abs.

It left nothing to the imagination.

But he looked so embarrassed, and she feels like a creep for having stared for so long, even if it was only for a second. If their roles were reversed, she would have been mortified.

She almost doesn't hear Nicole as she rides up on the grocery cart, braking hard with her sneaker to come to a stop right next to her.

"Dalisay? Hello? Did you hear me?" asks Nicole.

Dalisay starts. "What?"

"I asked if you knew where Mama is."

"Oh, um, deli, I think?" Dalisay puts the salt in the cart.

"You okay?" Nicole peers at Dalisay with a skeptical eye.

"Yep!" Dalisay grabs the front of the cart while Nicole balances on the back, riding it as usual. Dalisay's determined not to let the sight of Evan's perfectly adequate torso become a core memory, but sheer willpower alone doesn't seem like it's enough to erase it. She can't stop thinking about him.

After she got home from work, she decided to join Nicole and their mom to buy all the ingredients for Lola's famous oxtail soup, *kare kare*, that she's making this weekend.

Cal-Mart is like most American grocery stores, sprawling with wide aisles and bright displays. The first time Dalisay set foot in one, she was shocked by how big it was. If deciding between two bookcases in IKEA wasn't frustrating enough, the overwhelming array of choices between six different brands selling the same tomatoes, or cheese, or milk was almost paralyzing at first. She got used to it, of course, but she wasn't expecting culture shock at a *grocery store* for God's sake.

"So how's it going with you and Big Brown Eyes?" Nicole asks, stopping the cart at the tower of mangos. She squeezes one and holds it up to her nose. "He pass step two?"

Dalisay blushes. "Evan?" How is it she can get so flustered even saying his name?

"Who else?" Nicole tosses a couple mangos into the cart and moves on to the cartons of strawberries. Ever since Nicole met Evan that day at the birthday party, she's been teasing

Dalisay about how *so her type* Evan is, despite Dalisay's pro-tests that it isn't like that at all, that it's all for a bet.

"Stage two was sort of a dud. The first day he gave me balloons—"

Nicole barks out a laugh.

"He ended the week strong, though. He got me a candle that smelled like books." She didn't mention the note he'd written. It's still in her purse.

"So is he moving on to stage three?"

Dalisay idly organizes the disheveled rows of blueberry cartons, giving her hands something to do. "I don't know."

"What's there not to know about? I'm starting to think you're chickening out . . ."

"I am not!"

"Well then, don't you think you're being a little unfair? He went through stage two. I think that means he passed."

Dalisay narrows her eyes. "You just want to hear what he does for stage three."

A devilish smile spreads across Nicole's lips. "Maybe I do. I want to see how he does. I like him."

That, coming from Nicole, is a lot.

Dalisay smiles and puts some blueberries into the cart, and they make their way toward the back of the store. "I'm going to check on Mom," Dalisay says, and Nicole splits off to keep shopping.

When Dalisay gets to the deli, she watches helplessly as her mom cuts in front of a man already standing there, his arms folded firmly across his chest.

Dalisay rushes over and puts a hand on her elbow. "Mom, you can't cut here."

Her mom looks around like it just occurred to her what she did. "Oh! Well, then." She turns back and continues ordering from the person behind the deli counter.

Heat rushes up Dalisay's cheeks as she apologizes to the man for her. "I'm sorry. She'll be quick."

The man glares at her, obviously miffed, and Dalisay can only give him an apologetic smile.

As if disproving Dalisay's point, her mother whips out a piece of paper and peers through the glasses perched on the end of her nose at the long list of sliced meats and cheese. Thankfully, another person appears behind the counter to help the man. When her mom is finally done, Dalisay steers her away from there before she can cause any more social slights. In Manila, it was common for older women to cut the line. Old habits die hard. "I'm sure he didn't mind. Besides," she says, and gestures with her wrist in a cast, "I should go first because I'm injured."

Last week, her mom tripped and fell on an uneven patch of sidewalk while taking a walk around the block and fractured her wrist. Yet another cultural shock coming to America— after the hospital visit, getting the bill later was a real blow. It cost thousands of dollars, even with insurance. Everything in America is so much capital-M More.

It's no use arguing with her mother, especially about something as trivial as line etiquette, so Dalisay takes the deli items from her mom's hands, and they meet up with Nicole again in the cereal aisle. Nicole is checking her phone and smiling and only notices them coming when they're a few feet away.

"Who are you texting?" Dalisay asks as she puts the items in the cart, but Nicole slips her phone back into her jeans.

"No one. Just work."

Nicole's cheeks are pink, and her eyes are bright, so Dalisay is pretty sure it's not "just work" but she says nothing.

Together, they follow their mom through the rest of the store, but someone catches her eye, making Dalisay's heart leap before she does a double take. *Evan.*

Except, no. He has the same dark hair, the same broad shoulders, but it's not him. Dalisay's heart sinks a little as she watches the stranger, who actually doesn't look like Evan at all, pick up a giant pack of toilet paper and head to the front registers.

This isn't the first time she's thought she spotted Evan outside of work, and every time it happens it feels like her heart is going to leap out of her chest. Last week, it was when she was at Pinky's game store.

She's not sure why, but the idea of seeing him out in the wild, as it were, feels like a secret she needs to keep from her mom. If her mom found out Evan was doing the stages for a bet, and not with any intention of actually dating, she would throw a fit. It's the kind of cultural ritual that is supposed to be sacred, not something to play around with. Dalisay knows more than most that playing with hearts is a dangerous game, and she also knows that it's hypocritical of her to treat the Five Stages so carelessly, but what she and Evan have isn't real, so it can't count.

And yet, she'd be kidding herself if she wasn't a little disappointed that she didn't see Evan just now. She can't seem to get him out of her mind.

While the truth might upset her mother, she wonders if her father would have felt the same way. He was always the more playful one of her parents, the one who saw humor in life, who would have been curious to see if a guy like Evan would even try, for the fun of it. She can almost hear his laugh if he were still here, and—with a jolt—she wishes he could have been around to meet Evan. What would he have thought about him? Would he have liked that Evan is smart? That he's not going back on his word? That he makes her laugh?

"You never answered my question earlier," Nicole says, stealing the cart back while Dalisay isn't paying attention. "About if he's going to move on to stage three."

Dalisay considers it a moment, then she pulls out her phone.

Unknown Number:

Congratulations, Mr. Saatchi. You're moving on to stage three. ;)

Me:

Dalisay?

Unknown Number:

Bingo.

Me:

Who gave you my number?

Dalisay Ramos:

I have my ways. Mwah-ha-ha. >:)

Me:

Never took you for the type to still use . . . what are these called? (It was Pinky, wasn't it.)

Dalisay Ramos:

Emoticons, duh. It's a superior art form. You wouldn't understand. (Yes.) Coffee stain come out?

Me:

All clear. What's stage three theme

Me:

then*?

Dalisay Ramos:

And ruin the surprise?

Me:

I'm quaking in my boots.

Dalisay Ramos:

0:-3

Me:

Is that an angel face?

Dalisay Ramos 💬:

hehe ;3

Me:

:-p

Evan's heart hammers in his throat as he stares at the tongue-sticking-out emoticon before hitting send. Is that coming off flirty? He deletes it and opts for a safer exaggerated frown face. :-c

But in his haste, he hits the "x" instead and on autopilot his thumb hits send.

Me:
:-X

He stares in terror as an accidental kissy face text stares back at him. This is ten times worse.

Three dots appear next to Dalisay's name, then disappear. They don't appear again after another second. What is she thinking? Did she just assume—?

"Shit." Evan starts typing again, heart hammering, making the edit.

Me:
:-c*

Dalisay Ramos 🦋:
See, this is why you have so many spelling errors. :-p

At The Basement for D&D that night, Evan asks what comes next. After the flop that were all his gifts in stage two, frankly, he's surprised he's made it this far.

"Let me guess," he says while JM sets up for the campaign, aligning all the enemy figures on the grid. "For stage three, I have to sing a song about my undying love?"

JM and Pinky share another knowing look.

Reality sets in. Evan shakes his head. He was just being facetious! "No. *No, no, no.*"

"For real?" Riggs asks. "Evan's gotta sing a song?"

JM nods. "It's the stage called 'The Serenade.' The potential suitor gathers friends and serenades the lady with a song about his love for her."

"And," chimes in Pinky, "if she likes it, she will sing back. It's mega romantic."

"We didn't want to tell you in case . . . ," JM says, smiling awkwardly.

Of all the possible things he could have to do . . . He's always been a terrible singer, and singing in front of a gorgeous woman is a special kind of nightmare, right up there with ones about taking a test he didn't study for and his teeth falling out.

"It won't be that bad," JM says.

"Yeah!" says Pinky. "It's just like cosplay. You aren't nervous then."

"Cosplay is different, and you know it! Dressing up like Spider-Man is not like singing in public!"

Evan is confident in a lot of things, and that confidence allows him to know his limits. Singing is one of them.

"It's all about mindset," says Pinky. She presses her hands overhead, like she's unfurling an invisible banner. "Positive thoughts!"

While it's easy to slip into character at a convention, performing for Dalisay feels like a cruel and particularly unusual punishment. Cosplay is fun. But this? Evan might puke. "I *actually* have to sing?" His voice sounds pathetic even to him.

"You don't have to be Freddie Mercury or anything," says Pinky. "It's about the passion. Confidence! Kurt Cobain had one of the worst voices ever, but it didn't stop literally everyone on the planet throwing their underwear at him."

"In case you haven't noticed, I'm not Kurt Cobain!"

"Oh, we noticed," murmurs JM.

Pinky shushes him. "Do you want to win this or not?"

She's right, of course. He can't back out now because of a tiny little fear of looking stupid or sounding bad. "Can't I just—I don't know—pull a Lloyd Dobler and stand outside her window holding a phone above my head playing a Taylor Swift song or something?"

Everyone boos him.

"Come on, Evan," Pinky says. "Go big or go home! We can help you again!"

She looks at JM and Riggs, but Riggs is already typing away on his phone, a devious smile on his face.

"Who are you texting?" JM asks.

"No one!" Riggs says, innocently enough. Everyone knows that's a lie. "But I don't think you're going to do it."

Evan tries to smile, but the sweat on his palms is a dead giveaway. What did he get himself into? *Tokyo, think of Tokyo*, he tells himself. He has to win this. *Whole-ass.* "Fine! I'll do it. But I can't break out into song at work, can I?" Evan asks, surreptitiously wiping his hands on his thighs.

"Hey, it might shake up the editorial meeting," Riggs says, still smiling.

JM says, "No, Evan's right. He can't do it at work. It needs to be someplace personal, someplace meaningful. You can't skirt by like you did in stage two. I think it was *generous* that she let you move on to stage three."

Evan thinks about it for a moment. The community center is out, for sure. The office is a no-go. What's another place he can meet her? He remembers their first meeting, talking about the mochi-making demonstration. "How about the Asian Art Museum?" he asks.

Pinky claps loudly, once. "Brilliant! I'll text Dalisay, make it a girls' day, and bring her next Saturday afternoon."

"That's not a lot of time to practice," says JM.

"Love doesn't need practice," says Pinky.

"Who said anything about love?" Evan asks.

Pinky raises a shoulder and smiles.

A moan catches in Dalisay's throat and her eyes snap open.

Evan . . .

Her insides undulate, pulsing with the rhythm of her rapid heartbeat, even as the dream fades. She squirms, her body curling with pleasure, still half in dream. But when she stretches her arm out, she finds no one beside her.

Of course. He's not here.

Dalisay squeezes her eyes shut, blocking out the morning light creeping through the curtains, and still she sees his face. Those hooded eyes, the straight line of his jaw, the way one corner of his mouth lifts when he smiles like he knows something she doesn't. It's infuriating in real life, but in that dream . . . She presses her hands to her eyes and blots out his face, trying to scrub it from her brain.

That's never happened before. Like most dreams, it made no sense, but it felt so real.

She was on her old street in Manila, in her childhood backyard digging for something, but it wasn't really her yard because it was a bed, and Evan was there, fully clothed, and he didn't say anything as he leaned in and kissed her and then they were naked. She remembers the way his kiss deepened and how his hands searched her until the pressure built and hammered through her. She clung to him as . . .

Dalisay swallows thickly. They had sex. No, that's too neat to describe what they did.

They fucked. And it was incredible.

She puts her hands to her sweaty forehead and fists her hair, telling herself to get a grip. It wasn't real, it was only a dream. It doesn't mean anything. It doesn't mean *anything*!

It's not her fault Evan's been on her mind. He's made it hard for her to ignore him, intentionally or not.

That stupid coffee incident.

She's always prided herself on having a brain, some sensibility, measured control over herself for God's sake, and here she is, being driven half-insane by the first six-pack she sees.

Forget her comfort zone, Evan's flung her out of orbit.

This is not how it was supposed to go. Plus, she's getting worked up over nothing. He's not interested in her since she said she's not interested in him, she knows that. He said so when they first made the bet. Abs or no abs, that shouldn't matter. She will not let him get to her like this, even if her body has other ideas.

She can still feel the ghost of his hands as she wrenches herself into a sitting position. Behind her closed door, she can distantly hear the clatter of breakfast being made in the kitchen. It's Saturday; that means it's *tapsilog* for breakfast, and she can already smell the garlic fried rice. That snaps her back to reality.

She checks her phone. There's a missed text from Pinky last night, something about a girls' day, but Dalisay is too wound up to pay attention to the details. She can still feel Evan's breath on her neck, and she stands up so abruptly that, if he were actually here, she would have smashed his nose.

In the shower, she lets the hot water pour over her face and forces herself to take deep, calming breaths, but the thought of him follows her. What would Evan's hands feel like for real? The stubble on his cheeks? The softness of his lips?

"It doesn't mean anything!"

She must have said that out loud, though, because Nicole bangs on the door. "What?"

"Nothing!" Dalisay calls back, sputtering on shower water.

"Hurry up! Breakfast's getting cold!"

Dalisay sighs and drowns herself in the shower once more. There's only one way she can snap out of this.

She wrenches the shower knob to the right and the instant change from hot to freezing cold water makes her yelp, and she forgets all about Evan Saatchi.

The next day, Evan meets up with JM at a dance studio owned by their old college friend Yoon-gi in Central Market. JM texted everyone he knew who might have space for them to practice, and Yoon-gi delivered. His studio, Dance on Main, specializes in teaching K-pop dance classes for all ages, and he has some rehearsal rooms with huge mirrors and sound systems.

When Yoon-gi was young, his parents enrolled him in a K-pop trainee boot camp in Seoul where he learned everything from dancing, to singing, to speaking Korean. While their dreams of him becoming a star were short-lived, Yoon-gi was easily the best performer in their undergraduate class, show-casing his own choreography at every talent show and parents' weekend. After he graduated with a BS in business admin, he opened his own studio, and while they still live in the same city, Evan hasn't seen him since they walked across the stage at graduation.

But the second JM and Evan walk in the door, Yoon-gi rushes for Evan and drapes an arm across his shoulders, guiding him through the lobby toward the dance rooms as if no time's passed at all. "Well, well, well, look what the cat dragged in!"

Yoon-gi is a slender, Korean American man with a flop of shining black hair and a face that kind of reminds Evan of a fox with sharp eyes and a sly smile.

"JM told me everything! Who's the lucky guy or gal?" Yoon-gi says, teeth sparkling as he smiles.

Who doesn't *know at this point?* Evan thinks and smiles. "It's not that serious."

"Not that serious? You're doing the Five Stages! That's serious!"

"It's a bet," says JM.

Yoon-gi swivels his head to look at him. "A bet! No one goes this far for a bet." Not everyone is as serious a bettor as Evan. "Whatever you need, my friend, I am at your disposal. You just owe me dinner. A big dinner. Lobster."

JM shoulders his duffel bag. "Two lobsters, even."

Yoon-gi points a knowing finger at JM, then wraps his arm around him next, barraging him with questions about Pinky and what he's been up to, while Yoon-gi leads them to one of the dance rooms. Upon entering, Evan feels out of place in his basketball shorts and T-shirt. A crowd of slender, fit dancers are finishing up practicing in front of a large mirror, their sneakers thumping on the polished wooden floor in sync to a bass-heavy K-pop song. They're all women in their thirties of all ethnicities and they move with confidence and strength. He knows just by looking at them that they've been dancing for years.

The song ends and everyone claps and cheers for a job well done.

A dark-skinned Asian woman at the front pauses the music from the speakers. She seems like the instructor for the group as she turns around and addresses them all. "Good work, ladies! Excellent job! Same time next week. Don't forget to stretch and hydrate." When the group moves to gather their things, she looks over at the three of them. To Yoon-gi she asks, "Need the room?"

"Take your time, Mari. My friend here is going to be practicing a song to woo the love of his life," says Yoon-gi, gesturing to Evan.

Evan refrains from snorting incredulously. No one seems to understand.

While the group packs up and Yoon-gi and JM set up the audio system, Mari says to Evan, "You look nervous."

Evan tilts his head, casually. "What makes you say that?"

Mari smiles with tight lips and scans him. "Let me guess— The Serenade."

"How'd you know?"

"My boyfriend did it for me way back in the day. He had that same look. Deer in headlights."

Evan's smile gives him away, but he lets out a breathy laugh. "It's not what you think."

"No?" she says, grinning. "You wouldn't be so nervous if you didn't care."

Evan's about to protest, but music blares from the speakers, and Yoon-gi and JM scramble to turn it down. The shock of it sets Evan off kilter, and he struggles to find the right way to explain why he's here, but it gets scrambled on the way from his brain to his mouth.

Yes, he's still drawn to Dalisay, but it's not like he's in love with her.

But Mari just smiles at him knowingly, like she's already got him figured out. Before she leaves, she says, "An old stage trick to get over your nerves is to imagine that your audience is naked. It helps. Especially when your audience is a gorgeous girl of your dreams." She winks at him and exchanges a few words with Yoon-gi before she too leaves, giving them the entire space to practice and leaving Evan feeling exposed.

He can't help it. Dalisay, naked, pops into his mind. How smooth her skin would feel, how good she would smell when he presses his nose against the slope of her neck, how soft her breasts would be in his palms—

The song starts up again, this time much quieter, and it snaps Evan back into himself. He can't help that he's physically attracted to her, but fantasizing about Dalisay won't do him any good. Mari is wrong. She doesn't know the situation at all. Dalisay isn't interested in him. He can't let his own feelings get in the way.

He forces himself to think of anything else that can redirect the blood flow back into the rest of his body. Basketball. Airplane tray tables. How they make stop signs.

"What song are we doing?" Evan asks a little too loudly.

"'Maharani' by Alamat," says JM. "They're a Filipino boy band."

"Ooh," says Yoon-gi as he stretches his hamstrings and rolls out his shoulders. "I don't know that one. Now it'll be three lobsters."

"You're doing it with us?" asks Evan hopefully.

"Look, I've got the voice of an angel, but I'm only here for backup. We gotta make it a good show. You're the face of the group."

"We'll take it slow," says JM. "The choreography is basic, but there's a lot of moving parts."

JM shows them what to do, reminding Evan that he is going to have to learn the dance as well as the Tagalog lyrics. It's as hard as it sounds, but Evan will try his best. He's in too deep to give up without a fight.

The sky is starting to darken, but it doesn't close the farmers market on Fulton, just around the corner from the Asian Art Museum. Dalisay and Pinky slowly make their way down rows of white tents, taking in the sights and smells. It was Pinky's idea for the two of them to grab something to eat before heading inside, and it seems like everyone else has had the same idea since the market is bustling with crowds of people carrying tote bags full of produce. The smell of fresh-baked bread settles nicely in the afternoon air and reminds Dalisay of going to *palengke*, the public markets in Manila, with her grandmother, Lola, where she would pick the firmest fruit and help carry bags of fish home for dinner. The only difference is that here in San Francisco, it's a lot quieter. Dalisay wonders if it's because of the promise of rain.

Dalisay loves the rain. It always makes her feel giddy with something . . . she can't quite explain. During the rainy season in Manila, one of her favorite memories is of coming back from school, her uniform soaking wet, only to change into comfy dry clothes and bury herself in bed with a good book. Rain means warm blankets and stories. Rain means home.

She tips her head toward the sky and is about to ask Pinky if she checked the forecast, but Pinky is furiously texting away on her phone.

"What's going on?" Dalisay asks.

Pinky starts and looks up, cheeks flushed. It takes her a moment too long to come up with something. "JM. Just giving him updates!"

Dalisay smiles, leaning in. "About what?"

Before Dalisay can see the screen, Pinky cries "Oh, look! Pickles!" and bounds to the stand lined with huge glass jars full of them. She buys them each a pickle, failing to answer Dalisay's question, but Dalisay won't let her get away that easily.

"If this is about The Serenade . . ."

"Who said anything about a serenade?"

Dalisay gives her a look.

Relenting, Pinky takes a deep breath and rolls her eyes. "Okay. Fine. Yes, Evan is waiting for you outside the museum right now—" Dalisay bursts into laughter. "He's worked really hard for this! The least we can do is make an appearance."

Dalisay cackles. This is absolutely the point at which she expected Evan to back out. She can't believe he's attempting

The Serenade! He's proving a lot tougher than she thought. But Pinky looks at Dalisay with large, hopeful eyes and Dalisay can't resist.

"If you say so. And here I was hoping that you honestly wanted to see the shipwrecks and Japanese tattoo exhibit just for fun."

"Oh, I still want to see that! But our pre-museum entertainment awaits."

Dalisay lets Pinky drag her through the market and they walk toward the museum entrance. "If nothing else," Pinky says, "we can get a video of it and use it for blackmail later."

When they round the corner, Dalisay hides her laughter behind her hand.

"There they are!" Pinky says, squeezing her other hand tightly.

Indeed, there they are.

The music sounds tinny coming from a small portable speaker by one of the bronze lion statues near the entrance as Evan, JM, and another man—Yoon-gi, a college friend, according to Pinky—start to dance in sync with each other and wearing matching *barongs*, traditional long-sleeved white shirts from the Philippines, each embroidered with white leaf patterns.

Dalisay covers her mouth to keep herself from dissolving into giggles and holds in a snort. She recognizes the song, but she's well beyond her boy band days. She used to dance and sing with Nicole in their room in Manila, loud enough that Daniel would storm in and tell them to keep it down.

This song had to have been either JM's or Pinky's doing. Heat rises in her cheeks, and it's not because of flattery. Evan sways his hips and swings his arms to the choreography, singing along to the tune, and Dalisay can't tell if she wants to make him stop for his own sake or hers.

To make matters worse, the sky opens up. At first it's a single drop, then another, until it's a downpour. In seconds, everyone is drenched. The guys' thin white *barongs* instantly become transparent, but the trio stick to the routine.

A group has gathered to watch and Dalisay realizes some aren't strangers. They cheer Evan on by name, hooting and hollering like it's a sporting event, and a separate group of teenagers films everything on their phones, but still Evan doesn't break eye contact with Dalisay as he sings to the song in Tagalog, a language he obviously doesn't know. When she looks back, she sees his eyes burn with a spark that ignites something in her chest.

Perhaps because it's raining, or maybe because she's had a nice day so far, or because the imprints of that sex dream still linger on the outskirts of her thoughts, but her heart actually skips for a moment.

It's like Evan's looking only at her, trying to say everything he wants to with his body, with his eyes, and—damn him—her smile grows wider. But she presses her fingers to her lips harder.

When the song ends, Evan is totally soaked. She can see his chest through his shirt and can't help but stare as he strikes a finishing pose. If it were anyone else, what Evan is doing might be cheesy and a little ridiculous, but her smile falls as she stares at him, her breath trapped in her chest, as she's overwhelmed by something akin to walking up to the edge of a cliff. It's scary but exhilarating and it makes her feel a little crazy to even entertain the idea that she could jump, because right now she feels like she could fly.

Oh, she thinks. *Oh no.*

She's into him. Like, *really* into him.

Desire washes through her like a giant wave, exactly as in her sex dream. The same swirling tension in her gut, the gooey wobble of her knees, the pulse pounding in her ears . . . She could march right up to him, rip his sopping wet shirt off, and kiss him—

It takes superhuman strength to stay right where she is.

Evan rakes his hand through his wet hair and gives her a boyish grin. "Hey," he says to her.

All at once, the spell is broken. What was she thinking? Heat creeps up her face. She's being ridiculous and totally embarrassing herself. *Get a grip, girl!* she thinks.

"So? Did I pass stage three?" Evan asks, a little breathless.

Dalisay's eyelids flutter as she remembers to breathe too. She has to restrain herself from looking at his chest, visible through his wet shirt, just like that day in the office. For some reason, she's shivering. She blames the rain.

"Your Tagalog is terrible," she says. Then, innuendo unintended, she takes a huge bite of her farmers market pickle.

At work, Dalisay acts as if The Serenade never happened, but Evan finds that he can't keep his eyes off her, especially during their collaboration meeting. She also seems to sense that he can't stop looking, because she keeps glancing up from her laptop, and Evan tries his best to focus on his own screen while being aware of her every movement. It's like they're circling the last seat in a round of musical chairs, waiting for the other one to be caught on their heels. Being alone in the same room with her is making him fidgety.

To her credit, Dalisay hasn't edited his articles since that one time, but he's been taking care to read and reread his work, knowing full well that she might be reading it too. Either she's taken pity on him or his writing's gotten cleaner. He finds himself wanting to impress her and is paying more attention to his style, something he finds both aggravating and confusing. Why does he care what she thinks so much?

"Good job the other day," she says, not looking up from her laptop, typing away with lightning speed. It makes him look up from his own computer, shocked that she brought it up.

"The Serenade?"

She raises her eyebrows, then drags her eyes up to meet his. His heart thumps in his throat. "It was adequate enough. Your performance would make any other girl swoon."

Any *other*? He remembers the way her face fell when he finished the song, the way she stared at him, and he thought he was done for. Hope blooms hot in his chest.

"I can't wait for stage four," she says and smiles wickedly.

That smile sticks with him like glue.

CHAPTER SEVEN

Evan's sanctuary, outside of The Basement, is the bookstore. Hooked On Books, a little independent shop just down the street from his condo in Noe Valley, is one of the only bookstores in town that allows dogs. He and Tallulah can often be found wandering the aisles of the cramped shelves together. Evan likes it because it has an extensive collection of case-bound classic fantasy novels that make him feel like a wizard reading from a spell book when he holds them, they're so heavy; Tallulah mostly likes it because it has free treats. The women running the front desk always coo and fuss over her and give her too many. Today, they can't get enough of Tallulah's flower-print coat. It's Evan's duty to make sure that Tallulah never gets too cold when the temperature drops below fifty, and he honestly can't blame them for melting down and taking a bunch of pictures. She's too damn cute.

It's the perfect weather to go to the bookstore. Granted, he believes any kind of weather is perfect for shopping for books, but on a gray, chilly day like this, it's almost a cliché. Besides, Evan's in search of some comfort. His eyes glaze over as he skims the titles, looking at nothing in particular as his mind is still squarely back in front of the museum after the disaster that was stage three. He really thought he had something there. Her smile, the way the skin around her fingers turned pale from pressing them to her mouth so hard, the gleam in her eye, the snort of her laugh . . . He knows he looked like a fool, but he really tried. He didn't have to, but he did. For the sake of the bet, of course.

Rationally, he knows that it doesn't mean anything whether it changes Dalisay's opinion about him or not, he just has to complete all five stages to win, but a part of him wants her to look at him like that again.

He still can't believe Riggs told Kyle, Noah, and Leo—old classmates of theirs—to come catcall him while he was dancing. He hasn't seen them since college. Obviously, when Riggs found out what Evan had to do, he texted them immediately that night.

"Riggs is just teasing you," JM said at the gym the next day.

Despite their best efforts, Evan thinks he handled the embarrassment pretty well, even if Dalisay told him his Tagalog was terrible. It's not in Evan's nature to quit, especially not after he looked like a complete tool in front of everyone. He doesn't know when to cut his losses.

Every day this week at work has been like a game all on its own. Work has been so busy for both of them now that they're working on a bunch of separate pieces from their finished analysis. But simply being near her is practically driving him crazy. The scent of her lavender lotion overwhelms him, the ring of her laugh across the office always makes him perk up, and the look in her eyes when she catches him staring . . . Evan tries hard not to look at her, but each time he breaks from typing notes on his laptop, his eyes lift to Dalisay, and he must force himself to look away again. Like Perseus fighting

Medusa—if he meets her gaze, he might as well be turned to stone.

Being around her makes his heart thump with anticipation.

No matter what he does, she's the only thing he can think about. She's everywhere. He doesn't want to believe he's obsessed with her but . . .

The bells at the front chime as the door opens and he turns to see silky black hair sweep inside. For a moment, Evan's heart stops. *Dalisay.*

Daniel said she likes bookstores. What are the odds that she's here now? She's new to town, maybe she's checking out all that San Francisco has to offer.

But the woman says something to the others at the front and just hearing her voice, Evan knows it's not Dalisay. He was mistaken. Seeing her now, as she moves farther into the store, he realizes the only thing they have in common is hair color. Unless Dalisay moonlights out of the office looking like a goth vampire in fishnets and a choker, which he highly doubts.

He lets out a sigh of relief.

And for a brief, baffling moment, disappointment follows. He can't seem to get Dalisay out of his head. Even in his sleep, he can't get rid of her.

This morning, when he woke up, still hovering in the warm haze of a dream he can't remember, he rolled over in bed, and wrapped his arm around Dalisay's body sleeping next to him. Except his arm passed through cold, thin air, and he jerked awake feeling like he'd lost something.

It wasn't real, he reminds himself. He can't lose something he's never had.

Dalisay Ramos 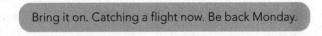:

> Ready for stage four?

Evan's in line to board his flight when he gets the text. He's headed to London for a weekend trip for work, but seeing Dalisay's name makes him feel like he's already in the air, defying gravity.

> Bring it on,

he types.

> I'm heading to jolly ol' London now, though. Be back Monday.

Before he hits send, he winces at his own words. He sounds like such a dork. Who says 'jolly ol'? Really? He edits the middle sentence and hits send.

Me:

> Bring it on. Catching a flight now. Be back Monday.

Dalisay Ramos:

> The anticipation is excruciating. ;)

"This is her house?" Evan asks.

JM shifts the car into park and nods. He offered to drive Evan, seeing as Bettie decided not to start today. She might be on her last legs.

Evan still doesn't know what stage four entails, and JM and Pinky keep mum about it, even after he asks them a million times. He wants to prepare as best he can, but they're resolute. They told him it's not fair if he googles it either. He'll find out soon enough.

After work, JM drives Evan to Outer Richmond, a neighborhood on the north side of the city. Despite Evan having lived in San Francisco most of his life, he's never visited this side of town before, and for some reason it makes him nervous. Maybe it's because now he's on her home turf.

The Ramos home is a robin's-egg blue, single-family house with a large bay window overlooking the driveway leading up to the front door and garage. It's one of the nicer houses on the block, and like Dalisay, he knows that there's more behind the facade than meets the eye.

"This is the address Pinky gave me," JM says. "All you have to do now is knock on the front door. Prepare for servitude, my guy."

Evan whips around to look at him. "Servitude? You're making this up now. Are you and Dalisay in on it together?"

With a laugh, JM shakes his head.

"Why didn't you say anything earlier?" Evan asks.

"Because I know you can do it, no sweat," replies JM. "You need to serve to prove that you're useful, that you can take care of things, that you're not lazy. Shows that you're willing to make an effort."

"I'm not lazy. Haven't the first three stages proven that?"

"Now you gotta prove it to her family."

Evan puffs out his cheeks. "Family." For some reason his heart pounds in his chest. Why is he so nervous about meeting her parents? "Can you at least tell me what kinds of things I need to do? Like, run a few errands?"

JM just chuckles and says, "Whatever they ask you to do, you do it. No complaints. Good luck, bro."

He holds out his hand and he and Evan complete their elaborate handshake, one they crafted way back when they started Berkeley together before finals. Old habits die hard. Their good luck ritual never failed them before. Evan doesn't want to think about the fact that he might need it today more than ever.

"Let's get this over with. Thanks, man." He gets out of the car and JM pulls away.

No one's at the window, and he can't see a shadow moving at the door, so Evan takes a beat to gather himself while he walks up to the house. As he smooths out the front of his sweatshirt, thinking he should have worn something nicer, he finds his palms are sweaty. Why is he so nervous? Is he really that worried about making a good impression on her family? Of course, he always wants to make a good impression. He's a people pleaser. But for some reason, the idea that he's meeting her parents makes the stages feel . . . real. He shakes his head and forces his heart to stop hammering in his chest.

At the door, he rings the bell and Daniel opens the door, greeting him with a big smile.

"Evan!" he says. "You're right on time."

"Oh, uh, okay!" Evan says. He didn't know Daniel would be expecting him.

Daniel lets Evan inside and has him take off his shoes, leaving them on a rack full of others. The entry area leads to a split-level, one small set of stairs going up while a door nearby leads to the garage. For a foyer, the entry is heavily decorated, with dozens of different kinds of crucifixes and family photos in gilded frames covering every inch of the diamond wallpaper. Based on their number, the Ramos family loves taking photos. Christmas, vacations, weddings, baby photos—each happy moment preserved. One thing is clear, the Ramos family is close. It occurs to Evan that he can't remember ever seeing a framed family photo in his parents' houses. They're all saved on phones or computers. Daniel hands Evan a pair of slippers to wear in the house and beckons him up the stairs.

The main floor is even more decorated and lively than the entryway. Evan isn't sure there is a single white object or straight line in the entire house. The first thing he sees is the kitchen and the living room. The smell of cooking onions and garlic washes over him, and a crowd of people—all women, Evan notices—are standing in the kitchen, yelling over one another. An old woman hunches over the kitchen island, tasting a pot of something steaming with a wooden spoon, and scowls, speaking quickly in Tagalog. A pregnant woman leans on the counter, her hand on the small of her back as she gesticulates wildly with the other hand as she tells Nicole a story. A toddler no taller than Evan's knees crawls on the polished wood floor pushing a large fire truck. A woman with salt-and-pepper hair nearly trips over the toddler and she scolds him for getting underfoot. Five other older women chat and gossip, holding on to each other as they laugh.

To say the room is chaotic is an understatement. It's loud. At first, Evan's so overwhelmed by everything, his feet root to the spot.

"Evan's here!" Daniel announces to the house.

Everyone spins around to look, then roars in approval. They descend upon him like a flock of birds.

"Finally!"

"What took you so long?"

"Open this for me."

Someone hands him a jar of pickled papaya and without thinking, he twists it open and hands it back. He's not even sure who it went to. It's a flurry of introductions by Daniel.

"Evan, meet the family. Our cousins, who live out in Richmond—"

The gossiping women smoosh his cheeks and crow about how handsome he is, and his face goes hot as he remembers what JM talks about when he visits family in Cebu City.

"You remember Nicole," Daniel continues.

Nicole appears, pats him on the cheek, and hands him a vacuum.

"This is our Lola." Daniel gestures to the elderly woman. He can surmise that "Lola" is the Filipino word for "grandmother." She elbows her way through the crowd and inspects Evan with a stern eye, like she might inspect a piece of furniture for scratch marks. In contrast to her glower, she wears a bright, floral button-up shirt and matching skirt. She says something in Tagalog, but Evan distinctly hears the word "Dalisay."

Evan holds out his hand. "*Mano po.* I'm Evan." Sure, he might be doing the Five Stages for a bet, but he's determined to get it right. He's done his research. He's not phoning any of this in.

Whole-ass, like he promised.

Lola's eyes widen, and she looks at his hand, then back at him. She takes his hand and shakes it. She says something else, though it doesn't have the bite it did before, and when she leaves, someone uses the opportunity to fill his empty arm with a toddler.

"This is Little Luis," says Daniel, nodding at the squirming child, "and cousin Melinda."

Melinda, the pregnant woman, looks like she's about to collapse with exhaustion. "Baby needs changing," she says.

Evan can smell it already, and his eyes start watering. Little Luis flails and cries, and Evan has to hold on to him for dear life; otherwise, the toddler will pancake onto the floor.

"The list, where's the list!" the salt-and-pepper-haired woman in her sixties calls out. She's got her arm in a sling, a cast on her wrist.

"On the counter here, Mama," Dalisay says.

Finally, through the crowd swarming him, he spots Dalisay near the sink. When she's at home, she wears more comfortable clothes than the ones she wears to work. Her hair is piled on her head in a messy knot, and she's wearing yoga pants and a loose-fitting shirt that makes him think she's just finished a workout. She smiles at him and shrugs, as if to say *Sorry, not sorry* and Evan smirks back.

The woman hustles over to them and hands a notepad to Daniel.

"This is our mom," Daniel says.

"Yes, yes," Mrs. Ramos says, barely looking at Evan. She's got her glasses on a delicate gold chain, looking fashionable in just a knit sweater and long floral skirt. He notices her cast is decorated in flowers in permanent marker. "This is all I could think of off the top of my head. I'll probably add more, don't worry!"

Daniel hands Evan the list, and Evan isn't sure where to keep it. His hands are full, so he pinches it in his armpit while Little Luis tries to crawl over Evan's head, screaming the whole time.

"Bro, you better roll up your sleeves," says Daniel with a sly grin.

CHAPTER EIGHT

Dalisay winds up, hefting the ax behind her head, and hurls it toward the target. With a solid *FUMP* it lands squarely on the wall at the end of the lane. Pinky cheers behind her. "Yeah! Bull's-eye!"

Dalisay spins around, fist pumping, and laughs. Pinky invited her after work to Axe Me About It, a recreational ax-throwing center near Fisherman's Wharf. It's a giant warehouse stacked like a bowling alley, with several private lanes for people to practice their throws without worrying about hurting anyone else. It's a good thing too, because Dalisay's aim wasn't so great at first. On her third throw she lost her grip and let the ax fly behind her, nearly hitting the burly, tattooed instructor. She's gotten better with practice. The world's best-kept secret stress reliever, Pinky told her. Everything with Evan, and Nicole's secrecy, and the fact that Dalisay's still adjusting to life in America has made Dalisay feel like she's juggling axes for real. For once, it feels like she can finally think about something else. It's frustrating not being able to talk to Nicole. Dalisay would never want to put her on the spot, or out her before she's ready, and yet at the same time she isn't sure how she can tell Nicole what she knows. It's a tightrope walk, one that Dalisay isn't sure she has the dexterity to maneuver.

But throwing axes for fun seems to put that pent-up energy to better use. If only everything in life made her feel this good.

"You're kind of scary!" Pinky says. "Dalisay, warrior princess." Then she gasps. "You would look so good in a Xena cosplay."

"Consider it . . . considered. I've never done anything like that before."

"It's so much fun! JM, Evan, and I, we go to Comic-Con every year. We get a hotel room and make a whole weekend of it and everything. You should come! It's the best."

Dalisay smiles, dubious. "Evan does cosplay?"

"Yeah! Mostly superheroes. He and JM lift weights at the gym together to get in shape."

It makes sense then why he looked so good without his shirt. Dalisay bites her lip to keep herself in check. "He's never struck me as someone who does that kind of thing."

"What, being a total nerd? Looks can be deceiving. Speaking of . . . ," says Pinky, smiling over the rim of her beer. "Spill."

"What?"

"Spill. The tea. I have to know. What torture did you put him through? How'd Evan do with his servitude?"

"Infuriatingly well. He never complained once, not even when my mom had him unclog the shower drain."

Pinky grins toothily. "He's all-in, that's for sure."

"It's nice having an extra pair of hands around the house."

"Is that all Evan is? A pair of hands?"

"Yes." It's not a convincing lie.

Even though it's been days since the dream, Dalisay can't shake how it made her feel. How *good* it made her feel. She hefts another ax, appreciating how heavy it is in her palm, how it gives her something else to focus on.

"You're really not coming around about him?" Pinky asks, skeptical.

"He's fine . . ."

Pinky's lip curls knowingly because Dalisay might as well be made of glass, she's so transparent. Dalisay blushes and Pinky throws her head back with laughter.

"Hey!" cries Dalisay, brandishing the ax. "You want to laugh at the person holding this?"

Pinky holds up her hands, still cracking up. Dalisay is laughing too, despite herself. Is she really so obvious?

"I won't tell, I promise," Pinky says. "Your secret crush is safe with me."

"Thank you." Dalisay turns back to the target. "But I'm not sure I'd call it a crush."

"What else would you call it? You're into him, right?"

Dalisay doesn't know. She mumbles, "I may have had a sex dream about him . . ."

Pinky nearly spits out her beer. "What!"

"It doesn't mean anything, though, right? I have weird dreams all the time."

Pinky's eyebrows are in the stratosphere. "I guess, but . . . whatever you gotta tell yourself!"

A shadow of guilt gnaws at Dalisay's insides. She hasn't even told Nicole yet that she might have feelings for Evan, but then again Nicole hasn't exactly been an open book either. Besides, talking with Pinky about Evan is a lot easier than it is with Nicole. Pinky doesn't break out into song, teasing her to no end, like Nicole does.

But none of this means Evan has any feelings for her. He asked her out, she said no; that's all there is to it.

With a huff, Dalisay raises the ax and takes aim at the wooden target. "It doesn't matter anyway. He's only doing this so he can have the Asia tour."

"I wouldn't be so sure. Have you two actually, you know, talked?"

Dalisay throws the ax and it lands with a solid *thunk* in the wood. "No."

"Then you don't know."

Pinky might be right. She's just assuming how he feels. She's left wondering unless she asks, but does she want to risk the disappointment?

That dream was so real, she actually *could* see herself being with him. But Evan from her subconscious is very different from the Evan of real life. What if he doesn't feel the same way? Does she really want to open her heart like that again?

"This isn't just because Evan's my friend," Pinky says, "but I genuinely think you'd be good together. For real."

Dalisay turns back around and takes a sip of her beer. "He's . . . definitely not what I thought. He's stubborn, in a good way."

It *is* admirable he didn't complain at all during his servitude. He scrubbed all the floors in the house on his hands and knees, got on a ladder and cleared the gutters, got rid of a wasp's nest in those same gutters, and repainted the shed in the backyard. A man of lesser character might have given up by now.

Pinky nods. "When he says he'll do something, he does it. I could have told you firsthand what you were in for. He's the only friend I know who will say he'll pick me up from the airport in the middle of the night and actually follow through. In his piece-of-shit car, no less."

Dalisay's heart softens a bit. "Say, hypothetically, I felt differently about him. And he felt differently about me. I would still want to take things slow, and take my time, but I realize for Americans maybe that's too slow."

"Don't worry about all that. Play by Manila rules. JM and I dated for four months before we slept together," Pinky says, waving her hand like she's shooing away a fly. She says "four months" as if it's a long time.

"Who said anything about sleeping together?" Dalisay asks, her voice a little shrill.

Pinky's eyebrows shoot up. "Are you a virgin? Oh, wait—of course you are. Good Filipino girls don't have sex till they're married!" Pinky rolls her eyes.

"It's not that I don't want to have sex, it's just . . . complicated."

When her dad died, dating had taken a back seat. She was more worried about what her family needed than what she needed. Besides, if her parents found out that she wanted to have sex before marriage, they would have freaked out. All three of them—Daniel, Nicole, and Dalisay—were forbidden from dating anyone until they graduated, and dating Luke in secret was one of the only times she rebelled.

She remembers a time back in Manila when Daniel was caught in the theater kissing a classmate from high school. The rumor mill churned, and news reached the Ramos house before Daniel even crossed the threshold. Their parents ranted for hours about how it was inappropriate and low class and unbecoming for him to gallivant with a girl as if he was some Casanova. And it's even worse for girls. If they had known Dalisay was dating Luke—her first real boyfriend—she would have been grounded and forbidden from going out for the rest of her life. Daniel merely got a slap on the wrist for his dalliance. Of course, this was before their dad got sick. Priorities changed after that.

Sometimes Dalisay wonders if her parents realized how differently they treated her. How her mom *still* treats her. Guilt is the first emotion she feels whenever she does something remotely selfish. But can she really call what she wants "selfish"?

She never wants to hurt her family, and at the same time she can't deny the twist in her gut sometimes when she sees Evan at work, as he laughs with Riggs, when he types so fast his fingers are a blur, the way a crease forms between his eyebrows when he reads . . .

Her desire feels like a dangerous thing, like something that she needs to control, to tame. It's come from a lifetime of growing up to be a polite, respectable woman. One sex dream cannot throw off that delicate balance.

"What about your family?" Dalisay asks. "Don't they worry about you dating?"

"Sure they do! Like any other parents. But I guess mine are more culturally American than they are Filipino. They sort of pick and choose what to hold on to, and with me and JM, it's a little more relaxed. It's like the pressure is off."

Although Filipino, Pinky's perspective seems totally different from hers, and it makes Dalisay almost envious. Dalisay's not sure she's in a position to be able to choose what she wants at all. Concern draws her eyebrows together.

Pinky must notice, because she cracks a smile. "Look, I know you and Evan didn't start out on the right foot, but you can trust me. He's not a player. He's not looking to rush into anything. He's not going to pressure you or anything, if that's what you're worried about."

That surprises her. "He's had girlfriends. He might be disappointed."

"Oh, please. He's had one serious girlfriend. Becca. But it ended . . . messy," she says, cringing.

Dalisay's mind races. She's about to ask what happened, but then she reminds herself that she doesn't care about Evan Saatchi. Apparently, she can't even be honest with her own heart.

How many times is she going to lie to herself?

"I might be speaking out of line, so feel free to ignore me," says Pinky, "but he's worth a real shot."

Maybe Dalisay doesn't know what she wants. Her mind is telling her one thing, while the rest of her body is saying another.

Besides, Pinky is doing a good job of convincing her. She's one of Evan's closest friends, so she would know what he's like, right? Dalisay trusts her.

The only problem is, Dalisay isn't sure she can trust herself. She's too attracted to him to think straight.

CHAPTER NINE

After-hours, the office at Overnight is dark and quiet, and Dalisay and Evan stay late to work on their project. Naomi has some last-minute additions she wants them to include in one of the pieces, so to make the deadline, they need to put in extra hours.

"You can't let them overwork you, especially so close to the holidays," her mom says, when Dalisay called to tell her why she would be late.

Dalisay sighs and glances through the large windows lining the conference room, watching Evan as he rests his cheek on one hand, scrolling on his laptop with the other. His eyes flick up when he notices her looking, and she turns away, drawing her attention to the indoor Christmas tree, which she now notices is made of plastic. "It's okay, Mom. May I remind you, I actually like this job."

"I didn't forget. I am proud of you, and I love that you're happy, but I want you to have a life outside of work."

"I do! I won't make this a habit, I promise. This is just part of the job."

Calling her mom now, especially in front of Evan, makes her feel a little immature. A part of her still feels like she owes it to her family to tell them where she is, while another part of her knows that for an American, the idea seems ridiculous. Of course, it's nice to know that her family cares enough to worry, and calling them to tell them is the least she could do, but at the same time, shouldn't she have a little independence?

"Is Evan there?" her mom asks.

Dalisay swallows a lump in her throat, panicking a little. "Uh, no!" She has to lie. What would her mother think if she was alone with the guy who was "supposedly" courting her?

"Who's there with you?"

"Just a couple other editors. Don't worry."

"Oh. Well." She almost sounds disappointed. "Leftovers will be waiting for you in the ref."

Dalisay smiles, relieved. "Thanks." It's the little kindnesses that contain the most love.

When Dalisay comes back into the conference room, she notices now how Evan's cologne fills the space, spicy and warm, and she has to remind herself that they're at work. She needs to be professional. She can't let him distract her. But first—food. Naomi gave them the company card so they could order whatever they wanted.

As she passes behind Evan to get to her seat at the table, he asks, "What are you in the mood for? I was thinking tacos."

"Oh! Me too, actually . . . How about the place down the block, La Taqueria?"

Evan spins his laptop around to show her his screen as she sits. He's already got La Taqueria's menu pulled up. "It's like you read my mind," he says, one corner of his mouth raised in a half smile.

Funny. Never did she think they could agree on anything, even about something as simple as tacos.

Evan takes the initiative to place the order for both of them and when he does, he says, "Food'll be ready in twenty. I'll pick it up."

"Thanks," she says, and they get back to writing. On her laptop, she sees Evan working in their shared document and she watches his words as they appear on her screen. Despite the speed with which he types, she can tell he's tired. He looks like he didn't sleep well last night; his hair is extra mussed and his eyes a little glassy.

With the office empty, she can't help that her mind starts to imagine all the things that could happen without worrying anyone would walk in on them. She's seen enough trash TV to easily picture the way he could press her up against the wall, kiss her neck, hold her hips . . . The image invades her mind before she can stop it, and she scrambles for anything else to think about in a desperate effort to gather her wits.

"How long do you think this will take?" she asks, a little pitchy.

Evan sighs and rocks his head to the side, still not looking up from his computer. "As long as it needs to, right? Got somewhere to be?"

"No. I just . . . You look tired."

"Thanks?" he says, with a hint of a smile.

"I didn't . . ." She catches herself and licks her lips. "I just know you've been working hard lately. With servitude and all."

"Are you taking pity on me?" When he looks at her, with those dark eyes lit up by the glow of his computer screen, that smile of his takes center stage. Damn him. Something inside her coils up, a heated pressure below her navel. How can he turn her on with just one smile? The back of her neck feels sunburned.

"I'm saying," she says, forcing her gaze to the keys on her laptop, "we can get an outline at least, figure out our main points, and then take another stab at it tomorrow. I'll ask Naomi for an extension if we need it."

Evan seems amenable to that idea. "All I want is to get home to Tallulah," he says and glances at his watch.

"Tallulah?"

Evan's eyes flick up to her and a hint of a smile creases the corners. "My dog."

"Oh." The pressure below her navel dispels the longer she sits in silence. Is she really starting to feel something for him? She rolls her teeth across her lower lip. For some reason, she never expected that he would have a dog, let alone a dog with such a delicate name. "What is she? Tallulah?"

"Dachshund. Wiener dog."

Dalisay actually laughs.

Evan raises his eyebrows. "What?"

"I didn't picture you'd have a dachshund, or a dog period, for that matter."

"Why?"

"I figured you were more of a cat person because you're also independent, aloof, and stubborn."

This time when Evan smiles, it's the kind that melts into Dalisay's skin like sunshine. "Then I guess you don't know me at all."

Her heart sinks a little. Pinky was right, she really doesn't.

All Dalisay can do is try to smile, but she knows how unfair she's been toward him these past few days. She realizes this is the first time they've had a conversation, a *real* conversation, since he started doing the Five Stages. Normally, they wouldn't be alone in the same room together if they were playing by Manila rules. But nothing, when it comes to Evan Saatchi, is normal.

Dalisay draws her eyes back to her computer, as if she's about to start working again, but she can't, not when it feels like everything's been set off-balance between them. He's had to learn so much about her to go through the stages, and here she is, not knowing anything about him, even something as small as him having a dog. If their roles were reversed, and she was the one doing the Five Stages, how would she go about winning his affection? What music does he like? What kind of gifts would she give him? How could she be helpful to his family? Where does he even live? The answers are all infuriatingly blank.

And it's her own fault.

The Ramos family goes all out for the holiday, it would seem.

Evan stands in the driveway while Mrs. Ramos opens the garage to reveal plastic boxes upon boxes labeled *Christmas*. Evan is certain there isn't room left to park a car, there are so many.

"Wow," he says as he looks at the two-dozen or so boxes labeled Lights. "They must be able to see your house from space."

His attempt at a joke falls flat. "I don't think so," she says, earnestly. Just like her daughters, Mrs. Ramos has dark eyes and hair, but unlike them, when she smiles at him it's pure, simple warmth. Her wrist is still in a cast, so he does all the work carrying the boxes to the driveway for her. As if he'd let her do it anyway, even if she wasn't hurt.

"Use a ladder," she says, "and hang the lights on the outside of the house. Then bring the *parol* from the garage to hang in the bay window."

"What's a *parol*?"

Evan's not sure if he should explain that his family never gets into the holiday spirit like the Ramoses do. The most the Saatchis ever did to decorate was hang a "Christmas tree" made out of driftwood on the wall. No lights, no pine needles, no candles. And then after the divorce, his dad didn't keep up with that tradition either.

"A *parol* is an ornamental star lantern," Mrs. Ramos says.

"Oh. Okay, then leave it to me!"

Mrs. Ramos goes back inside, and already Evan's wondering if it's too late to run home to grab a jacket. The sky is unusually gray and chilly for the Bay Area. If he'd known he'd be working outside all day, he would have worn more layers. His hoodie does a poor job keeping out the rain as it barely falls—spits, really—on Evan as he climbs the ladder, balancing precariously, to hang the lights across the gutter on the roof.

It's slow-going, and his fingers are numb by the time he's secured one string of lights to another, but he won't be caught dead complaining about it.

Shivering, his whole body tense from the cold, Evan climbs the ladder again with another bundle of lights. This high up, he's level with the bay window on the second floor, and he can see right into the living room, where it looks so warm and inviting. Their Christmas tree stands in full view of the window, capturing the spirit of the holiday with pale twinkling lights.

He doesn't mean to be a creep, but he keeps watching as Dalisay comes into view carrying a box of ornaments. She completes the welcoming scene in her cozy sweatpants and hoodie, and unprompted, his chest tightens with longing. Through the glass, he watches her laugh and joke with Nicole as they hang up some handmade ornaments, likely from their childhood, on the tree. When she reaches up to hang one on a higher branch, Dalisay's hoodie rises and reveals the small of her back. Her skin looks warm and soft, and a thrill goes up Evan's spine. He looks away, for her sake.

Like the changing of the season, there's been a shift inside of Evan. He's been thinking less and less about the bet. Seeing Dalisay every day for servitude has done something to him, made something malleable. He can't quite place what exactly it is, just that he knows it's different than before and that it wasn't one thing that made it happen but a matter of time.

Whatever change this is, Evan isn't sure what to make of it.

While he gets back to hanging the lights, Dalisay notices him through the window and her face brightens as she smiles at him. A real smile. And all at once, he can't help but wonder . . . Is she actually starting to like him?

He can't be imagining it, can he? The way her dimples get deeper and her eyes light up like that when she sees him, what else could it be? If anything, they've become friendlier toward each other, but—Evan reminds himself—that doesn't mean anything. They were both clear that there weren't any strings attached to this bet, and he intends to uphold his side of the bargain.

She said no; he would always respect that. After this is all over, they can go their separate ways. He can't read into anything so simple as a smile. It wouldn't do anything good for his heart.

By the time he's done, the Ramos house looks like it belongs on a Christmas card festooned with warm yellow lights. All that's needed to complete the picture is snow. Of course, there's no chance of that, but Evan amuses himself with the idea of flakes falling from the dreary gray sky. Crazier things have happened to him recently.

By the time he brings the ladder back into the garage, it's already dusk, and Evan can't feel his fingers anymore. He breathes some feeling back into them by cupping them over his mouth and blowing. All he wants to do is get indoors to warm up, but he remembers he has to bring the *parol* to the living room. He searches everywhere in the garage, opening and closing seemingly every box labeled "Christmas" until finally he finds it inside the last one, cradled with packing peanuts and copious amounts of tissue paper.

When Mrs. Ramos said it was ornamental, he expected something small, but the *parol* is huge, the diameter as long as his forearm, and fragile. While the frame is made of aluminum, the faces are made of some kind of translucent pink shell and there's a lightbulb inside. It'll look incredible when it's lit up, that's for sure.

Eager to finally get warm, Evan carries the *parol* into the house with numb fingers and Daniel stands with a mug of hot chocolate, greeting him from the top of the stairs. "All set?"

"Thanks for all your help," Evan teases as he kicks off his shoes.

"You had it covered," says Daniel. "Careful with that."

"I've got it. No problem." He climbs the stairs and spots Dalisay and Nicole still in the living room, debating what kind of Christmas music they should play, and Dalisay smiles again when she sees him. Evan's body feels just like his fingers, tingly.

"That's a family heirloom," says Daniel to Evan.

"I said I got it."

Just then, Little Luis comes tearing from around the Christmas tree, running full tilt for Evan as he chases his fire truck rolling across the floor. Evan's too busy staring at Dalisay to notice quick enough. By the time he does, it's too late.

The toddler knocks into his shin, and Evan pulls back before he can do any harm, but he loses his balance.

Evan tips forward, and so does the *parol*. It slips from his numb fingers and the star hits the floor, fracturing into pieces like glass.

Little Luis's screams bring Melinda running. Everyone's asking what happened.

Evan tries to apologize, but the toddler is inconsolable. At least he's unhurt. Evan doesn't know what to do as Melinda carries Little Luis to another room to calm him down.

"What is it? What happened?" Mrs. Ramos appears, wide-eyed. She must have heard the commotion. Then she gasps and covers her mouth at the sight of the *parol*.

Pieces of shell glitter on the floor, the bulb inside broken too. The only thing that remains is the skeletal frame of the star, but it's dented now.

"I am so, *so* sorry," Evan says. His brain finally starts working again as he scrambles to pick up the pieces. But Mrs. Ramos rushes to him, hands fluttering.

"No!" she says. "Don't cut yourself!"

Evan repeats his apology, over and over. "I'm so sorry. I'll pay for it. It's my fault—"

Everyone in the room assures him that it's nothing to fret about, but Evan feels like they're only saying it to be polite, maybe to make him feel better. Guilt crushes him like a ten-ton weight on his chest. He's a complete oaf, and they trusted him with a family heirloom.

While Mrs. Ramos and Daniel hurry off to get a broom and dustpan and the vacuum, Evan kneels to pick up the pieces. Most of the shell has shattered into bits, but he does what he can to gather the larger fragments into his palm.

Dalisay kneels next to him and helps.

"I'm so sorry," he says again.

"It's okay, really."

He can't bear to look at her. He has to fix this somehow. Memories of being a little kid again, scrambling to piece together his mom's favorite vase because he was tossing a baseball in the house when he knew he wasn't supposed to. And knowing how angry she'd be with him, that she had enough problems to deal with already, and thinking that it was his fault his parents got divorced—

Panic bubbles up. He can't breathe.

"Hey, look at me," Dalisay says. Her dimples come out when she smiles. "It's just a *parol*."

Evan feels helpless. He swallows thickly. "What about Little Luis—?"

"He's fine," Dalisay says, smiling assuredly. She reaches out and touches his wrist, and the warmth of her fingers makes Evan's breath catch in his throat. "You're okay too. No one's angry. I promise."

Looking into Dalisay's dark eyes, Evan forces himself to breathe, hissing between pursed lips. Dalisay's fingers slowly slip off his arm. He misses their heat right away. "Sorry," he says. He's got more than one thing to be sorry about.

Whether she understands or not, Dalisay simply nods, still smiling, and helps him clean up without another word.

CHAPTER TEN

Dalisay ties off the final balloon with string and adds it to the bundle already tied to the back of the chair.

"Who decided on the fiesta theme?" Daniel asks, hefting a stack of chairs across the hall. It's Melinda's baby shower and everyone's been tasked with helping set up St. Mary's recreation hall for the big event, a seemingly all-hands-on-deck sort of emergency, so the shower can happen before everyone is occupied for the holidays.

"It is a little odd for a baby shower," Dalisay admits. "But it's Bernila's vision!"

Bernila, Melinda's best and extraordinarily loud friend, is in charge of everything. She is a taskmaster, putting everyone to work to get the place ready for fifty guests. Evan, fortunately, is spared the servitude. After his near panic attack with the *parol*, Dalisay is glad the family is giving him a day off.

She wishes *she* could get a day off, but she'd rather die than admit it out loud.

Working at Overnight is exhausting. American work culture is a lot more demanding than she ever expected. After spending eight hours at the office, sometimes she comes home to do even more work, on the weekends sometimes too; checks her work email on her phone in the middle of the night; is always aware of the unspoken rule that she must be reachable at all times, especially before deadlines.

In Manila, there is a concept called *pakikisama*, the closest English translation being "camaraderie," and it's a foundational part of office life. Teamwork and cohesion and social harmony. It's a value she's brought with her since starting at Overnight, but in America, office life is a lot more individualistic. Everyone seems to be looking out only for themselves, but Dalisay still feels the need to go above and beyond to make sure that everyone in the office is happy, pulling extra weight just to ensure that everything gets done. She truly stands by the concept that if the company looks good, everyone looks good. She will not be the weak link in the chain, even if it means she has to sacrifice her own free time to do it.

She barely feels like she gets any time to breathe anymore, with both work and home responsibilities. But Evan coming over to the house for Servitude has been more helpful than she cares to admit. She's grateful, truly.

Her mom sets up games, like a blindfolded diaper-changing challenge and a baby bump balloon pop; Daniel raises a pacifier-shaped piñata on a rope in the corner of the room; and Lola brings out the ice-cream cake, and tells Melinda not to eat any. "Cold food equals big baby!"

Melinda holds her belly. "It's too late for that, Lola!"

The party hasn't even started, and yet Little Luis is taking full advantage of the fact that Melinda is so pregnant and about ready to burst that all she can do is sit on a chair and scold him from afar. He runs through the empty church hall, whacking anyone unfortunate enough to stand nearby with the piñata stick.

"Perhaps a fiesta was not the best decision," Dalisay says, wincing, as Little Luis thwacks her in the back of the knees.

"Come here, you!" Daniel growls and chases after Little Luis, grabbing him by the torso and putting him under his arm like a football. "You are being a monster."

"Monster! Monster!" Little Luis squeals and struggles to escape, but he's no match for Daniel, who plops him down on a chair near Melinda, telling him he's in timeout, and Little Luis screams. His tiny but powerful voice echoes off the walls.

See, Evan? she thinks. *He's perfectly fine.*

Evan was so worried about breaking the *parol*, Dalisay has been thinking about his reaction since last night. The way his eyes got so wide, how the color totally drained from his face, the way his hands shook. She's never seen someone so upset over such a small thing before. He was acting like he'd done something terrible, like he was holding on by a thread. When she touched his wrist, she wasn't sure if it would help, but the way he looked at her made her feel like it did.

Pinky was right. She hasn't even begun to understand him. She wishes there was an easier way to find out what goes on in someone's head.

While she's been with the family setting up for the party, she's thought about Evan almost the whole time. A part of her almost wishes he were here, just so they could talk about what happened.

Then again, she can't even talk to people who are right in front of her.

Across the hall, Dalisay watches as Nicole stands on a ladder, hanging the last of the streamers across the door as a curtain. She's been quiet all morning. Of course, she's been working hard these past few weeks. The holidays are always hard at hospitals—broken bones, knife lacerations, food poisoning, firework burns. Hospital visit rates skyrocket this time of year, no matter what part of the world, and staff can only try to keep up. It's almost a never-ending tsunami of emergencies. Their dad, a heart surgeon, always said that the holidays were the most stressful for people. It's why he never made a fuss when he was in the hospital himself. He always understood. But Dalisay wonders if Nicole's looking tired for other reasons. If only she could just talk to her, but Dalisay hasn't been able to have a moment alone with Nicole yet, they've both been so busy. Overnight and Kaiser Permanente might as well be on different planets.

Before she can think of what she'd even say to her, Bernila marches over to Dalisay. "The balloons aren't even done yet? People will be here in five minutes! Chop-chop!"

Before long, the party is in full swing, but something doesn't seem right.

"Bernila said there were just fifty people, right?" Dalisay asks Daniel. Daniel silently counts them too.

"Yup," he says. "This doesn't look like fifty."

There are at least two hundred people packed into the church hall. Either Bernila miscounted the RSVPs, or everyone decided to invite plus-threes and then some. The hall buzzes with conversation and laughter. There aren't enough chairs for everyone, so pockets of people stand around the room or line up to play games in rounds. They totally underestimated how many people were going to show up.

"We're not going to run out of food, right?" Daniel asks.

"I hope not . . ." She glances at the buffet table and sees that most of it has been picked clean. Nicole helps dole out desserts, but it won't last long.

As if summoned, Bernila appears. "Dalisay! *Saklolo!* We're all out of food! This is a disaster!"

"What do we need?" Daniel asks.

Bernila looks desperately at the hall. "Everything!"

"I'm on it."

Just as he leaves, a new face enters the room, and Dalisay's eyes immediately linger on the flash of auburn hair.

It's the woman from the hospital. She's wearing jeans and a leather jacket, and her hair is braided loosely down her back. A motorcycle helmet is tucked under her elbow. She lingers at the door, standing on her tiptoes, and cranes her neck, looking for someone. Probably looking for Nicole.

Nicole, meanwhile, notices the woman too, her eyes flicking to the door furtively, but she doesn't go to meet her.

Dalisay counts out the seconds, waiting for her sister to go to her, but Nicole doesn't move. It's like she's frozen in place.

"Come on, Nicole . . . ," Dalisay murmurs, but Nicole looks like she's seen a ghost.

Dalisay doesn't want this woman to feel like she's unwelcome, so she winds through the crowd and greets her. The woman's eyes land on Dalisay for a beat, doing the usual double take at the sight of Nicole's twin, and then she smiles curiously.

"Hi!" Dalisay says, extending her hand. "I'm Dalisay."

"Dalisay," the woman repeats, shaking her hand. "Nice to meet you. I'm Claire."

"Claire! Welcome! Come in! Don't be shy."

Claire smiles and her freckled nose crinkles when she does. She's stunning.

"Are you looking for someone . . . ?" Dalisay is fishing, seeing if she'll get a bite.

"I know, it's rude. I wasn't invited. But, yeah, actually. I was in the neighborhood and wanted to stop by to see someone."

"Oh! Well, this place is pretty crowded. I'm sure we'll find them sooner or later. It's no problem! Everyone is welcome."

"Thanks!" Claire seems like a genuinely sweet person. Dalisay glances in Nicole's direction, and Nicole remains frozen, watching the two of them.

"So what do you do, Claire?" She sounds so American asking that, she almost laughs at herself. Maybe she is feeling more at home here than she thought.

"I'm a med student, actually," Claire replies.

"Oh! Funny, my sister is a med student too! Where at?"

"I do clinical rotations at Kaiser Permanente."

"My sister does rotations there too! What a fun coincidence!"

Claire doesn't stop smiling. No doubt she starts to realize the game being played. "Wow! Crazy happenstance!" she says, her eyes twinkling. Claire finally sees Nicole standing on the other side of the room, and Dalisay can actually see Claire melt. Her eyes widen, her smile gets bigger, and her whole body relaxes with a sigh. She's in love with Nicole.

"Would you like some ice-cream cake?" Dalisay asks.

"Sure!"

Before Dalisay can guide Claire toward the dessert table where Nicole is, Nicole makes a beeline for them, elbowing her way through the crowd and intercepting them. Dalisay can see the whites of her eyes, and all the color has drained from her face.

"Hey!" Claire says, beaming.

"Hey," says Nicole, slightly sharper, teeth clenched so her mouth barely moves. She tries to smile, but it looks strained. "What are you doing here?"

"I came to see you," Claire says.

Nicole's eyes dart back to Dalisay and she leans in to Claire. "Can we talk about this outside?"

Claire furrows her brow. "I . . . I thought I'd surprise you. Wanted to take you for a ride." She shows her the motorcycle helmet tucked under her arm.

Nicole's face is turning so pale, Dalisay is worried she might pass out. She keeps looking around, as if she's waiting for a clown to pop out like the one who scared Evan at Angel's party.

"Is this your sister?" Claire asks. "We were just chatting—"

"Yes, this is my sister," interrupts Nicole, sharp and staccato. "She is needed at the dessert table."

"It's fine, Nicole!" Dalisay says. "Claire and I were just getting to know each other. She's welcome to stay—"

But Nicole interrupts Dalisay now. "She's just a friend from work."

Claire reels back, staring at Nicole with a frown. She looks hurt.

Too late, Nicole sucks in a breath, like she knows she said the wrong thing. She freezes, waiting, and clenches her fists at her sides.

None of them say anything for a moment, and Claire clears her throat. "Right! Just a friend," she says, eyes darting to Nicole.

Dalisay desperately wants to tell them it's okay, that she knows, but she can't. If Nicole wants to tell her, she will on her own. All she can do is put on a smile and say, "Well, you're welcome to stay anyway."

Claire gives Dalisay a tight smile, then looks at Nicole. "You know what, I'm going to . . ." She juts her thumb over her shoulder, spins, and leaves before she can finish her sentence.

Nicole drops her shoulders and groans. "Claire, wait!"

Before she can run after her, Dalisay grabs Nicole by the wrist. "Hey, it's okay—"

"Not now, Dalisay." Nicole rips her arm out of Dalisay's grasp and chases after Claire.

Alone, Dalisay stands wringing her hands, spinning her silver infinity ring on her finger. It was a gift from Nicole when they were teenagers. It was supposed to symbolize that together, they were forever, and now it feels like a brick wall has been erected between them, and Nicole is filling in the holes with cement.

CHAPTER ELEVEN

Late on Sunday evening, Evan's on the couch reading with Tallulah curled up on her pillow beside him when he gets a text from Daniel.

Can you call me? it says.

Evan's heart pounds. That's never a good sign. Usually if everything is okay, it can just be in a text. If Daniel wants to call, this is serious.

He doesn't text back. He calls Daniel right away.

"Is everything okay? Is anyone hurt?" Evan asks the moment Daniel picks up. Immediately, he wonders if Little Luis might be in the hospital.

"Oh yeah, no, everyone's fine," Daniel says. Evan can hear the TV going in the background, and distant conversation growing more muffled as Daniel gets up and leaves the room. "Sorry, I should have just texted you what it was."

Tallulah looks up from her pillow, head tilted to the side, curiously listening to Evan's conversation. He scratches her behind the ears as his heart settles back down from his throat. "Okay, good. I'm still a little shaken up after what happened."

"It's just a *parol*, dude," says Daniel, laughing. "Seriously, everything's good."

"Really? Your mom's not mad?"

"She's not mad, seriously, she's the whole reason I'm calling. She has officially invited you to Simbang Gabi."

"Invited me?"

"She asked about you specifically, and I quote: 'Will Evan be joining us?'"

"Oh!" Evan blinks a few times, processing. He knows, objectively, that Mrs. Ramos knows his name, but he never expected that she would actually use it in conversation without him present. He realizes he truly cares if she approves of him.

"Is this part of Servitude?" Evan asks.

"Not officially, no. Unless you want it to be."

Evan closes his book, using his finger as a bookmark. "Not particularly."

"Figured as much. So is that a yes?"

"Yes! Yeah! I'm so thankful she thought of me." He licks his lips. "Does Dalisay know?"

"As a matter of fact, she does."

Evan doesn't know what to do with this information, but his heart upticks a bit.

He can practically hear Daniel smile. "So I'm guessing you have no idea what Simbang Gabi is."

"Uh, no."

Daniel laughs again. "Don't worry. It's a series of nine Masses held each day leading up to Christmas. The church we go to holds them at six in the morning."

"That early?" Evan repeats, balking.

"You're lucky we're not going to the ones at midnight."

The only time Evan's ever gotten up that early was to catch a flight. It's not part of the Five Stages, and he could still say no, but he realizes he doesn't want to. "No sweat. I look forward to it."

St. Mary's church, a Spanish revival-style cathedral in the Marina District on the north side of the city, is already bustling with parishioners making their way through the front doors by the time Evan arrives ten minutes before Mass starts.

He stands on the sidewalk, looking up at the bell wall lit up with Christmas lights and an illuminated *parol* ten times larger than the one he shattered. He's never been to a Catholic Mass before and he's not sure what to expect. When he told JM and Pinky what was happening, they reminded him to follow what everyone else did and he'd be golden. He needs to make it up to Dalisay's mom somehow, even if she kept telling him the *parol* wasn't an issue. Going to Simbang Gabi is the least he can do.

Near a giant church bell with a plaque on it, the Ramos family stands chatting in a small group, except Little Luis and Melinda. Probably being a toddler and a heavily pregnant woman gets them a free pass to stay home. Dalisay stands apart from the rest, craning her neck, seemingly searching for something.

Or someone, Evan thinks.

She's wearing a modestly cut floral dress and black tights with a long-sleeved white cardigan, and her hair is pinned up behind her ear with a clip decorated with jasmine flowers. When she spots him, she smiles and Evan's stomach flops with nerves.

He adjusts his suit jacket and tugs at his tie. It's suddenly too tight.

When he comes over, Mrs. Ramos's smile lights up like the decorations above. "Evan! Good morning!"

"Morning! Morning, everyone," Evan says, a little breathlessly, smiling at the group. "Thanks for inviting me."

Mrs. Ramos is bursting with energy, despite the early hour. "Of course! We're so glad you came. You look very sharp."

Cheeks hot, Evan's eyes dart to Dalisay, who's slightly turned away from him to look at the nativity scene. She tucks her hair behind her ear and Evan notices that she hasn't stopped smiling since he arrived.

"Let's go inside," Daniel says around a yawn.

Nicole too looks like she's just rolled out of bed, and she grabs Dalisay's hand, dragging her to the front doors.

Lola bursts through the group to stand next to Evan, snaking her thin arm through his.

"She'll walk with you," says Daniel as Dalisay and Nicole walk ahead of them. Evan secures Lola's hand in the crook of his elbow and escorts her inside.

Exposed wooden beams stretch across the ceiling overhead, drawing his eye to the front of the cathedral where a statue of Mary stands in front of the largest golden crucifix Evan has ever seen. Three giant Christmas trees are on the altar, flanked by bouquets of white peace lilies and ornate wreaths, and a solemn but excited hum permeates the air as people take their seats in long wooden pews.

Mrs. Ramos chooses an empty row, and everyone files in, leaving Evan at the end. He tries not to stare, but every so often, he catches glimpses of Dalisay when someone shifts or turns their head. Evan's not sure what to do with his hands, especially during church, so he chooses to leave them clasped in his lap.

The entire Mass, Evan can hardly think about anything else but her.

Every day for the next week, Evan gets up bright and early to meet the family at St. Mary's. After the third Mass, he starts to get into the rhythm of the service, knowing when it's time to stand, or pray, or hold hands, even though it's all in Filipino.

Despite that, he actually looks forward to spending more time with the Ramoses. They make him feel like he's part of the family, opening their arms and welcoming him into their world. Some days he sits next to Daniel and they talk comics, other days he sits next to Melinda (who makes an appearance with Little Luis now and again), or Nicole and they talk dogs (she's always wanted one), or Mrs. Ramos and she asks him about his writing, but he never gets to sit with Dalisay. Still, no matter how far away she is from him, it's like she's a radiator, drawing him in from the cold. All he wants to do is be near her, but the family finds ways of keeping them apart.

On the ninth day, Christmas Eve, Evan sits next to Daniel again.

Before Mass starts, Daniel gently nudges Evan with his elbow, startling him. He hopes Daniel hasn't noticed that he was staring at Dalisay.

But, sneakily, Daniel holds out his fist and drops something in Evan's hand. A peppermint. He must have taken it from the bowl in the vestibule before coming in.

"Thanks," Evan whispers. "Does my breath smell that bad?"

"No, you're good," Daniel says. "It makes these services not so unbearable."

Evan slips the mint in his mouth. "Why do you say that?"

Daniel shrugs. "Once you've been to one of these, you've been to 'em all. We're not supposed to eat anything before Communion, so I'm always starving. I've been up all night, studying. I'd rather be in bed. Oh, look, the delegation is here."

Daniel's gaze draws Evans to a prim, silver-haired couple in matching gold outfits.

"That's the Consulate General from the Philippines and his wife," says Daniel, switching the mint from one side of his mouth to the other, making it click on his teeth. He laughs. "My mom is practically foaming at the mouth to talk to them. Look."

He's right. Down the pew, Mrs. Ramos is craning her neck to get a look at them and whips out her compact mirror to check her makeup.

Evan smiles and his eyes flick back over to Dalisay. She and Nicole are talking quietly. Her eyes are bright, and she's wearing an "ugly" Christmas sweater today. It's covered in button-sized bells, puffballs for snowflakes, and neon-green reindeer running down the sleeves. It even has built-in lights, like a real Christmas tree. Somehow, she makes it look good.

"Yo," Daniel says, nudging Evan again. "Insider tip. If you really want to impress my mom by being here, you should know that the last Mass today is called *Misa de Gallo*, Mass of the Rooster. Afterward, it's tradition to ring the bell out front to commemorate your first *novena*."

"Are you serious?" Evan asks, scrunching his brow.

"Hell yeah, I'm serious." Someone gasps behind him, hearing him curse, and Daniel makes the sign of the cross. He leans back into Evan. "They say the sound is supposed to scare away any spirits that might want to do harm in the coming year. I did it when I was old enough to finally sit through all morning Masses. It's a rite of passage."

Evan's never heard of anything like that, but who is he to question it? It's not his culture. "But I'm not Catholic. Am I allowed to?"

Daniel nudges him again. "It'll be big brownie points with my mom. Trust me."

When Mass finally ends, and the congregation floods out of the building, Evan steps into the bright morning sunlight with the rest of the Ramos family. Dalisay and Nicole are talking with Melinda, and Little Luis tries to bolt into the grass to play before Dalisay catches him by the collar.

For a brief moment, Dalisay glances his way, holding Little Luis back, and a smile brightens up her face. She off-loads Little Luis to Melinda, color apparent in her cheeks.

Forget butterflies; Evan's stomach plops over like a bag of sand, heavy and solid. Does he really have a shot with her? Why is she smiling at him like that? Is he reading too much into things? He's made it this far, and Daniel is even helping him, so did she change her mind about him after all? Have they really changed their minds about each other?

Daniel catches his eye, tipping his chin up ever so slightly, and gives him the thumbs-up.

Right, the bell. Maybe after this he'll have earned his way to stage five.

Most people mingle in small groups, chatting with one another, and small children run between the groups like frogs jumping from rock to rock in a river. Daniel gives him another encouraging thumbs-up while Mrs. Ramos discusses a course of intercept for the Consulate General and his wife.

Evan takes a breath and adjusts his suit jacket.

Whole-ass, he thinks. All or nothing.

Evan approaches the bell and looks around, waiting for someone to beat him to it, but no one does. He tries to read what it says on the plaque, but it's all in Filipino. He wonders if it's some kind of prayer. Without thinking much else about it, he reaches for the hammer underneath, pulls it back, and lets it go.

The second he does it, the deafening sound of the bell makes everyone on the block fall silent. People stare at him with mixtures of shock and befuddlement. The priest shakes his head, mouth open. The Consulate General and his wife stare, baffled. A child gapes at him, picking his nose.

Daniel covers his mouth in silent laughter and Lola rounds on him, scolding him in Tagalog. It was a prank.

Heat rushes to Evan's face as the priest steps forward. He points a finger to the plaque on the bell.

"That is the original bell from this church after it burned down in 1906," the priest says, his tone curt and disapproving. "It is not for ringing."

Evan's blood runs cold. He's never been scolded by a priest before; it feels surprisingly like being scolded by his father. Panicking, he looks over at Dalisay, whose face is bright red. She looks at Evan, then at Daniel, her jaw set and her lips pinched. When she looks at Evan again, his heart drops.

What has he done?

CHAPTER TWELVE

"**E**van!"

It's Dalisay. Evan doesn't turn around. He's too embarrassed. He rushes down the block, his hands tucked firmly in his pockets, shoulders hunched as he hears her footsteps hurrying after him, the bells on her sweater jingling as she jogs. It would almost be funny if Evan didn't feel so miserable.

"Evan!" Dalisay says again, breathless.

She catches up to him just before he gets to the bus stop. He can't take it anymore. He turns around to face her.

"I'm sorry, Dalisay. I—That was so stupid of me."

"It's okay!" she says, breathless. "I know Daniel was teasing. It's just how he is. I'm the one who should be sorry."

"You didn't do anything," he says. Evan licks his lips, toeing the sidewalk with his boot. He can't bring himself to look her in the eye, and he's afraid that if he does, he might break. He's so ashamed. "I should have realized."

"Jokes are supposed to be funny," Dalisay says. He's surprised how sharp her tone is. She's furious, but not at him. "It's not your fault. Daniel went too far. He's trying to protect me because he thinks . . . He does this with all the guys I'm . . . It's his way of testing you."

"Like you were testing me? With this bet?" he asks.

She's silent, the straight line of her mouth saying more than any words she could speak. Regret pulls at his gut. He's lost the bet. He can't do any more, not after today.

The Five Stages was a complete failure, but for some reason, the bet is the last thing he cares about because there's only one thing he wants, and now he can't have it.

"My mom knows what Daniel did. You wanted to impress her."

He almost says it's not her mom he wanted to impress but stops himself. He's been reading everything so wrong, and it hurts more than he can say.

When Evan still doesn't say anything, she says, slowly, "Listen, are you busy this afternoon? I know it's Christmas Eve and all . . ."

"No. Do you need me to do any more chores?" He doesn't mean to sound so blunt, but he's had a rough day. He regrets it the minute he says it. "Sorry."

Dalisay shakes her head. "It's not about that. Can we meet at the Union Square ice rink?"

"The ice rink?"

Dalisay nods. "Please?"

Evan lets out a breath and tucks the corners of his lips down. "Sure," he says.

Evan doesn't know how to ice-skate to save his life. The last time he came to the Union Square ice rink, it was for Yoongi's twenty-first birthday, and everyone was drunk and falling over one another. Evan barely remembers the day at all. He woke up with the worst hangover the next morning and so many bruises, he couldn't walk right for a week.

The rink at Union Square is outdoors, surrounded by white tents selling hot dogs and hot chocolate under the shadow of the giant Macy's Christmas Tree decked out for the holidays. The square is already packed with families as Evan waits near the gate, looking for any sign of Dalisay.

His insides squirm as he tries to figure out why she would want to come here. After everything that's happened, he's sure this is the end. While Dalisay may have warmed up to him a bit, he's certain that she's not the type to change her mind about things, especially when such things made her family look like complete fools in front of their community.

He's not upset he lost the bet, he's upset he lost her.

At the far end of the square, Lola and Dalisay appear, arms linked together, walking toward Evan. They're speaking in Tagalog while they approach, and Lola's face splits into a grin when she sees Evan.

She says something to Dalisay, and Dalisay translates. "Lola says she's never ice-skated before, and she's excited for you to teach her."

"Oh!" says Evan. He wasn't expecting Lola to be here. He thought when Dalisay said to meet at Union Square, she'd be alone. He recovers quickly. "I'll do my best."

"I've never ice-skated before either," says Dalisay. "You're probably an expert." When her eyes sparkle like that, it makes Evan feel like he really is standing on ice, weak-kneed and prone to falling over.

Evan laughs nervously. "Right." He doesn't have the heart to explain that the opposite is true. Why is she dragging out the inevitable?

With their rented skates, they sit on a few benches under one of the tents to tie their laces. Lola and Dalisay chat happily in Tagalog, but Lola is having some trouble bending over to tie her laces.

"I can do it for you, Mrs. Ramos," Evan offers, unsure if she understands him. But Lola stares at him with one eyebrow raised, so similar to the way Dalisay does it, then nods. When he kneels down and ties the laces on Lola's skates, she says something to Dalisay, and the back of Evan's neck feels like it's caught on fire.

He's failed every single stage. He fumbled their first meeting, she threw away all his gifts, she didn't sing back during his serenade, he broke a priceless family heirloom, and he made an ass of himself today. Regret tugs at his gut as he lingers behind as Dalisay and Lola wobble their way to the ice, gripping the wall for support. Other skaters whiz past in a giant oval on the rink but Lola and Dalisay are fearless.

The moment Evan steps onto the ice, he nearly falls. The ice is smooth, and he slides across the surface, arms thrown wide for balance. Dalisay's smile is huge as she looks back at him, her own arms flapping beside her. His instinct is to reach out and hold her upright, but someone else's hand slips into his—Lola's.

"I can hold your hand," Lola says, her voice gravelly and stern. "But Dalisay cannot."

It's like she's read his mind.

Heat creeps up Evan's face. All this time, he had assumed she only spoke Tagalog. He opens and closes his mouth a few times, speechless, but Lola doesn't let go.

Without them, Dalisay takes off, getting the hang of ice-skating quickly enough to join the flock of skaters around the rink, smiling the whole time.

Sweat breaks out on Evan's back as he helps keep Lola upright. Once, Evan nearly loses his balance and throws his foot out, almost tripping a couple of women skating by.

"Watch it, dude!" one of them yells at him.

"Sorry!" he calls.

Lola's hand grips his like a vise, and his fingers start to lose feeling, but if it means losing an arm to keep her safe, Evan will do it.

"So," Lola says, "you have had quite a journey to this point."

"Yeah. The stages were a lot harder than I thought."

"Not for the faint of heart." The wrinkles on her face deepen with a smile. He thinks this is the first time she's directed one at him. "What are your intentions with my granddaughter?"

Evan finds that he can answer truthfully for the first time out loud. "I like her. A lot."

Lola nods. "You are in good company, because I like her a lot too." She winks at him. "Dalisay is one of the kindest, most clever people on earth. Her heart is true, but she is protective of it. She does not let it free so easily. One must truly be exceptional for her to give them her heart."

He catches a glimpse of Dalisay through the crowd, coasting on one foot with a huge smile as her hair billows out behind her, and he feels his heartbeat in his throat and a longing he didn't know existed tears through him.

"Many don't put in the effort," Lola says.

Evan's heart feels like it's being squeezed as tight as his hand, and he means it when he says, "She's worth it."

"Yes. She is."

Later, after a tentative few laps around the rink, Evan guides Lola safely back to dry ground. Her smile is huge, full of child-like wonder, and her cheeks are pink with joy. A photographer near the Christmas tree offers to take their photo for ten dollars, and Lola can't pass it up even though Dalisay *tsks* at the price. Lola hands the photographer the money and she brings Dalisay and Evan close on either side of her. She's so small, Dalisay and Evan's shoulders bump together above Lola's head. Evan catches a whiff of Dalisay's perfume, and his smile twitches as the camera flash goes off. She's so close to him, and yet she feels so far away.

When Evan helps Lola untie her skates, his own feet sore and aching from being so confined, Lola says, "I need to do some shopping at Macy's. Dalisay, will you walk me there?"

At first, Dalisay looks confused, but then the expression disappears. "Evan, will you wait here?" she asks.

Still in servitude mode, Evan nods.

He's leaning on the fence by the Christmas tree for twenty minutes when Dalisay reappears alone, holding two steaming paper cups. "I hope you like hot chocolate," she says, holding one out.

Evan takes it, their fingers brushing for the slightest moment before she pulls away. She wraps her fingerless gloved hands around her own cup and leans on the railing, just as the tree lights come on to the gasp of the crowd.

"Oh!" she says, excitedly pointing. "So pretty!"

Evan barely notices. He's only been watching her, and it's as if the rest of the world has melted away. The lovely slope of her nose, the gentle waves she ironed into her hair, the shiny pink lip gloss . . . When she glances back at him, he looks down at his hot chocolate and grips it tighter.

How can there be one more stage after this?

"Lola spoke very highly of you," Dalisay says. "She said you were quite the gentleman."

"I was prepared to use my body as a shield in case we fell."

Dalisay laughs and when she does, her hair falls over her shoulder. It's such a stupid instinct, but Evan wants to touch it, to tuck it behind her ear. The need to touch her is all-consuming and holding himself back becomes an Olympic-level endeavor. How can something so simple drive him so crazy?

They fall into silence for a few seconds, sipping their hot chocolate and people-watching. The skating rink is a lot more crowded now with families and couples enjoying the muggy winter evening. A young couple skate by holding hands, smiling, and Evan's heart drops a little. They make it look so easy.

Everything he's gone through these past few weeks has made him feel like he's coming up short. The thought eats away at him, and he can't stop himself when he finally says it.

"I'm sorry I've wasted your time," he says. He can't look at her. "I thought I could do it, but . . ."

"The five stages."

Evan nods, and despite everything smiles. "I've been try-ing my best, and to do everything the way you expect in the Philippines." He swallows and looks up at the tree, anything so he doesn't have to see her face. "But I guess I'm a blunder-ing American who can't even manage four stages."

Dalisay laughs, a sort of snort-hiss that's so cute, he could explode. It's a totally new feeling, and Evan feels like he might be going insane. Out of the corner of his eye, he sees her shake her head in disbelief. "You think you're still on stage four?" she asks.

"Well . . . yeah." There she goes, laughing at him again, but Evan is too tired to fully understand why.

"There are five stages," she says, waving her hand, fingers splayed. "The last is this one." She reaches for his hand and slides her fingers in between his. The tips of her fingers are warm, the touch of her wool gloves soft. Her eyes sparkle and she squeezes his hand. "The Acceptance."

It takes a second for it to sink in. "That's it?"

"When we hold hands in public, it means I've accepted you as my suitor," she says. When she looks away, the dimples deepen in her cheeks. "Don't look so surprised."

He doesn't know what to say. Dalisay seems amused by this. Her gaze slips back to him. Her lips are closed, but her smile is bright, and her eyes have so much color, with flecks of gold and mahogany, deep and rich. He never allowed himself to see it before, and now he can't look away.

"You won," she says. She lets go of his hand, and Evan realizes too late that he didn't want her to. "I thought you'd chicken out. I didn't think you'd see it through. But you proved me wrong. You earned it."

Evan doesn't know what to think. A part of him wants to be thrilled that he did it, that he passed all five stages, but another part of him has moved way beyond that.

"I don't care about the Asia tour," he says.

Dalisay's eyebrows shoot up.

"I . . ." He looks at her, weighing the words in his mind before releasing them. "I want this, us, for real."

There, it's out in the open. He can't take it back.

Dalisay looks at him for a long second, her dark eyes wide and surprised. She still doesn't say anything.

But Evan's nerves get the better of him and he can't stop. "I know we said there weren't any strings attached or whatever to date after the stages were over but I can't help the way I feel about you. Forget the tour, forget the bet. I want to be with you. I stopped caring about winning a long time ago. And I know you don't have to change your mind about me or anything, but I figured you should know." She still doesn't say anything, and that's all he needs to get the message. He winces. "And I made this really awkward! I . . . I'll see you at work."

He turns to go but Dalisay grabs his wrist. "Wait."

His skin burns where she touches him, but he doesn't pull away. Her touch is grounding him to the spot.

"Evan, I . . ." She can't seem to find the words, and his heart pounds so hard, it actually hurts. Her fingers twitch, holding on to him tighter. Finally, she says, "I feel the same way about you too."

Relief is like a drug coursing through his veins. "Why didn't you say anything earlier?"

"Why didn't you?" she laughs, eyes bright.

This whole time, he should have known . . . They'd been circling each other, neither knowing that their feelings for each other had become mutual. The revelation is as clear as a ringing bell. He takes her hand, the one on his wrist, and holds it. Every nerve in his body is electrified.

A smile creeps onto his lips. "I want to kiss you so bad," he says, a little breathless.

Dalisay sucks in a tiny breath, like maybe she's a little breathless too. She raises an eyebrow and a playful smile lifts one side of her mouth. "I *bet* you won't kiss me."

Evan's heart is beating like crazy. "I'll take that bet."

His eyes drop to her lips and desire fills him up. He wants her. He's wanted her for so long, and now that she's right in front of him, all he has to do is close the gap. She goes still, as if waiting to see what he'll do; then Evan lifts his other hand, resting his palm on her cheek. Then he pulls her toward him.

He kisses her, pressing his lips against hers so gently, it makes his head spin. She melts against him, leaning forward, and her breath tickles his cheek. Her lips are so soft, and he can taste her cherry lip gloss mixed with chocolate on her tongue. He deepens the kiss and feels her whole body respond, matching his urgency now that they are finally doing what he's dreamed about for weeks.

After a second, he pulls back and remembers to breathe as Dalisay's eyes flutter open. Those beautiful dark eyes take him in and it's easy to forget where they are. He lifts his hand off her cheek, dumbstruck. Is this really happening?

Dalisay licks her lips, her pink tongue peeking out for the briefest moment, before she looks at him with a shocked expression that Evan can only assume matches his own. His blood pounds in his ears as they stare at each other. It's like the temperature of the air between them got cranked up a hundred degrees.

Deftly, Dalisay twists her hand out of his and she grabs him by the front of his jacket, her gaze returning to his mouth with a kind of desperation that makes him feel like he's a Hershey's bar placed in front of a chocoholic. She might eat him alive.

Holy shit. She wants him. Now.

"Should we . . . go somewhere else?" He barely recognizes his own voice, low and hoarse with desire. "Somewhere private?"

She nods, meeting his gaze once more. Color rises in her cheeks, and her eyes sparkle with Christmas lights from the tree as another smile spreads on those insanely kissable lips. "About time."

CHAPTER THIRTEEN

Dalisay's back slams the bathroom door open, and she and Evan tumble into the room, lips locked. Making out with Evan Saatchi in the public bathroom at the ice rink was not something she ever imagined herself doing, but she couldn't wait another minute to get her hands on him.

Evan uses his foot to close the door behind them as they kiss like they're making up for lost time. Fire burns between their bodies, and Dalisay's thoughts drown in the feel of him under her fingers. How warm his neck is, how soft his lips are, how strong his hands hold her as they knot in her hair. His mouth crashes against hers and her lips slide against his, taking him in with every breath. *God*, she thinks. *Finally.*

She kisses him, cupping her hands against the line of his jaw, her fingers touching the soft skin behind his ears. A small moan melts out of his throat, and she smiles against his lips.

Kissing him in the dream was nothing compared to the real thing.

She presses Evan against the bathroom wall and his hands secure her to him, firmly grasping her hips, like he doesn't want to let her go. The heat of his fingers burns through the yarn of her sweater. Although her eyes are closed tight, colors dance behind her eyelids. She loses all sense of time, of space, and the only thing that matters is the way Evan leans into her, strong and solid. Warmth floods her whole body. If it were possible, she wants to touch him everywhere at once.

Why did they take so long to get here?

She tangles her fingers in his curls. He smells like spice, he tastes like hot chocolate. Every time they touch, it's like new.

Evan's tongue eases her mouth open, and her head drops back. He sucks, and pulls on her lips, dragging his tongue across hers, stealing her breath away.

His hands trace her sides, and she lifts her Christmas sweater to let him touch her skin. If she had planned on doing this, she might have worn something less absurd than an outfit with built-in lights. But she hardly cares about that now. All she cares about is his rough hands sliding up her body, sending sparks of pleasure across her bare skin, before one hand finally lands on top of her bra and he squeezes her breast. It makes her moan.

Evan gasps a little, his eyes open now, half-lidded, his pupils blown out. She can't see his irises anymore, those gorgeous brown eyes lost in a black hole.

Dalisay nudges his head to the side with her nose as she drags her lips across his beard stubble and nibbles on his earlobe. The muscles in his jaw tighten and she kisses him there, feeling his pulse and the goosebumps that rise under her lips. He wants her, she can tell, the hardness pressed against her apparent, and pleasure rolls through her at the thought. His grip on her only gets tighter.

Dalisay's head knocks back once more as he squeezes her breast again, and he kisses the slope of her throat. His hand inches down, teasing the waist of her jeans, sending electric shocks of pleasure across her skin. The tips of his fingers skim against the soft skin below her hip bone. He dips lower.

"Evan," she says breathless. "Evan, wait."

He pauses, looking at her under his straight, dark brows, shoulders bobbing with every heavy breath.

"I . . ." It's like she's being torn in two directions. Her body pulses with want, but her mind tells her to pull back. To be patient. To take it slow. "I've never done *that* before. It's just . . . can we slow down?"

"Of course," says Evan. Not disappointed, not repulsed, not even turned off. He takes his hand back, the spot where it was now unusually cold, and a part of her regrets letting him go. "It's okay."

"Is it?"

"Yeah. We don't have to do anything else." He dives in to kiss her again, and it makes her eyes flutter closed. She's drunk off his touch.

They pull back for air and Dalisay swallows a lump in her throat. "You're not mad?"

"Why would I be mad?" His voice is husky and low, and he kisses her again, sending her mind spiraling down into the depths of pleasure.

She always thought that American men were far more promiscuous and sexually liberated, and dating a virgin would be like a professional baseball player pitching in the little leagues. She doesn't have an answer for him.

She can barely speak anyway, not when he kisses her like that. Open, craving, imploringly full of desire. A desperate moan escapes her, and she wants this, she wants this so badly, it almost hurts. She wants *him*. But she won't let herself have him. She shivers under his touch, despite the heat burning through her, and Evan pulls back ever so slightly; his grip on her hips tightens and then eases.

"Do you want to wait until . . ." Evan pauses before saying, "Marriage?"

"Uh . . ." A part of her wants to automatically say yes—the good, responsible Catholic girl in her—but another part of her isn't so sure anymore. She's hardly let that part of herself run wild, and it's been waiting for so long. Then again, does she really want to have sex in a public bathroom?

Evan hears her hesitation and nods, the smallest dip of his chin, and his eyes drop to her lips. She meets him there, pressing her lips to his, tugging his lower one between her teeth. He lets out another soft moan, and she swells with desire. He doesn't seem to be troubled by wanting to take it slow. He only tightens the grip of her body against his, and he drinks her in as he kisses the corner of her mouth, then her cheek, his breath tickling her ear, his teeth nipping into the soft skin of her neck. "Is this still okay?"

"*Ooh*, yes. Please." Her eyes roll back, and she feels his smile against her skin.

This is a good start.

Being with Evan is like being tipsy, all the time. It's all warmth, and lightness, and everything is funny for some reason. The days are brighter, the sky is bluer, and the air has never smelled so sweet.

Unlike when she was dating Luke, it's no secret that she's with Evan. Word spreads fast. The whole family knows within a day that he completed all five stages, because of course Lola would never let something like that stay quiet. Lola's approval alone at the ice rink was enough for Dalisay to solidify how she felt about him. She can't remember the last time she's felt this happy. She even told Pinky about it, accidentally letting slip that she and Evan hooked up in a public bathroom. Pinky almost upended the board game they were playing at The Basement, she jumped to her feet so fast, overjoyed. "*Yes!* Get it, girl! But also—ew, gross! A bathroom?" she cried.

To keep it professional at work, she and Evan maintain their distance, but Dalisay fantasizes too often about sneaking into a broom closet somewhere and tearing his shirt off. It would be totally inappropriate, but the fantasy makes her feel naughty and sexy, and the thrill alone makes her tremble. During meetings, grocery shopping with Mom, or staying up late at night working toward deadlines, all she can do is think about what she wants to do to him, what she wants him to do to her.

No one else at work, besides Riggs, knows that they're dating. If HR found out, it would be such a big deal, Dalisay's head would spin.

During the week, she tries to focus on her work, to lose herself in her words, but Evan can distract her in a way only he knows how. He can give her the lightest touches on the small of her back when he moves past her that make her spine tingle or bumps his knee into hers while they're sitting next to each other at the conference room table in a way that makes her bite the inside of her cheek to stop from smiling. He sends her emoticon texts throughout the day that say so much in so few characters. Every time times he sends her the kissy-face :-x, their new inside joke, she feels the ghosts of his lips on her skin.

Once, they crossed paths in the elevator going up to work and they spent the twenty-second ride up furiously making out, then breaking away a millisecond before the doors opened, pretending like it never happened.

It occurs to Dalisay that nothing about Evan has really changed, but she notices a slight shift in his demeanor. She doesn't believe in auras, but she gets the sense that Evan feels more at ease, as if he too is feeling something between them that's taken root. When he catches her eye across the office, his smile is contagious.

That Friday, Evan convinces her to take a half-day after lunch to see the Painted Ladies. It's their first official outing as a couple.

Once they turn the corner on Steiner Street, she immediately recognizes the row of historic Victorian and Edwardian houses from countless movies and TV shows she saw growing up in Manila. Their pastel color palettes and architectural cohesion is so aesthetically pleasing, she can't help but take a photo.

"I had a feeling you'd like them," Evan says, grinning as he watches her.

"They look like books neatly nestled on a shelf! I *love* them." She leads the way, taking probably a hundred photos as they walk together down the street.

"So, speaking of books"—he sidles up next to her—"you gave Maggie that candle I got you, the one that smelled like old books. You threw out every single thing from stage two."

"Yeah," she says, cringing.

"I thought you hated me."

"I know," she admits. "I was a little standoffish at first."

"A little?" His baritone laugh makes her smile. "That candle crushed me. I thought I had it in the bag."

"You almost did. I gave it away only because I didn't want it to be . . . I don't know, personal? If I kept the gifts, it felt too real. I wanted to remain impartial, for the sake of the rules."

"What changed?"

Dalisay thinks a second before answering. "It wasn't one thing in particular. I think I needed time."

Evan hums, tucking his hands into his front pockets, and turning his head to gaze across the Painted Ladies' white eaves. Dalisay can't help but admire his profile, the sharp lines of his face, the arch of his brow. His face belongs on a coin.

"No one's ever done what you did," she says.

"Not once?"

She shakes her head. Not even Luke. "I guess I misjudged you."

Evan's lips curl, amused, and an instinct to press her own lips to the shape of them overwhelms her. It's so easy picturing herself kissing him. He's magnetic.

"I didn't think I had a chance with you either," he says. "Not after our first meeting."

Dalisay grins. "And yet here we are."

"Here we are," he repeats. Evan shakes his head, grinning, and his eyes shine in the sunlight.

Two blocks down, he brings her to his favorite ice-cream shop. It's a small boutique, with a dozen homemade ice creams in aluminum bins in a glass display. While everything looks amazing, she gets her favorite, chocolate with sprinkles, and he gets cookie dough and pays for them both. Ice cream in hand, they sit at a small table on the sidewalk under the shady canopy of a nearby laurel fig tree.

They're halfway through their cones when Evan asks, "So what are your plans this weekend?"

"Mama, Lola, Nicole, and I were going to have a Ramos Family Bake-Off."

"What's that?"

"We watch a season of *The Great British Bake Off* and then try to re-create what the contestants make at home, just to see how hard it is. It's usually a disaster. A delicious disaster."

Evan laughs and it's easy to join him, but Dalisay's heart hitches a little. Things are still a little awkward with Nicole. There's a wall between them that Dalisay isn't sure how to navigate around. It's hard to accept that maybe it's not her place to do so.

She's been told she's a fixer, and it's true. When presented with a problem, her mind automatically starts working on a solution. Nicole has called her out on it more than once. Sometimes her sister just wants to rant about work, or school, or life in general, and Dalisay defaults to trying to find a way she can make it better, even though all Nicole needs in that moment is to be heard. Dalisay hates seeing the people she cares about suffer, and the only way she can think to help is to try to make everything better. It's gotten worse ever since the moment she sat down in the chair next to her father's hospital bed and realized she couldn't do a damn thing to help him. She'd never felt so useless.

One thing's for sure, it's not Dalisay's place to out Nicole. She can't tell Evan despite wanting to. And she's not sure how to help Nicole, especially concerning their mother.

Dalisay knows the world is changing, that family means a lot of things to different people, but their mother is a product of time and place. Her culture has always been a fundamental part of her identity and she doesn't exactly distinguish between the good and the bad aspects. She sees it as a foundation to lay the groundwork of their lives, a compass to guide them through the difficulties of life. All that matters is family. It's the one thing that can be relied on, and that means finding a husband, and settling down, with bunches of kids. And when Papa died, those traditional views felt like something that needed to be preserved, to ensure that he lived on in a way, because it was his culture too. But how would her mom react if Nicole came out now, being in America? Would she still uphold those narrow-minded opinions? The possibility is haunting enough without Dalisay's fear that she wouldn't have the courage to stand up to her mother and tell her that she's wrong.

"Hey." Evan's voice cuts through her thoughts. When he looks at her with that small smile on his face that crinkles the corners of his brown eyes, Dalisay's mind settles. His presence is like a warm mug of tea on a rainy night. "What are you thinking about?"

"Just . . . family stuff." Some ice cream dripped down the side of her cone, so she licks it before it can get on her hand.

"Everything okay? You know you can tell me anything."

"Oh, really?" she says, raising an eyebrow and smirking. "Does that mean I can *ask* you anything?"

"I'm an open book."

"Past girlfriends?" she asks, taking him up on the challenge.

"One. Well, one serious one. Becca."

"Oh right, Pinky mentioned that."

"What did she tell you?"

"No details. Just that it ended poorly."

Evan huffs a sigh and manages a grin. "Did she mention it ended with a champagne bucket full of ice dumped on my head?"

"She did not," Dalisay says, eyes wide. "What did you do?"

Evan shakes his head, still smiling, and says before taking another bite of ice cream, "We'll just leave it at that."

"Okay, Mr. Open Book," she says with a teasing grin.

"You got me. Becca is in the past. I don't want to distract from what's right in front of me."

Dalisay understands. She's not entitled to anyone's history, and when Evan's ready he'll tell her. She has to remember that, even with Nicole.

"What about you? Any boyfriends?"

Dalisay groans. "One. It ended pretty quick, though."

Evan hears the tone in her voice. "What happened? If you don't mind telling me."

Dalisay hesitates, then realizes it no longer bothers her to talk about it. Evan will understand. "He just . . . He was a little pushy and I wasn't ready. We did go pretty far, but I didn't want to have sex, even though I thought I loved him. He tried to pressure me into doing it by threatening to lie to everyone that I wasn't a virgin, so we might as well. He had some pictures . . . Anyway, Daniel found out and scared him off, and I was kind of relieved he did."

"Shit," Evan says. "I'm sorry."

Dalisay waves her hand. "It's fine. My parents didn't know about him. I was too afraid to tell them; dating him was a secret. My mom especially believes that I need to wait for marriage, to be 'pure,' and I think it would have broken my dad's heart." A lump forms in her throat and she swallows it down. "What about your parents? Are all American parents so chill about their kids dating?"

"Depends. My parents are both academics, so they were too busy with their work to micromanage my love life."

"What do they do?"

"My dad's in physics, and my mom's got a doctorate in engineering."

"That's impressive."

"They're divorced now, though."

"Oh," Dalisay says, frowning. "I didn't know that. I'm sorry."

Evan shrugs. "It happened when I was seven. No big deal. My mom lives in India now, teaching at an engineering school, so I don't really see her all that much, but at least I've got my dad."

She can tell by the way he says it that it was a big deal, despite Evan saying otherwise. "Are your parents divorced too?" he asks. "I haven't seen your dad around."

She knew this would come up eventually. "Papa died. Two years ago."

He was about to take a bite of his cone, but he freezes. "Oh, shit. I'm sorry. I didn't know, I shouldn't have assumed—"

"It's okay," she says. It's automatic saying that. She's not sure it'll ever be okay, really. "Lola is his mom. We look out for each other."

"Do you . . . ," Evan starts to say, but he changes course. "How did he die?"

"Cancer." And in an instant, she's teleported back to those long days at the hospital, sleeping in a chair at his bedside, watching as he withered away. "So then, what got you into writing? And traveling?" she asks, trying to lighten the mood.

Evan takes her in for a moment, perhaps wondering if he should let her change the subject, but she's too skilled at pulling herself back before the riptide of grief can take her under. Evan seems to realize that and answers her question.

"I always loved traveling. When I was little, I told my mom I wanted to be Indiana Jones. You can imagine how well that went over. Initially, she was excited that I wanted to be a doctor, but I wanted to be an adventurer. Writing is kind of its own adventure, you know? You?"

"I always loved reading, and started writing as soon as I could hold a pencil. I guess I was really good at it. In high school, I entered a creative writing contest at a local independent publisher with this story about a girl who clones herself so she can live two different lives, and I won. I was first published at fifteen."

"That's amazing! You're selling yourself short." He makes a *psh* sound, forcing air between his front teeth.

Dalisay blushes and looks at her shoes. "Well, the thing is, my parents took that as a sign that I had peaked, and it was time for me to start being serious about a medical degree." When Evan bobs his head in understanding, she says, "You too?"

"Yeah. My dad didn't really see the point in studies outside of applied sciences at first, but he came around in the end. But my mom keeps asking me when I'm going to stop writing and get a serious career."

Dalisay huffs out a laugh through her nose. Turns out parents are the same everywhere in the world. "My family just thinks they know what's best for me, without really asking me. Like what Daniel did to you at Mass. He was trying to protect me. He wants to make sure I don't get hurt."

He reaches over the table and brings her free hand up to his mouth and kisses her knuckles. His lips are cold from his ice cream, but they feel nice against her warm skin. "Family is important. But we need to live our own lives, you know? We can respect what they say because they want what's best for us, but the only thing that's right is what *we* want."

She couldn't have put it better herself. She wants *this*, being right here, right now. With him.

Evan's eyes playfully light up. "And what *I* want, is to kiss you till I can't feel my lips anymore."

"Funny," she says, failing to suppress her grin. "That's exactly what I want too."

CHAPTER FOURTEEN

In the dark of the movie theater the following weekend, she can feel Evan next to her. She doesn't need light to know he's there. The warmth coming off him being so close, the smell of his cologne, it's all so uniquely him, she wishes they weren't in a packed movie theater, just so she could have more of him to herself. They've only just started officially dating, and she wants to take things slow, but her body betrays her sometimes, a tightness below her gut that coils with lust and makes it hard for her to notice anything else.

Horny, she's horny. There's no other way around it. And it's driving her insane.

Breathing the same air he does makes her feel like she needs to handcuff herself to the nearest stationary object or else she might jump him because she wants him so badly; it would be the easiest thing in the world to give herself over to him. But she usually manages to hold herself back, finds ways to calm herself down, to stay in control for one more day. But she's always had an active imagination, and now it's too easy to imagine what they would do if they were alone in the theater. How she would leap into his lap and yank his sweatshirt over his head, how he would squeeze her ass, pulling her closer. How his hands would wind under her skirt, how his fingers would tease at her skin. How she'd kiss him so long and hard that both their lips were swollen and pink and they would—

Jolting her out of her fantasy, Evan's hand slips into hers, sweet as can be. By the pale glow of the movie screen, she can see his profile and the smile that lifts his cheeks. She knows he can't read her mind, but for a brief, panicked moment she wonders what if he could and how embarrassing that would be. Heat on her face lets her know she's blushing hard, and she gives him an embarrassed smile in return. She's being so ridiculous, but he doesn't have to know that.

He doesn't let go of her hand for the rest of the movie, or even after the movie ends, or as they walk outside.

"Tonight was really great," Evan says. He tips his head back, breathing in the night air. Only then does he let her hand go as he tucks his in his jeans pockets against the brisk wind that sweeps down the street. He does that a lot, tucking his hands into his pockets.

It's easier to notice those quirks more often. How he can only raise his left eyebrow or both—never the right on its own—or how his ears lift when he smiles, or how he twists his wrists before he starts typing a new article as if he's warming up. But her favorite is when he steps up to any bookshelf he comes across, picks up a random book, and flips to an equally random page to read a couple of paragraphs before setting it back in its place and moving on, like he's sneaking into a show during intermission and sneaking back out again before he's caught.

What feels like ages ago, she thought she had him all figured out, and still he has ways of surprising her. Like now, when he asks, "Would you like to come over to my place tomorrow? You can finally meet Tallulah."

Dalisay's smile falls a little. That coil inside of her winds up again. "I don't know."

Evan's brows knit together, concerned. "You don't like dogs? Are you allergic?"

"No! It's not that . . ." She licks her lips and looks off to the middle distance, as if there she'd find a way to explain it.

Why did she say that? *Why* is she still holding back? Why is she so afraid of being happy? What is she afraid of? Evan isn't Luke. She's a tangled mess of conflicting desire. She doesn't want to disrespect her family's wishes and have sex before marriage, but she wants to lose her virginity to Evan. And yet she isn't sure she's ready to physically bare herself to someone yet, but she knows deep down she can trust Evan not to hurt her. And to make everything worse, she's terrified of the desire that rages through her. It's a brand-new feeling, and she doesn't know how to wield it. She's never felt like this about anyone, not even Luke. And she's certain that being with Evan is everything she wants, but she won't let herself have him. It's such a mess inside her brain, it's a miracle she's still standing. "I'm sorry," she says, after what feels like an eternity.

Evan looks surprised, then lets out a breathy laugh and shakes his head. "If you think I'm trying to get you in bed—" He holds up two fingers in some sort of salute that Dalisay doesn't understand and crosses his heart with his other hand. "Scout's honor, I'm not. I've been over to your house dozens of times by now. I thought you'd want to . . ." He trails off, biting his lip, because he notices the way Dalisay's face is bright red. Another quirk of his, lip biting when he's trying to think of what to say.

Evan looks confused, and he shifts his weight from one hip to the other.

Why is her heart pounding so hard?

Gently, Evan takes her hands and looks deep into her eyes. Sincerity is always in style, especially on him.

"It's normal for people who are in a relationship to see each other's homes," he says, gently nodding and smiling. "But you don't have to come over if you don't want to."

It occurs to Dalisay that she hasn't the faintest idea what "normal" means in America.

Dalisay steels herself, standing on Evan's porch. Her nerves twist and turn inside of her, competing for the warmth spreading in her belly at the thought of finally going into his home. Alone.

It's only lunch, she reminds herself. She checks her reflection in the glass of his front door and smooths out the creases of her sweater, a last chance to make sure she looks her best for Evan. She curled her hair, put on lip gloss, even used some of her favorite jasmine perfume. Why is she so nervous suddenly? The coil in her gut feels like it's about to spring.

She rings the doorbell with shaking fingers. Immediately, she hears a small dog barking.

"It's okay, Tallulah! It's just Dalisay!" she hears Evan say behind the door. He opens it and immediately she's overwhelmed by the smell of fresh-baked bread. Evan stands in an apron, wearing a smile and a black T-shirt with a smudge of flour around the neck.

A little brown dog leaps at Dalisay, tail wagging, jumping up on hind legs to greet her.

"Hello!" Dalisay says, leaning down, letting the dog sniff the back of her hand. "You must be Tallulah. I've heard so much about you."

Tallulah takes kindly to that, licking Dalisay's hand enthusiastically.

"Come in!" Evan says, beckoning her inside. Tallulah leads the way and Dalisay follows.

Evan's condo is, strangely enough, exactly how she imagined: minimalist and monochromatic. Evan likes his whites, blacks, and grays. Everything is neat and clean, save for the towers of books leaning against the walls. A plush dark gray couch stands opposite a large TV and dozens of maps of all different sizes, origins, and orientations decorate the walls. His home is simple, but not boring; mature, but not cold; organized, and yet somewhat chaotic. Most importantly, it's all Evan.

"I was just making some focaccia," Evan says. "You'd better be hungry."

"I'm *starving*." She had no idea Evan could cook.

He brings her to a kitchen where glass double doors overlook a small patio garden. The garden is bursting with color, the only place in his house that isn't monochromatic, and he brought some flowers inside to sit on a small vase on the table. Evan went all out making lunch. Caesar salad, pancetta and pesto pasta, antipasto skewers, shrimp-stuffed avocado. Everything looks delicious.

"I mistimed the focaccia, so it'll be a few extra minutes until it's ready," Evan says, leaning down to peer through the oven window. "Hope you don't mind waiting."

Dalisay's heart swells. "I don't mind. I never figured you were the home chef type."

"Traveling so much, I crave foods from all the places I go. Sometimes the only thing I can do is learn how to make them myself."

"You'll have to teach me sometime," she says. Her heart skips when he smiles at her and pours her a glass of red wine. When he hands it to her, he swoops in and kisses her, tasting like olive oil and salt. Like a proper cook, he's been tasting the food.

After stealing her breath, he leans back and smiles. "Hi. Can't believe I forgot to do that earlier."

The blush creeps its way up her face. The pressure below her gut builds and she searches for a distraction. "Want to show me around?"

"Sure, we've got time." He unties the apron, then takes her by the hand.

His condo has a lot of space for one man and his tiny dog. It has two bedrooms, one for himself, and the other he's turned into an office. His office is the messiest, most chaotic room in the whole house. Seemingly every wall is covered in maps.

"I collect them," he says when he notices her looking. "Kind of a weird hobby, I know."

"It's not weird."

Evan grins. "It's a little weird."

His office has a desk stacked with books, a lamp, and a wide filing cabinet as large as one wall. One of Tallulah's dog beds is situated in a corner, surrounded by even more books. It smells like paper here and immediately Dalisay feels at home.

"Sorry about the mess," he says.

Dalisay sets her wine down on top of the filing cabinet. "Do you work in here?"

"Sometimes. Write, read, research."

"Using maps?"

"Maps can tell you a lot, not just about the place charted, but the people who charted it. Here, look, let me show you." He goes to a cabinet and pulls one of the thin drawers open. The drawer is about an inch deep, but Dalisay can see a stack of maps laid out inside. He flips through a few and brings one out, laying it flat on the desk. It's of Ancient Greece, with Greece surrounded by Africa, Europe, and Asia and then the oceans like rings, the dimensions completely skewed from modern satellite imagery. "It's not so much a map as it is the idea of one," says Evan.

"Navigation by vibes only."

Evan laughs. "Exactly." His gaze lingers on her for a minute, and then he clears his throat and turns back to the cabinet drawers, pulling out another one. It's an explosion of saturated reds, blues, and yellows with hundreds of detailed geographic illustrations and illuminated texts. "Fra Mauro. It's one of the biggest maps from medieval Europe. Notice how south is oriented at the top."

Dalisay traces her fingers over the print. The lines look so textured, she almost thinks she can feel them popping out of the page. The world seems so different turned upside down.

Evan pulls out another map. "Now this one is my favorite."

It's a map of North America, or rather, it looks like some-one's best guess at what North America looks like, as if they'd heard about it from a friend of a friend of a friend. Notice-ably, the western part of America is labeled as an island.

"Cartographers used to think California was this magi-cal, mythical island," Evan says. "Like, early European col-onizers mistook the Baja Peninsula for one, and the rumor spread as other cartographers kept copying the same map. California became this fantastical place, separated from the rest of the land, as more and more maps were re-created based off that misconception for hundreds of years."

"People didn't check?" Dalisay asks, amused. "Could have asked the natives."

"It only took them two hundred years."

Dalisay laughs and so does Evan. Seeing him like this warms her heart. He's so excited to show her the maps, she can tell he doesn't get to talk about his collection all that often. They riffle through more maps, and Dalisay lets Evan rattle off historical details, realizing she could listen to him for hours. This whole time she thought cosplay and D&D was the geekiest thing about him. He's a lot nerdier than he lets on.

"Growing up, with my parents' work schedule and stuff, we didn't really travel all that much. And I think they kind of hated each other by the time I was actually making memories anyway." He lets out a small laugh. "So the only way I could travel was through books or movies. I remember being fasci-nated by the first Indiana Jones and those map sequences, and how they had so much texture and how the soundtrack made everything feel so . . . epic. I would rewind that part over and over and learned everything I could, and I even got to a point where I found mistakes, like anachronistic country names. I was so obnoxious when I was little, I would tell anyone within earshot that Siam wasn't Thailand until 1939." He smiles at her, his whole face bright, and Dalisay can't help but smile back.

It's clear he could talk about this forever, but the timer on his phone goes off. "The focaccia. I'll be right back."

When he leaves, Dalisay brings out another huge map, this time a map of the world. She spreads it over the entirety of the desk and her eyes glaze over all the words, simply taking in the shape of the world, and her mind drifts. It's crazy to think that she started on one side of the map, and now she's on another. She traces her hand over the archipelagos of the Philippines. It feels so small on the page, only an arm's length from Manila to San Francisco. It doesn't capture the enormity of the distance. Sometimes it feels like she left so much behind . . . and yet there's still so much more of the world she wants to see. While her father always said, *remember where you came from*, that was only half the saying. When she won that writing contest, he said to her, his hand warm on her shoulder, "Remember where you came from, but also remember where you're going." It's easy for Dalisay to forget that last part, especially since he's not here anymore.

When Evan returns, Dalisay is still looking at the map, her thoughts a million miles away.

"Do you think we could make our own map someday?" she asks, lifting a shoulder.

Evan comes to her side, bringing the smell of bread with him. "Like, go on a trip together?"

"Why not? Cartography can't be too hard, can it? I bet we wouldn't make California an island."

Evan's smile goes wide. "No, we would not."

"So then, where would we go?"

Either the wine is getting to her head, or it's getting warm in here.

Evan looks at the world map in front of him, his brown eyes catching the light and turning to honey. He points, tracing his finger down the boot of Italy. "Rome. It's the most romantic place in the world."

"Oh," says Dalisay. "The *most* romantic? How do you know if you haven't been everywhere else first?"

Evan's large hands splay on the map, and Dalisay's eyes linger on them before Evan says, "You're right. I haven't seen everything. Where would you take me?"

She puts her hand over his and draws it across the paper, using his finger to point. "Hoi An, Vietnam. The Old Town, beaches, paper lantern festival." She leads his hand again, appreciating the warmth of his skin. "Kyoto, Japan. Temples, yakitori, bright pink cherry blossoms." She leans over, and her hair brushes against Evan's forearm. "Bhutan. Tiger's Nest Monastery, natural hot springs, snow-capped mountains."

Evan teases, "I thought you didn't like going on hikes. You'd want to trek the Himalayas?"

"With the right person," she says.

And all at once, he goes still, realizing what she means. It's only after she says it does *she* realize what she means.

She could fall into his eyes, they're standing close, so close now, she can see every detail of him, each hair in his stubble, every single one of his eyelashes, a small scar above his upper lip.

This is what she was worried about. This feeling right here.

Evan's eyes flick back and forth a few times, looking at her, taking her in. He moves as if to pull back, but she doesn't let his hand go. She wants him to read her like a place on a map.

"Should we . . . ," he asks, his voice barely a breath. "Do you want . . . ?"

And she kisses him.

CHAPTER FIFTEEN

Dalisay pushes Evan against the table, and the maps go fluttering to the floor. His hands cup her jaw, and his breath is as ragged as tearing paper when he takes her in. Color pops behind her lids as Evan's lips slide down the length of her neck, his teeth nipping at her skin. A whine escapes her throat and all she can think about is him and where he's touching her. She needs to close the gap where he's not. Evan leans, as if falling backward, then straightens up and spins them around. He lifts Dalisay so she sits on the table. She wants him closer.

She crosses her arms at the hem of her dress and pulls it over her head. Evan lets out a low groan as he swoops in, his mouth hot on the skin of her chest above her lace bra. She grabs the side of his head, arching into his touch, and gasps. "Take it off," she says.

With deft fingers, he unclips her bra. It tumbles to the floor and Evan kisses her, squeezing her breast and rubbing his thumb over her other nipple. It's unlike anything she's ever felt before, and her whole body shakes with anticipation. She wants more.

All that runs through her mind is Evan. Only Evan.

She grabs the back of his shirt and pulls it over his head. He looks as solid as he feels, the slight taper at his waist easy for Dalisay to wrap her legs around, and he pulls her closer. She drags her fingers up and down his back, feeling his muscles flex as he holds her, exploring the dip of his spine and the smoothness of his skin as he kisses her with crushing force and hungry eagerness. His tongue eases her mouth open, and a moan escapes her. Each kiss is sloppy, and wet, and hot.

Slowly, Evan's lips move down her throat, down her chest, down her soft stomach, and his breath tickles. He kneels in front of her, pressing his mouth to the smallest, most sensitive places on her legs, between her thighs.

"Evan," she says, panting. On his knees, Evan waits, looking at her under his hooded brow as she burns with desire. "Are you sure . . . ?"

"I want to do this," he says. "Only if you'll let me."

"Okay," she barely manages to say. Evan smiles and watches her face as he slides her underwear down her legs. He drops it to the floor and presses his lips to the soft, bare places of her thighs, marked with panty lines. His fingers dig into her skin, and her whole body throbs with need. His touch is sure, resolute, but he's taking it slow, teasing her with each lick in the groove of her hips, and she's not sure she can take much more.

She leans back on the desk, ready to give herself over, and a tower of books topples to the floor. She laughs, then squeals, as Evan's lips press at the crest between her thighs.

Her brain melts.

"Is this okay?" he asks.

She palms the back of his head, unable to speak. She thinks she says yes, but her body definitely does. Evan's mouth works and her knees fall open. She presses herself into him, uncoiling and unwinding with every flick of his tongue. Her eyes roll back, and she lets out a choked gasp. This is what she's been missing.

She doesn't have a body anymore. There's only heat, and the tattooing of her heartbeat, and building pressure. Evan's hands grip her tightly, even as she arches against him, and her body moves with him for more, more, more. Until finally, she unravels.

A second lasts an eternity. Lights pop behind her eyelids, and she twists, writhing under his touch. Pleasure pumps through her, meeting the rapid-fire pace of her heart, hammering away every single thought in her mind as a cry bursts out of her.

Too soon, the rush subsides, like a receding tide, leaving Dalisay covered in sweat. It was so intense, tears blur her vision, and she stifles a sob. She breathes, gasps, and looks down.

Smiling, Evan rises, dragging his lips up her body once more, and meets her face. She kisses him, smiling back, despite tears running down her cheeks.

She wipes them away and he asks if she's okay, and she can only nod. "I've never made a woman cry before," he says.

Dalisay lets out a laugh, thick with tears. Happy tears.

"You tell me when you want to stop," he whispers.

"Don't stop," she says, undoing his belt and tossing it away with unbridled need. "Don't." She unzips his jeans and slips her hand down his briefs. He's rock hard.

She's never touched a man like this before, and she's too gentle at first; she doesn't want to hurt him. He guides her hand and helps her, and he lets out a gasp as she strokes. She smiles as his eyes fly open, and his jaw drops, staring at her, almost pleading. She has him, literally, in the palm of her hand. She can tell, he's close. They've been waiting so long.

She's not done with him yet. "Take me to bed," she says.

Evan doesn't speak. He rests his forehead against hers, his eyes half-lidded. He's melting under her touch. Then, in one move, he grabs her, lifting her against him. She laughs as he carries her from the office and into his bedroom, kissing the whole way. Together, they fall onto his mattress with Evan on top. Evan kicks off his underwear and fumbles in his side table for a condom and Dalisay teases her lips up and down his ribs. No thinking, only feeling.

"If it hurts, tell me," he says. "We'll go slow."

"Not too slow," she says. She burns for him. Evan hovers over her, one hand braced by her head, and the other running between her legs. One of Evan's fingers slides inside of her. Dalisay's eyes go wide and she lets out a surprised, "Oh my God!"

Carefully, Evan watches her, then he puts in another finger. It's even better. Dalisay squirms with pleasure as he searches inside her with his fingers. A desperate noise rises out of her that sounds a lot like, "Yeah."

Evan readies himself and slides the condom on. He's naked, exposed, and she can't stop staring. *God, he's beautiful*, she thinks. *And he wants me.* Slowly, he positions himself and Dalisay gasps as the fullness of him slides into her.

He waits, checking to see if she's okay, but she kisses him, forcing him to stop thinking for once. They move together.

"Oh, *fuck*," he groans against her mouth, his voice hot and low. "Dalisay."

He turns his head, as if he can't bear it any longer.

Dalisay nips her teeth on his earlobe, wrapping herself around him, leveraging her hips against his. She buries her face into him, breathing him in, tasting him, kissing him. She can feel his heartbeat thrumming through his whole body, the tension of his neck, the curve of his biceps.

Evan reaches down and rubs his fingers between Dalisay's thighs, and she arches.

"Oh, God," she gasps. It's happening again.

How can a simple touch be so amazing? The pressure builds, and he looks down at her, his face inches from hers. All it takes is one more smile, one more push, and something loosens in Dalisay's gut and she's unwinding in his arms and so is he, and for once, words aren't enough for either of them.

A few hours later, they lie, sticky with sweat, exhausted in bed. It's dark outside, and the sheets have long ago been kicked to the floor, and Dalisay isn't sure where any of her clothes are, but she doesn't care.

The shape of Evan next to her is almost unreal.

He traces his fingers over her shoulder, brushing her hair away, and she nuzzles deeper into his pillow. She never wants to leave. If she's not careful, she could fall asleep.

"I've thought about doing that with you for a long time," he says, his voice low and soft, sleepy too.

Dalisay smiles. She's about to say the same, but she'd be incorrect. She couldn't imagine it being half as good as it actually was. She rolls over and kisses him, and his lips are soft, and gentle, and sweet.

She can't tell anyone about this, but a thrill rushes through her at the prospect of keeping it a secret. It feels naughty, and a little dangerous, and exciting. If anyone in her family found out, there might be hysterics.

The digital clock on Evan's bedside table says it's almost nine. So much for only coming over for lunch. She totally lost track of time after her third orgasm.

"It's getting late," she says.

Evan rolls over and looks at the time too. She loves watching the way his chest muscles move when he does, and she touches her hand against them, to feel for herself. He takes that hand and brings it up to his mouth so he can kiss her knuckles.

"Stay," he says.

"I wish I could," she says. "But my family will start asking questions."

"I know." His eyes sparkle in the dark. "It was worth a try."

She kisses him again, deeply, and breathes him in, remembering this moment. She was saving herself for the person she loved most, and she thinks, maybe she fell in love with him a long time ago.

CHAPTER SIXTEEN

"Evan, can I see you in my office?" Naomi asks as she passes his desk early Monday morning.

He looks up from his computer with a start, heart hammering in his chest. Immediately, he thinks she knows about him and Dalisay, and he has to swallow the bite of his croissant hard, it's suddenly so dry.

"Uh, yeah, sure," he says, trying not to look at Riggs as he follows her.

Even in heels, Naomi is a brisk walker and she's already sitting at her desk by the time he gets to her office, which always smells like lemon Lysol. Normally when he's in here, it makes his nose itch, so he constantly feels like he has to sneeze, but now his dread has shut down his senses. His armpits are already sweating.

Naomi won't even look at him, eyes cast down to her desk. That can't be a good sign. He can't lose this job. There has to be something he can do, something he can say that will fix this, but what if it's not enough? He has to think of something that won't get Dalisay fired either. If one of them has to go down, it'll be him.

"Close the door," Naomi says. He does, robotically.

When she indicates for him to sit, he does, and she slides the paper in front of him. He always thought a pink-slip was, well, pink, but the one in front of him is just a regular sheet of paper. And as he reads the words on the page, they don't make sense at first. He has to read it a few times for them to sink in.

"'Senior editor'?" he asks, looking up. "Me?"

Naomi leans back in her high-backed chair, one corner of her mouth lifting in a smile. "Eliza put in her two weeks—it's still not announced yet—but she suggested we replace her with someone internally, and your name was the first that came to mind. You're a good fit to lead the European team in her stead."

Evan's whole body starts tingling. He didn't even know Eliza, his senior, was leaving. This is the absolute last thing he imagined would happen right now. "A promotion?"

Either Naomi doesn't notice that he's been rendered dumb, or she doesn't care. "That analysis you wrote with Dalisay really impressed us. Those kinds of articles will be a staple going forward. Of course, you'll have to travel more, but it comes with a significant raise and title change and . . . Is this something you're interested in?"

Evan blurts out, "Hell yeah!" And then he clears his throat, gathering his professionalism. "I mean, yes." He can barely sit still.

Naomi smirks. "Good. We'll iron out all the details later, but for now get whatever projects you're working on done, and then we'll start talking about next steps."

Evan thanks her profusely, standing on shaking knees, and leaves before he explodes with joy.

On the main floor, the first thing Evan does is look for Dalisay. She's not at her desk, but he catches a glimpse of her back as she heads toward the storage closet. Without moving too quickly, he follows her while glancing around for anyone who might notice him, trying his very best not to sprint.

In the cramped closet, he finds Dalisay humming while she reorganizes the untidy shelves. He ducks in after her, pulling the door closed behind them. The single bulb above them is dim, but it still catches the brightness of her eyes when she turns to face him.

"Evan, what are you—"

He kisses her, holding her head in his hands, and her initial surprise fades as her arms lift, pressing her hands against his back. He sucks on her lower lip, dragging his teeth in a way that makes her sigh. Kissing her here and now feels dangerous, and it makes it all the better.

After a moment, she pulls away, having the same thought. "But we're at work! Someone might see!"

"I'm gonna be a senior editor," he whispers, his face close to hers. "Senior editor!"

Dalisay's eyes widen "What!" she whispers back. "Evan! That's amazing!"

"You're the first one I wanted to tell! No one else knows!" He kisses her again, and he can feel her smile against his lips. Excitement pumps through him, making him feel like he could fly. This is all he's ever wanted, and now he has it. Without Dalisay, this moment wouldn't be so sweet. He wants to remember this day forever, brand it in his mind with the taste of Dalisay's cherry lip gloss, the pinch of her nails as they dig slightly into his back when she grabs his shirt, the smell of her lavender lotion when he kisses down her neck. Sharing this small victory, even in secret, makes him feel unstoppable.

He's getting hard being this close to her, especially at work. He knows it's risky doing this right now, here, but he doesn't care. He wants to hold her, touch her, taste her. He imagines all the things he could do right now: lift her skirt, pull aside her underwear, and push himself inside of her. Every muscle in his body tightens with anticipation. A small voice in his head tells him to take it easy, but when she winds her hands up his neck, cradling his head in her hands, the voice fades away. What's the worst that could happen?

Dalisay seems to have the same thought, because she lifts one of her hands off the side of his head and guides his hand under her blouse. He squeezes her breast and lets out a breathy laugh against the goosebumps rising on her neck. This feels too good to stop.

"We might get caught," she whispers, but he can hear the throatiness in her voice. He nips her neck, and she stretches it for him, undermining her caution with a soft moan. She throws her arms out, keeping her balance against the shelves.

"Only you come in here to organize things," he says, stroking her ribs under her blouse.

"Someone has to."

"And someone has to kiss you until you stop thinking about organizing things."

He braces one hand on the shelf behind her, letting the tips of his fingers trace the outer edge of her lace bra while he meets her lips again. Is it the same one she wore the first time they slept together? He wants to see for himself. There's too much padding between them; he wants to tear it off her.

She traces her hand on his pants, against his erection, and—

The storage room closet door whips open and Dalisay practically pushes Evan away and Evan's stomach drops. Dread makes his whole body go cold as he blinks at the shadow in the brighter office light.

It's Riggs. He just stares at the two of them, hand still on the doorknob, his expression surprised at first before settling into a performative flatness. Dalisay meets Evan's eyes as she uses the back of her wrist to wipe her mouth.

The sight of Riggs is a distinct boner killer.

Evan knows that Riggs knows he caught them, but—like a good wingman—Riggs plays it cool. His gaze looks beyond them, pretending like he doesn't see them as he reaches past their heads, grabs a box of red pens, and then slowly he closes the door.

After a beat, Evan and Dalisay smother their laughter behind their hands, relief making both of them giggly.

"Okay, yeah," Evan admits, grinning. "That was too close."

Dalisay closes the gap between them and fists the front of his shirt. "Let's press pause and pick up where we left off tonight." She drags her hands down his chest, firmly placing them against the front of his pants in a way that makes his spine go rigid, especially when she looks at him like that with pouty lips and half-lidded eyes. "I'm not done celebrating with you yet."

"My place?" he asks, barely able to breathe. There's too much fabric separating them, and he might go insane not being able to touch her.

"Yes, your place. I'll be drawn and quartered if my family heard the noises you'll be making coming from my bedroom."

Oh, God . . . Evan automatically moves in to kiss her again, but she presses her hand to his mouth and smiles, stopping him in his tracks. His lips smoosh against her fingers.

Her dimples deepen before she spins away, leaving the storage room so Evan can regain his composure alone. It's impossible to stop smiling. This woman drives him crazy in all the best ways.

The next week, when she comes over after Mass, Evan watches Dalisay—naked, warm, soft—sleeping next to him. He was supposed to make brunch, but they had sex instead, and she fell asleep almost immediately after. He's not complaining. She's exhausted, obviously, so he tries not to move to avoid waking her up so he can be this close to her as long as possible. He likes looking at her slightly parted lips, watch as her soft, slow breathing makes her chest rise and fall, how her eyelashes just barely rest against the soft skin under her eyes when they're closed. It's in that moment that Evan realizes the truth.

He really likes Dalisay. Like, *really* likes.

He doesn't know exactly when it happened; it's not like it was a definite lightning-strike moment. It just did.

It could have been so easy to ignore these feelings and win the bet, go their separate ways. He goes cold at just the thought.

He hasn't felt this way about . . . well, about anyone. Not for a long time. It's a kind of certainty that's almost tangible, like a solid fist behind his rib cage that refuses to unclench.

Evan has invited her into every aspect of his life. They go on long walks with Tallulah, spend hours in bookstores and libraries, and she's even started coming to D&D nights. Despite never having played before, she picks it up quickly, and she really gets into character as a barbarian half-orc, which Evan would be lying if he said didn't turn him on just a little bit. Pinky's the first to remind him that he never invited Becca to D&D nights, and that realization had rung through his head like a bell. He's serious about this woman.

Riggs threw a pen at his head the day after his promotion was announced, saying that he can't keep walking in on them getting hot and heavy in storage closets forever, and while Evan feels bad that Riggs had to cover for them, he can't get enough of her.

It's little things that make his heart soar: how, when she laughs too hard, she snorts; that she has a habit of tidying the table whenever they go out to restaurants, adjusting her glass and plate just so before she can eat; how unconsciously she drums out beats on any flat surface she can touch, even sometimes tapping out a paradiddle on her hips when she's feeling awkward. He doesn't know if she realizes she does it, and he'd never point it out in case she became self-conscious about it and stopped.

She's so expressive, like when he tells her something that catches her off guard, and her eyebrows shoot up and her eyes get big and that when she smiles so wide it stretches across her face, like she wears what she's thinking. Even when she's reading, he can see the emotions flick across her face, reacting in real-time to the events on the page. Everything in him makes him want to ask her what she's thinking about.

She's sharp, and clever, and he loves how she's all his . . .

Whoa. He actually thought it. *Loves.*

It shouldn't come as that much of a surprise, especially when yesterday, as he was walking Tallulah, he found himself standing in front of a jewelry store, staring at rings in the display window. He laughed about it, thinking of himself as Gollum drawn to the One Ring. Of course, it's still so early in their relationship to seriously be considering marriage, but he can't help that he is already imagining spending his whole life with her. He didn't buy the ring. But the fact that he considered it says more than he's willing to admit.

Of course, he's serious about her. Every chance they get, they've been having sex at his condo, but she's never stayed the night, always choosing to go home before it gets too late. She says she doesn't want her family to know they're doing it, that it's hard for her to feel normal about dating because she wasn't allowed to for so long.

Her family is a lot different than his. They're way stricter, for one, and he knows it comes from a place of love, that they care about her well-being, but it's a stark contrast to his own upbringing. Most of the time he felt like he was raising himself, not because his parents were neglectful, but because they wanted Evan to be more independent. But what would Dalisay's family think if they found out he's looking at rings already? What about his own parents? Would they say he's being too hasty? That he's getting caught up in his feelings? Would they try to talk him out of it?

He's deep into a thought spiral when Dalisay stirs. When her eyes crack open to look at him, he smiles. All his worries melt away.

"Did I fall asleep?" she whispers.

"Only for a little bit," he says and brushes the hair out of her face to plant a soft kiss on her forehead.

"Sorry."

"There's nothing to be sorry about." She does that a lot, apologize for things that don't require it. It's so distinctly Dalisay, it's almost become a punctuation mark she uses.

With a cute groan, Dalisay wraps her arm over him and pulls him closer, nuzzling her cheek into his chest and draping her leg over his so he's enveloped in her warmth. Her hair smells like vanilla and her smooth skin like lavender. Out of habit, he places another kiss on her crown.

"Were you watching me sleep like a creep?" she asks.

"I wasn't trying to."

"Okay, creep."

"You were snoring so loudly, you're kind of hard to ignore." She playfully slaps his chest. "I was not!"

Evan chuckles, and Dalisay twists to look at him, digging her chin into his sternum as she smiles. It kind of hurts, but he would never tell her that. He doesn't want her to go.

"So . . . ," he says, "you can say no if you want to, but my dad and stepmom want to meet you."

Dalisay lifts her head ever so slightly and drags her hand up to rest on her chin, sparing his ribs from the surprisingly sharp power of her bone structure as a serious look crosses her face. "Why would I say no?"

Evan shrugs. "Maybe I'm a little nervous and I'm hoping you'll say no for me?"

"Nervous? What do you have to be nervous about? They raised you! I want to see where all this comes from." She waves her hand over his face. "I want to meet them. Where do they live?"

"Carmel. When I told him about my promotion, my dad mentioned it was a good enough reason for us to take a day trip to visit them this weekend."

Dalisay hums. She isn't as familiar with the geography, but it thrills Evan that he can show her where he grew up. "Where's Carmel?"

"A little ways south. Couple hours driving. We could borrow JM's car. I don't trust Bettie to make the trip."

"What's wrong with Bettie?" Dalisay asks, her eyebrows creasing. She looks as concerned as if Bettie were a real person.

"What isn't wrong with Bettie?" he asks, grinning. "But I don't want us getting stranded on the side of the road somewhere. It's not half as fun as it looks in the movies."

Smiling, Dalisay's fingers trace thoughtfully over Evan's chest, tickling him with her silky touch. "Should I bring something?" Despite her smile, he can hear an edge of nervousness in her voice.

"You don't have to."

"I'd feel rude coming empty-handed," she says.

"It's not rude. Really, they won't expect anything of you."

Dalisay lifts herself up on her elbow and looks at him. "I want to make a good impression."

"It'll be great," Evan says, assuring her with a peck on the lips. "We'll make it a road trip, drive down the coast, our first couple's vacation."

He sees the fantasy light up her eyes, no doubt imagining driving the coast with her hair blowing in the wind. "Okay.

Then I'll make leche flan," she says. "It's my mom's specialty. Always a hit at parties. I'll use her recipe."

"You don't have to try to impress them," Evan says, smiling. He kisses her again. "They'll love you no matter what."

Like I already do, he thinks.

Late winter in San Francisco is cold compared to Manila, but Dalisay rolls the windows down and lets the wind whip through her hair as Evan blasts classic rock hits for them to drive along to. The sun rises through the gray, misty morning air, and by the time they get through Half Moon Bay, it's warm and bright as they follow the coastal road, curving and winding through green farmlands and cliffs that overlook sandy beaches.

With her leche flan tucked carefully in a cooler at her feet, Dalisay can relax for a little bit. Her mom helped her make it, a sign that she wants Dalisay to impress Evan's parents as much as Dalisay does. But all of Dalisay's worries go by the wayside as Evan drives, singing along with the music. Smiling is easy when she's with him.

The views are spectacular, sometimes literally taking her breath away. It's not every day she sees a pod of whales breeching the ocean surface, a couple of seals sunbathing on the rocks, and—the best one yet—a raft of sea otters holding hands in the surf. Dalisay nearly yanks the steering wheel so they can stop and get a better look.

By the time they reach Evan's parents' house, it's a little after noon. Unlike the picture-perfect fairy-tale-like cottages

Dalisay saw in the rest of Carmel, the Saatchi house is a little more subdued. It's painted a soft, buttery yellow with a nut-brown roof. Large windows overlook a neatly kept lawn, and a balcony on the second floor rises above a patio shaded with a large green umbrella. Like Evan's condo, it's neat, stylish, and orderly—Dalisay can tell even just by looking at the exterior.

Her stomach sits high with nerves. She clutches her cooler and glances at Evan, who smiles at her, softening her heart a little, and leans over to kiss her forehead.

"Let's go," he says.

She takes a deep breath and exits the car.

Mr. Saatchi is already on the porch. He must have heard them come up the driveway. Seeing him, Dalisay knows where Evan got his full head of hair and strong jaw from. Good looks run in the family. He's a white man in his sixties, similar in age to her own mom.

Evan bounds up the steps and greets his father, giving him a huge hug and slapping him on the back.

"There's my senior editor!" Mr. Saatchi says, his voice low and booming.

Evan pulls back, grinning, and turns to Dalisay. He holds out his hand for her and she steps up. "Dad, this is Dalisay Ramos."

"Of course! So good to finally meet you, Dalisay," he says. His handshake is firm and well-practiced. "Evan's been talking nonstop about you."

Heat spreads up Dalisay's face. Hearing that Evan talks about her to other people is a wonderful feeling even if she knows she should be used to it by now. It's surreal in the best way possible to know that he thinks about her even when she's not around. "It's nice to meet you too, Mr. Saatchi."

"Please, call me Jim."

"Sure, Jim." Dalisay smiles, feeling more at ease now.

Jim waves them inside and Dalisay immediately begins to take off her shoes in the entryway.

"Oh, don't worry about that," says Jim. "You can leave them on."

Dalisay is taken aback. When Jim disappears deeper into the house, Dalisay leans into Evan and whispers, "You don't take your shoes off in American houses?"

"Sometimes you do, sometimes you don't."

"They're not bothered by dirt?"

Evan shrugs. "It's their house. I wouldn't worry."

But Dalisay does worry. She would feel awful if she tracked in something from outdoors that could ruin the rugs or scuff up the hardwood floor. Evan takes his shoes off at his place, and she figured his parents would share that practice.

"It bothers me. I'm taking them off," she whispers, doing so before she and Evan head further into the house.

The Saatchi home is pristine, full of sunlight that bounces off egg-shell-white walls and sleek, monochromatic mid-century modern decor. The living room is furnished in a way that reminds Dalisay of a dentist's office, all neat and tidy, and she starts to wonder if that's the Saatchi way. Order and uniformity. The kitchen is new and shiny, sparkling as if it's never been used before, and Dalisay figures they must clean it a lot to keep it looking that nice. It's like something out of a magazine.

She hears a woman's voice coming from the patio. "They have arrived! Hello, hello, hell*oooo!*" Evan's stepmom appears from the patio, Jim in tow. She's a tall, thin white woman in her sixties wearing a tailored dress, gold hoop earrings, and a big sun hat.

"Hey, Jenny," Evan says and hugs her. Dalisay notices that while he smiles, and greets her, his shoulders are stiff. "It's good to see you again."

"And you must be Dalisay!" Mrs. Saatchi says and gasps. "Look at you! You are beautiful."

"Thank you," Dalisay says, blushing. "It's really nice to meet you, Mrs. Saatchi."

"Oh goodness, calling me missus makes me feel old. Please, call me Jenny. Oh my, are you barefoot?"

Dalisay looks down at her painted toes, still bright blue from the pedicure she got with Lola last week.

"She didn't want to get the floors dirty," Evan explains.

Jenny goes slightly pale, lips pursed, and she tries to smile, but it looks like she swallowed a fly. "I have a terrible thing about feet, especially on the floor. It's just that feet are so disgusting, um—Would you mind putting your shoes back on?"

Dalisay's mouth opens and closes several times, stunned. Her whole face is blazing hot. She looks at Evan, who looks equally stunned. Blinking rapidly, she turns back to Jenny. "Oh, uh, yes. I'm sorry!"

Dalisay hurries back to the front and slides her shoes back on. She can hear conversation happening in the other room, Evan probably explaining, and Dalisay lingers in the entryway for a moment to gather her wits. Jenny practically called her feet disgusting. But she washes her feet every day; they're not disgusting. And aren't shoes from outside grosser than bare feet anyway?

Dalisay closes her eyes and takes a breath. Her pounding heart feels like it's going to leap out of her chest, but she reminds herself it's not the end of the world. She can do this.

When she comes back to the living room, she can hear Jenny saying to Evan, "I understand that, it's just that the cleaners already did the floors, and I don't want to call them back for—" Her face lights up with a smile when she spots Dalisay. "Oh! Thank you, Dalisay! I really appreciate it. I love your shoes! Super cute."

Evan looks beleaguered, the skin around his eyes tight, but Dalisay just smiles and says, "Thank you!" Jenny beckons them all to the patio where the table is already set.

"I also wanted to thank you for having us over," Dalisay says, "so I brought some leche flan." She lifts the cooler slightly.

"Leche flan?" Jenny asks, looking at Evan for clarification.

"Ah, yes," says Dalisay, "it's kind of a custard. Eggs, milk, sugar."

Jenny sits at the opposite side of the table. "Oh, dear, that sounds lovely, but we're vegan!"

"When did that happen?" Evan asks, surprised.

"We heard some program on NPR a while ago about how important it is—for the environment, et cetera—to go vegan and, well, we were already halfway there with vegetarianism, so we figured might as well go the whole way!"

Dalisay's heart sinks. Evan notices the look on her face, and he leans in closer to her as Jim brings out a bowl of salad and Jenny pours everyone glasses of sparkling water. "It's no big deal," he whispers. He must see the look on her face and adds, "They're not offended."

"What do I do with this? I can't bring it home," Dalisay whispers back. "If my mom finds out her famous flan was a failure, she'll be devastated."

"We'll keep it at my place and bring it to work on Monday. Everyone at the office will eat it in ten minutes, I promise."

Dalisay sighs and nods.

"I didn't know. I'm sorry," he adds. "About the shoes or any of it."

"It's okay. I know for next time!"

He squeezes her hand, and she sets the cooler at her feet.

The Saatchis are more restrained, quieter, than the Ramos family. They're polite, and kind, and they ask Dalisay about herself, but Dalisay is so used to the chaos at home, it feels more akin to a job interview than meeting her boyfriend's parents.

Evan tells them how they met, the stages he went through in Filipino tradition, and how it took some time to win her over.

"You two are simply adorable," Jenny says, leaning back in her chair with a smile. "Simply adorable! You haven't looked this happy since Becca, Evan."

Evan deflates a little at that. His eyes dart to Dalisay, as if to apologize, and she can tell he's nervous about how she might react.

"Did Evan tell you about his last girlfriend?" Jenny asks, sensing the shift in the air.

"He did not," Dalisay says.

"We don't have to . . . ," he mumbles.

"What?" Jenny cries, clearly not getting the hint. "I mean, you *were* going to marry her. Isn't that something you two should talk about?"

Now that makes Dalisay's eyebrows shoot up. *Marry?*

Jim clears his throat.

The muscle in Evan's jaw jumps. "It wasn't like we were making plans or anything. It wouldn't have worked out anyway." Evan's eyes dart to his father, but then lower to his plate of food.

Jenny gestures with her fork. "Well, you wanted to! It's not nothing. I'm just saying!"

Dalisay glances at Evan, who looks like he wants to slide under the table.

Finally, Jenny seems to understand as her eyes go to Dalisay. "I meant no offense to you, though, dear, you're just darling." She looks at Evan, then back to Dalisay. "Wait, you didn't know?"

Dalisay puts on a smile but it's a reflex. The awkwardness is almost tangible.

"Dalisay knows about Becca," says Evan. "Just not all . . . this." He looks at Dalisay apologetically.

Jenny flounders. "Oh dear, I shouldn't have said anything. Ignore me. And don't read into that, Dalisay! You're just a delight. So much more . . ."—she rubs her hands together, searching for the right word before settling on "demure! All compliments, all compliments!"

"Jenny—" Evan starts, but Dalisay cuts him off.

"It's okay! I don't mind that Evan has dated other people. We're . . ." She's not sure if she should just tell his parents they're not that serious yet. They're just having fun. But she has a feeling that won't necessarily make things better. "It's okay," she repeats.

Jenny seems to sense this too, because she blinks, a smile still stretching across her face, and says, "Okay! Well then! Who wants some iced tea? Yes? I'll get it!"

When she excuses herself, making a lot of noise in the kitchen, Jim finally speaks up. "Don't be mistaken, Dalisay. When Evan told us about you, we were so happy he finally found the right person. What he had before?" He bats his hand. "The logistics of it just didn't make sense. Besides, then he never would have met you."

The word "logistics" sticks out to Dalisay, but Evan's face is fully red by this point. Whatever happened between him and Becca still bothers him. A part of Dalisay wishes he would tell her, but she would never want to pressure him. Clearly he didn't tell her for a reason. She's surprised by how insensitive his parents are when he's obviously uncomfortable.

When Jenny comes back carrying a fresh pitcher, Dalisay says brightly, "This salad is delicious, Jenny. I'd love to know the recipe."

"Oh, we never cook," Jenny says, sitting back down. "We always order in, don't we, Jim?"

Jim nods, digging into his kale.

So that explains why the kitchen is spotless. It's hardly ever used. Dalisay feels like she's met a roadblock, but Evan still looks like he wants to crawl out of his skin. She tries again. "Can you tell me more about the Persian roots of your name, Mr. Saatchi? That region of the world is a bit of a blind spot for me. What does it mean?"

Jim shrugs a shoulder and says, "I'm not really sure, to be honest. Never something I've asked about."

"You haven't been curious? Like, tracing back your family tree?"

"No. Just never had the inclination to, I suppose. I think of myself as more of an American anyway. It's not my culture."

The Saatchis are so unlike her family.

Her surname Ramos means "branches," a fact that was drilled into her brain at an early age. It's almost like her parents were preparing her for appreciating the literal branchlike family tree, a way to remind her where she came from and be proud of where they are now. To hear that the Saatchis aren't intrigued by the origin of their name is perplexing to Dalisay.

Her attempt at yet another conversation starter fails. But Evan swoops in, attempting a recovery.

"Dalisay's family are all from Manila," he says.

"Manila!" both his parents echo, impressed.

"We've always wanted to go there, haven't we, Jim?" Jenny says and Jim nods in agreement. "It must be so strange, moving here. What's your favorite thing about living in America so far?"

Dalisay thinks about it a moment and glances at Evan. "I can think of a few reasons I like it." Evan's mouth curls up and hers does too. "But I like working here. There are a lot of opportunities for me now."

"That's good," says Jim. "Overnight is a highly competitive company."

"Yes! I *really* wanted to work there. I didn't think I was going to get the position when I applied. I was up against a lot of qualified candidates." She reaches out and Evan takes her hand, smiling knowingly. "But I'm glad it all worked out."

Jenny lets out an "Aw!" and smiles at them holding hands.

Jim grins too. "I told Evan when he first started there, it was only the beginning. He'd be crazy to quit. I'm glad I'm right about something." He laughs deeply.

Dalisay remembers when Evan mentioned that his dad didn't approve of his career at first as Evan's smile drops a little, but Jim changes the topic this time, talking about wine, and Evan seems more grateful for the reprieve than she does.

On the drive home, Dalisay spends most of the time looking out the window at the passing countryside.

"My stepmom is well meaning," Evan says, "but she can be a little oblivious sometimes. She says things that can come off a little insensitive. Not a little. And not even 'insensitive,' just racist. Like 'demure.' Shit, I'm sorry."

"She must really like Becca," Dalisay says, amused.

Evan huffs a laugh. "Sometimes I think she wanted me to marry Becca more than I did."

Dalisay watches him for a moment, inspecting his profile. She can see through his smile that there's a tightness in his eyes, so she has to ask. "Is this the champagne bucket incident?"

Evan stares ahead at the road, and nods.

"Did you really want to marry her?"

Evan goes quiet, as if searching for the right thing to say on the road signs. "Yeah," he says, after a moment. "We were serious. No plans, or anything, but I . . . I thought I was ready." He squints, as if shielding his eyes from the sun, and drags his teeth over his lower lip. "I got talked out of it."

Dalisay doesn't say anything. Evan takes one hand off the steering wheel and reaches toward her so she can hold it.

"Seriously, Becca is in the past. I promise. Jenny might not be over it, but I am."

"I believe you. You don't have to talk about it if you don't—"

"It's okay," Evan says, glancing at her quickly before returning his eyes to the road and taking his hand back. "Really. I didn't mean to keep secrets, I just figured we'd talk about it later. But I guess there's no point now. Becca and I broke up because she got a job in Boston, working at the aquarium. It was her dream, and she wanted me to move with her. And I was going to. I would have quit Overnight and moved across the country."

Dalisay's eyebrows shoot up, surprised.

"I know, shocking, right? Me, quit my dream job?" He laughs, catching her expression, but his smile falls again. "When I told my dad about it, it didn't go over well. He thought I was valuing her career over mine, and that we weren't serious enough for such a big change, that I was dumping my future for . . ." He trails off. Suddenly, his dad's word "logistics" floats through her mind.

"Long story short, my dad talked me out of it," he continues. "Long distance was out of the question. It was either all or nothing. So I took Becca out to this fancy restaurant that made me wear a jacket, maybe to try to get her to stay so we could be together, or maybe I already knew it was too late and was trying to lessen the blow . . ." His smile is sad, as if he's amused by his own mistake. "She ordered champagne, thinking we were celebrating, but I . . . broke up with her. After she left, I grabbed the bucket of ice and dumped it over my head so I wouldn't cry in front of everyone."

"Evan, that's . . ."

"Ridiculous? You can say so. I think it's pretty ridiculous at least." He laughs again, but there's no joy in it. "I know Becca and I are over, it's done, but . . . if I'd done what *I* wanted, instead of listening to what my dad wanted, what could have happened? You know? Not to make it sound like I'm not happy with you right now, but it's one of those moments that you wonder what would be different if you'd gone right instead of left."

A lump forms in Dalisay's throat. "No, I know. Really. I do."

Her whole life, all she wanted to do was write, and if she'd listened to her parents when they tried to talk her out of it, where would she be? Sometimes she stays up at night and thinks about it. Just like she thinks about how she might have to pick between supporting Nicole and appeasing her mother one day.

Evan clears his throat. His words sound thick now. "Maybe I'm psychoanalyzing too much, but my parents' divorce was . . . rough. I know, being able to look back, none of it was my fault, but at the time I really thought that I didn't do a good enough job being their son, that I was somehow supposed to keep them together, that their fights were always about me. But when my dad told me to put my future first, it was like getting a sneak peek at the truth. And for a brief moment, when I watched Becca walk out that door in tears, I wondered if I was going to wind up like him and . . . it scared me. I never want to be that person who lets other people decide things for me. Never again."

Dalisay remembers how upset he was when the *parol* broke, like it was his responsibility to please the people in his life, and suddenly a lot of things about him start to make sense. The only son who bears the burden of a parent's expectation. Anything less than exceptional is unacceptable.

Dalisay lifts his hand to her mouth and kisses it. "Thanks for telling me," she says. "I'm sorry you sort of had to."

Evan laughs and groans.

"Hey," she says. "I'm glad I'm with you."

Evan glances at her again, his brown eyes warm, crinkling at the corners when he smiles. "Me too. I wouldn't change us for anything."

"Good. Because if you did, I'd be the one emptying a champagne bucket over my head."

"Don't get me thinking about you in a wet T-shirt until we get home," he says, narrowing his eyes at her mischievously.

She gawps at him and smacks his arm playfully as he laughs, and she laughs too.

CHAPTER SEVENTEEN

Pinky opens the door and breaks into a relieved smile. "You made it, thank *God*," she says, her voice rising.

Dalisay shushes her but can't help but laugh. "Don't make a scene. It's a wake."

"The body's not here. He's in a funeral parlor," Pinky says, offhandedly.

"As if that makes a difference?" Nicole whispers as she slides her shoes off at the entrance. "A funeral's a funeral."

The day after lunch at the Saatchis, Pinky invited Dalisay and Nicole over to her aunt's house to help make *pancit palabok* for Pinky's second cousin's stepfather's brother's funeral. The family tree may have a lot of roots, but no matter how far it stretches, family is family.

"You have no idea how happy I am that you're here," Pinky says, leading them into the house. "I think you're the only people under sixty to walk through those doors."

She isn't kidding. Dalisay counts at least a dozen older women sitting around on couches in the living room or at the table in the dining room, laughing and chatting as they make preparations for the funeral. It's far livelier than Dalisay expected, but it's still a wake. Most are talking about memories of the recently deceased.

Pinky introduces them to the house, and Dalisay and Nicole wave to the groups, before Pinky guides them to the kitchen where a woman is already there peeling garlic and shrimp.

"Auntie Tala," says Pinky. "Nicole and Dalisay are here."

Looking up from a bowl full of garlic slivers, Tala—an older woman wearing a bulky beaded necklace and huge, coke-bottle glasses—smiles at them. "Welcome, girls! Welcome! More hands the better."

Nicole and Dalisay get situated, setting out bowls and cutting boards, as they ready themselves to make enough *pancit palabok* for what they assume must be to feed the entire West Coast.

Tala leaves to attend to other things around the house while Nicole and Dalisay work quietly, sitting side by side at the table, not saying much of anything except "Pass the bowl?" And "Can you get some more garlic?"

When Nicole focuses, her whole face changes. Dalisay knows this look. She's lasered in on dicing the garlic, concentrating with furrowed brows and firm lips, maneuvering the knife like a surgeon. Right now, she looks much like she does when she's studying for exams.

It's been like this between them since the baby shower—the eggshells have been well trod upon. Nicole refuses to be alone in a room with Dalisay, and even when Dalisay tries to ask her innocent enough questions, Nicole finds any excuse to leave. She's clearly freaked out about Dalisay meeting Claire, but she won't give Dalisay one moment for them to talk about it.

The space between them fills up with all the things she wants to say, but here, with gossiping aunties within earshot, there's no chance of privacy. All Dalisay wants to do is grab Nicole by the shoulders, shake her, and tell her she's loved.

Pinky must sense that something is off, because every so often Dalisay notices her gaze flick between the two of them and she clears her throat, as if the garlic is to blame.

By the time Tala comes back into the kitchen, they've chopped so many cloves Dalisay's nose stings. "I need an extra pair of hands to help—"

Nicole stands up so quickly, Tala can't finish. "I can do it." She sounds almost relieved not to have to sit in the kitchen anymore. She exits, leaving Dalisay and Pinky at the table.

"Why is garlic so sticky?" Pinky asks, pinching her index finger and thumb like they're glued together. Dalisay doesn't reply, she just lets out a long sigh, and Pinky pauses in her garlic peeling to glance up. "What?"

Dalisay shakes her head. Pinky is like a German shepherd, ears perked and eyes alert with concern. She glances from the doorway to Dalisay and back. She gestures with her knife. "You wanna talk about it?"

"No," Dalisay says.

Pinky pinches the corners of her mouth in but gets back to peeling garlic.

Dalisay wishes she could ask Pinky for advice, but it's so hard. How is she supposed to confide in her without letting anything slip?

But things can't stay this way, and if anyone would understand, it was Pinky. She can trust her. Dalisay is so glad to have a friend here who gets where she comes from.

"I have this friend," Dalisay says.

Pinky's gaze slides toward her. "A friend?"

"A coworker. A friend who is also a coworker."

"Uh-huh," says Pinky, slightly narrowing her eyes. "At Overnight?"

"Yes! Well, this friend-coworker, she has a girlfriend. But she grew up in . . . Arkansas, yeah, and her parents are super strict, uh . . . Baptists."

"Right," Pinky says.

"I had one of those once!" A little old lady with a hunched back appears from the living room, shuffling into the kitchen. "Prickly fellow. Loved the sun."

"*BAP-tist*, Auntie Maria. Not *cactus*." The old lady makes a noise of understanding and shuffles back out, carrying a bowl to the living room. "So this friend," says Pinky, shaking her head, "she's not sure her parents will approve of her relationship?"

"I don't know. Maybe? But she definitely isn't telling the people who are closest to her. No one knows she's gay."

"Is this friend, coworker, whatever, feeling unsafe?"

Dalisay's heart sinks. "I hope not. I don't care that she's a lesbian. I just want her to feel confident in who she is. We used to share everything, and now it feels like . . ." Dalisay trails off. She may be giving away her hand.

Pinky nods thoughtfully as a threesome of aunties come shuffling in like a flock of colorful birds, clucking and hooting to themselves. "Lesbian, ruled by air, very good sign. All about balance and harmonious relationships. Plagued with digestive problems, though."

"Lesbian? You're thinking Libra," one of them says.

"No, I'm pretty sure I'm not."

"Lesbian is an *island*," says the last.

"Oh my God," Pinky groans, wielding the knife. "Can you eavesdrop somewhere else?"

The kitchen empties again as the ladies exit and Pinky takes a deep breath and leans back in her chair as she watches Dalisay for a long moment. Finally she says, "Is this . . . friend happy?"

Dalisay thinks about it for a second. "I think so."

That's what matters in the end, isn't it? Happiness? Dalisay doesn't care about anything else, so long as Nicole is well and truly satisfied with anyone she chooses. To be able to love someone, to be *in* love with someone, to be loved back, isn't that the best feeling in the world? The way she feels with Evan, she wants that for Nicole. Her mom should see that, and if she doesn't . . . it could tear the family apart.

After her dad died, her mom put on a brave face for the family, but Dalisay knew that it was a struggle to navigate life with the gaping hole that was her father's absence. But would she be able to accept Nicole's queerness?

"I think you're a good friend-slash-coworker," says Pinky. "You care enough to worry about her. I think it's sweet."

Dalisay tries to smile, but she's not sure it's enough. She doesn't know what else to do.

Pinky's aunt Tala returns, Nicole still absent. Dalisay spots her in the backyard winding up cords of lights that will be used at the funeral.

"I think this coworker friend of yours should be honest with her parents," Aunt Tala says, grabbing two sodas from the fridge. "Better to face the music than lie and sneak around. That is *much* more disrespectful to one's parents than being in love with the wrong person."

Dalisay's stomach twists uncomfortably. *Is it?*

"Staying in the closet isn't lying," Pinky says. "It's different. No one owes anyone else the intimate details about their sexuality."

Tala shrugs. "Family is the most important. It should come first. Everyone knows that."

Tala and Pinky argue about it while Dalisay watches Nicole outside as she closes the boxes and carries them around to the driveway, loading them into a car. Dalisay would do anything for her.

Pinky is fed up with the argument with her aunt. She throws her hands in the air. "If a family's love is conditional, what's the point? Being gay shouldn't matter."

"Family is all we have left in the end," says Tala.

Later, Dalisay drives them home. Nicole has her feet kicked up on the dashboard and Dalisay swipes at her boots.

"Sorry," Nicole says. "Habit."

A smile twitches Dalisay's lips. Nicole's always been one to do things her own way. "Hey, are you happy?" Dalisay asks.

Nicole looks at her, tilting her head. "Yeah . . . Why?"

"No, are you *happy*?" She's trying to lean on the word, trying to emphasize the point she's trying to make, if Claire makes her feel good.

Nicole blinks a few times, then disgust wipes across her face. "Oh! Christ, Dalisay! Is that your way of asking if I'm *gay*?"

Dalisay nearly jerks the wheel into oncoming traffic. "Oh no! No! I didn't mean it—"

"Well, that's how it sounds!"

"I swear!" Dalisay says, holding out a hand. "I didn't! I'm only asking if you're satisfied with how you're feeling!"

Nicole stares at her for a long second, her lips pulled into a sneer, but she scoffs and shakes her head, looking out the window to the dark night.

The silence between them is growing larger, swelling like an ocean, and Dalisay is caught in a riptide. It's pulling her even farther away from Nicole. She can't give up.

"Listen," she starts, "about the baby shower . . ."

"I don't want to talk about it."

Dalisay presses her lips together and taps her fingers on the steering wheel. "Claire seems—"

"I said I don't want to talk about it."

"Will you ever? I can't pretend I don't know."

"Try," snaps Nicole.

Dalisay takes in a sharp breath. If she pushes too hard now, Nicole will shut her down. She taps on the steering wheel again and decides it's time to close the gap between them. Enough not talking. "I saw you two, you and Claire, at the hospital."

Nicole goes rigid, staring out the window.

"I didn't want to say anything, even at the baby shower, but . . . You looked so happy. I thought you should know. I love you." Dalisay can't remember the last time she's actually said it. "I love you more than anything in this whole world. I don't want you to forget that."

Nicole continues to stare out the window.

"You deserve to be loved." Dalisay clears her throat. "That's all I care about."

Nicole doesn't say anything for a long time, even while Dalisay turns the car into Outer Richmond, past all the marina-style houses Nicole always says she wants to live in one day.

"I wish I could help you more than I can," Dalisay says. "I don't want you to feel like you're alone."

"I know. But it's my choice, my decision, to tell people or not."

That's fair, Dalisay thinks. Pinky is right. No one is entitled to know another person's sexuality. "I'm sorry I put you in a tough spot with Claire at the shower."

Nicole huffs out a laugh. "I knew I could only keep it a secret for so long . . . I didn't think Claire would mean as much to me as she does."

"I get it . . . I really do," Dalisay says. "How'd you two meet?"

Nicole shifts in her seat, like the subject makes her want to crawl out of her skin, but she takes a deep breath and finally says, "It's stupid."

"I bet it's not."

Nicole rolls her eyes, and the corner of her mouth lifts up as she relents. "I couldn't find the urine cups."

"Okay, that is stupid." Nicole slaps Dalisay on the arm and Dalisay laughs.

"I was in the storeroom and couldn't find the urine cups, someone didn't put them in the usual place, so I was practically tearing up the room to find them and Claire came in because she heard all the noise and helped me." As she talks, Nicole's face gets redder, and she trails off toward the end like she's run out of air.

Dalisay can't stop smiling. She's never heard her sister sound so sweet.

Nicole takes another shuddering breath and wrings her hands in her lap. "I don't . . . *know* what I am, okay?" she says, so quietly Dalisay almost doesn't hear her over the rumble of the tires. "I can't . . ." She pauses and takes a deep breath. "Claire is . . . special. We started out as friends at first, and I didn't think . . . She's . . . She makes me feel like I'm on top of the world. I . . . I don't want to have this defining thing, this capital letter adjective that everyone uses when they talk about me."

Dalisay doesn't say anything. She keeps her eyes on the road.

"I'm scared that if I do come out, it'll change . . . *everything*." She says it like she's gasping for breath. Dalisay's eyes flick to her and she sees Nicole's chin wobbling. Nicole furtively wipes her eyes on the back of her wrists and takes a shaking breath. She's always kept everything close to her chest, like she doesn't want the world to see her in a way she can't control. When they were little, she used to be the one who would scrape her knee and smile and say it didn't hurt, but Dalisay knew she would go into their room later and cry.

Dalisay has no idea what it feels like to carry that kind of burden. The world is a cruel, sometimes unforgiving place, and to be different in a world obsessed with categories and boxes . . . It must be terrifying.

"Maybe you should invite Claire over to the house."

Nicole whips her head, eyes wide, terrified. "What! Are you crazy?"

"Mom needs to get used to her, just like she got used to Evan."

"It's not the same!"

"You don't have to tell her anything!"

Nicole scoffs again and shakes her head. "She's not stupid."

"If you tell her, she'll be shocked at first, we both know that, but she'll see how you two are together. She has to understand."

"Does she? Have to?" Nicole asks.

Nicole has always been the one to say *yes*; Dalisay has been the one to say *no*, finding a million reasons not to do something. For once, their roles have reversed.

Dalisay takes in a deep breath. "Evan and I have been sleeping together."

Nicole's eyes go wide. "Don't tell me Mom knows."

"No, she doesn't."

"So then you know full-well why I can't just tell her my secret if you won't even tell her yours!"

"I'm saying that I'm on your side! I have your back! And now you have ammunition you can use against me, if you so choose."

Nicole doesn't sound convinced because she snorts and shakes her head. "Unbelievable."

"You never know unless you try," says Dalisay. "You were the one who encouraged me to get out of my comfort zone with Evan and look how that turned out."

Nicole lets out a huge, heavy sigh and groans. "What if it all goes horribly wrong?"

"What if it goes spectacularly right?" Dalisay's lip curls. "And I won't even make up a song about you and Claire either, because I'm *such* a nice sister."

Nicole actually laughs and it's like opening a window after a rainstorm.

They fall into silence again, but it's not the weighted kind that permeated the car earlier. It's a full silence, warm and affectionate. Dalisay knows Nicole isn't mad at her, and never really had been, but it's like a weight has been lifted from her shoulders.

"You really like Claire, don't you?" Dalisay can't help the sly smile.

"Yeah," Nicole says, then she sees the smile and slaps Dalisay in the bicep. "Shut up!"

Dalisay is so relieved to have Nicole somewhat back to her normal self.

"Did you ever find them?" she asks.

"Find what?"

"The urine cups."

"We did. And Claire slipped her phone number in my hand when she gave them to me." She's blushing again, like a teenager, and it makes Dalisay even more confident that their mom will see how happy Nicole is. That has to mean something. It has to.

Nicole seems to understand that too. "Okay," she says. "I'll invite Claire over."

Dalisay smiles, a little victorious.

CHAPTER EIGHTEEN

D alisay and Evan collapse onto his bed, glowing and smiling as they kiss again, Dalisay breathing hard as pleasure ebbs its way through her. Her body feels electric, relaxed and alive all at once.

"I . . . ," Dalisay says, hand on his cheek. She thinks about saying something else, but she settles on: "I love this."

Evan smiles. "Me too."

He kisses her again, his soft lips catching hers, and she sighs into his touch. His body is warm, his skin shining with sweat. The flush is deep in his cheeks, and Dalisay's heart thumps solidly in her chest. They've been having sex all evening, ever since they got off work. They could barely keep their hands off each other during the editorial meeting. Her trip through Asia is coming up, and they're already planning the stories she'll write. Everything is perfect.

When he kisses her, she rolls on top of him, leaning against the solidness of his chest and breathing in his spicy scent. She can't think of anything that could be better than this moment.

"Come with me," she says.

"Where?"

"On the tour."

Evan's eyes get round. "For real? Would Naomi even let me?"

"I bet we could talk her into it, especially since you're a senior editor and all too."

Evan laughs breathily and she kisses him, trying to capture it. "We could do *this* all over . . ." She kisses him again, dragging her hand along his torso, feeling his muscles constrict under her touch. "Hoi An . . ." Another kiss. "Kyoto . . ."

"On the side of a mountain."

"A must."

Why can't life always be as great as having sex with a man like Evan Saatchi? Effortless, incredible, and downright hot.

"Okay," he says, smiling. "Only because you asked so nicely." She kisses him again and again and again, before she throws herself off of him and sprawls in the sheets.

She buries her face in his pillow and moans happily. "I don't want to go home. I'm too cozy," she says. "Don't try to make me move."

Evan drags his lips across her bare shoulders, and she feels him press down on her, wrapping his arm around her. "Would you rather I kick you out? Who do you think I am?"

"But I have to go," she groans.

"I can think of a few ways to get you to stay." He nibbles her ear.

Dalisay lets out a snort and shimmies, loosening Evan's grip on her, but he laughs and buries his nose into the crook of her neck. She loves the way he holds her.

Sleeping with him still has the same rush she felt the first time. It's like she's a teenager again, sneaking off to see Luke, only this is a million times better.

As he traces a finger across her bare back with the lightest touch, his hot breath on her skin, Dalisay lulls into a daze. If she's not careful, she really could fall asleep in his bed. She told her mom she was staying late at work to finish a new article. What would her family say if she stumbled back home in the morning wearing yesterday's clothes?

Pinky's aunt Tala's words still echo in her mind.

Better to face the music than lie and sneak around.

Is that what she's doing? Lying and sneaking? She's violating her family's number one rule about waiting until marriage. Her parents always emphasized the importance of chastity in the eyes of God, practically drilled it into Dalisay's head. And yet, she's not hurting anyone by being with Evan. God forbid she have a little pleasure now and again.

At least things are better between her and Nicole. That's one small victory she can rest easy about. But Nicole's not the only one keeping things close to her heart.

CHAPTER NINETEEN

The next Sunday after church, Dalisay hears a knock at the door.

She opens it and is surprised to see Claire standing on the porch.

"Claire!" Dalisay says.

She smiles, a little shy. Today she's wearing a blazer, a T-shirt, and tight-fitting jeans. She's holding what looks like a plate of homemade cookies wrapped in cellophane. "Hey, Dalisay."

She had almost forgotten about Nicole's promise to invite Claire over. Work has been so crazy lately, other things in her life have been put on the back burner. She feels like a complete dunce for having forgotten, and it takes a second for Dalisay to realize she's left Claire standing in the doorway too long. "Come in!" she says, stepping aside.

Claire does and kicks off her shoes.

"You made cookies?" Dalisay asks, indicating the plate.

Claire gives her a little wink and leans in, whispering, "I bought them at Safeway. Wanted to look like I know what I'm doing in a kitchen because I know how important that is for your mom."

Dalisay can't help but smile. She likes Claire. She's a good fit for Nicole. And Nicole must have heard them come in, because she appears at the top of the stairs to the main area of the house.

"Hi!" Nicole says, a little breathless.

She takes the plate from Claire and introduces her to the rest of the family as they're getting the table ready for lunch. Everyone welcomes Claire with open arms, immediately showering her with compliments and food.

"You must be Nicole's friend! So good to meet you!" Mom says.

"Is that your motorcycle outside? So cool," says Daniel.

"Are you eating enough? Come, sit," Lola says.

Claire beams and glances at Nicole, whose ears are bright pink, but she's smiling so wide, Dalisay can almost see the rush of adrenaline pumping through her veins.

Everyone sits at the table and conversation flows as easily as the *buko* juice. Claire compliments Lola's cooking, and Lola takes kindly to that, speaking in Tagalog about how polite Claire is. "She knows what good food tastes like! Learn from her, Daniel," Lola says to Daniel in English, who looks slighted for being called out in front of a stranger.

"I like good food!" he says, mostly to Claire. "I just like certain good foods."

Claire tries all the food, and there's not a second that goes by that her plate is empty. Everyone shovels more food on it than she can keep up with. Dalisay wonders if Nicole will tell her she doesn't have to eat everything, that it's more of a sign of respect to fill a plate than expect anyone to eat all of it.

"So you know Nicole from medical school," her mom says. "Are you studying hard?"

Claire nods, wiping her mouth politely before answering. "I am! I really like it. It's really tough, though. Nicole makes it look so easy, she's so smart," Claire says, glancing at Nicole at her side.

On Nicole's other side, Dalisay nudges her with an elbow as if to say, *I'm proud of you.* Nicole's cheeks must hurt, she's been smiling so much.

"What specialty are you choosing?" Mom asks as she spoons another serving of adobo onto Claire's plate.

"Uh, pediatrics," says Claire. She looks at the food like she's climbing Mount Everest but hides it with a smile. She must be so full by now.

"Pediatrics! See, Nicole! That's what I've been telling you! I've been saying you should become a family doctor so you can work with the community here."

Nicole sighs and rests her forehead on her fist. "I know, Mom. It's what I'm going to do! I was just figuring things out. It hasn't been easy . . ."

"I know it's not easy! But Claire is setting a good example for you! You'd be wise to follow her path." She turns back to Claire. "Did you know that when Nicole was little, she was deathly afraid of needles?"

"Mom!" Nicole groans.

"It's true! She would scream and cry and hold on to me whenever we went to the doctor's office for checkups. Nothing like her sister. Dalisay was always an angel. Never complained, not even once."

Now it's Dalisay's turn to groan. The only reason she never complained was because she didn't want to embarrass her family. She was afraid of needles too.

"Trypanophobia is common," says Claire. "I think it'd be a good thing if Nicole became a family doctor. She'd know how scary it can be for kids. I think there's strength in empathy. But no matter what she chooses, it will only help people, and she'll be incredible at it."

Nicole's face is bright red.

Daniel leans back in his chair, arms crossed casually over his chest. "Well, I think Nicole should become a brain surgeon and make as much money as possible—that way we can all live in luxury."

"As if I'm gonna spend a dime on you," says Nicole with a smirk.

A child's scream cuts through the air—Little Luis. Melinda must be having a hard time getting him to settle down for his nap. He's been a whirling dervish all morning.

"Or," says Daniel, wincing at the sound, "you can send Little Luis away to boarding school back in the Philippines."

Their mom hisses at him and throws her napkin at his face. They argue in Tagalog, with Daniel saying it was just a joke and their mom saying it's not funny. Dalisay catches Nicole and Claire glancing at each other, hiding their giggles, and she breathes a sigh of relief.

By the time dessert comes around, the conversation circles back to Claire.

"So, Claire," says Mom. "Tell us about your family! Is there a lucky man in your life?"

Claire looks up from her plate, shocked. She glances around the table with wide eyes and then she smiles. "Actually, uh . . ."

Nicole's shoulders go stiff, but she stabs at her *carioca* with her spoon.

"No," Claire says.

"Really?" Mom says, impressed. "I guess I shouldn't be surprised. Nicole hardly has any time either. It's like she lives at that hospital. She's hardly ever home. All my children seem to want to work more than spend time with us."

Blink or you'll miss it, Nicole and Claire share a glance, but Dalisay is paying attention. Her stomach sits high in her gut, and her heart rate spikes. She can tell that Nicole isn't ready.

"You can't just ask people things about who they're dating here, Mama," Daniel says, coming to Nicole's rescue. Dalisay isn't sure if he's picked up on the truth, but based on the way he looks at Nicole, she thinks he might have. "That's private stuff."

"It's an innocent question! I'm sure being a doctor, you'll have all the men chasing after you soon enough," Mom says, laughing.

Dalisay pinches her lips closed. She isn't sure what to do, but their mom seems to be on a roll.

"Becoming a doctor is the most important thing. Being a married doctor is the second," she says with satisfaction, as if she's bestowing the table with great wisdom.

Nicole takes a deep, unsteady breath. Dalisay finds Nicole's hand under the table. She's nervous, her palm slick with sweat. Dalisay assures her with a squeeze. *You got this*, she means to say. Nicole squeezes back.

"Actually," Nicole says. Everyone turns to look at her. "Claire is . . ." Nicole trails off and she sits up straighter and levels her shoulders. She holds out her hand for Claire and Claire smiles tentatively before taking it. They place their clasped hands on the table.

"Claire and I are dating," Nicole says, eyes shining.

No one moves. Dalisay's pretty sure it's so quiet, they can hear a dog barking two blocks over.

"What?" Daniel asks.

"I'm gay," Nicole says, lifting her chin. "It's . . . I'm gay. Yeah."

Everyone stays frozen, like she's said a curse word. A second passes, and then another.

"But you don't look gay," Mom says. Nicole probably doesn't know how to respond to that. Her mouth works uselessly. "You're both too pretty!"

"It . . . it doesn't work like that, Mom," Nicole says. "I'm gay. I've known for a while. I'm telling you now."

"But . . . why?" their mom asks. Nicole almost laughs in disbelief. She looks at Dalisay for support and Dalisay gives her hand another squeeze.

"You're . . . Nicole, you're not!" Their mom's eyes shine silver with tears that are about to overflow.

Lola swirls her spoon in her dessert.

"I'm gay," Nicole says again. Dalisay can hear the wobble in her voice. Claire holds Nicole's hand so tightly, her already-pale fingers have turned white. The air feels staticky and full.

Dalisay can't help herself. She leaps in, playing defense. "It's okay, Mom. Nothing's changed, she's still our same Nicole."

"But . . . who—What about—" Their mom has a hard time finding any words before she bursts into tears, weeping into her hands. She's a blubbering mess as she gets up, rushing toward the bedroom. She slams the door behind her.

Daniel follows after her. "Mom, wait!"

Nicole's face turns red from a mixture of fury, embarrassment, and hurt. Her eyes shine with tears, but she's shaking so much, they can't fall. She gets up and storms toward the front door.

Claire wordlessly runs after her.

Dalisay throws her napkin on the table and chases after Nicole but by then, she and Claire are already gone. The front door slams closed, ringing through the whole house.

Dalisay's heart shatters into a million pieces. What an utter disaster.

"What's going on?" Melinda asks, appearing from the hallway. She must have finally gotten Little Luis to bed and heard the commotion. "Where is everyone?"

Dalisay goes back to the table and squeezes the back of the chair. Melinda stands at the head of the table, taking in everything with a confused shake of her head and her palms up, waiting for an answer, but no one says anything except for Lola.

"The *halo-halo* is delicious."

CHAPTER TWENTY

The second Evan opens the door and sees her, his smile drops. Ordinarily she would be smitten with his flour-smeared cheek, but now all she wants to do is cry at the sight of him.

"What's wrong?" he asks. He brings her inside and Tallulah runs circles around her, but Dalisay doesn't even have the heart to greet the dog.

Anticipating what's to come, Evan pours Dalisay a large glass of red wine and sits her down at the dinner table. It's already set and ready, the pasta in a large bowl, but she hardly registers any of it. Over the next half hour, she tells Evan what happened with Nicole.

"Yikes," Evan says, then again: "Yikes!" He takes a sip of wine from his own glass.

"It was horrible," Dalisay says miserably. Her cheeks feel hot and crusty from all the crying she did on the way over.

The two of them were supposed to have a romantic night together, with him making pasta from scratch, dining over candlelight, then inevitably falling into bed together, but she's never felt less in the mood for romance.

Dalisay's lower lip quivers. She stares at her plate without seeing it at all. All she can see now is Nicole's heartbroken face. "Daniel tried talk to Mom, but she wouldn't listen. And when Nicole finally got home later, they had this huge blow-out argument. Nicole kept saying this is who she is, but Mom doesn't want to listen. Either Nicole goes back in the closet and never talks about it again, or she moves out."

Evan asks softly, "What is she going to do?"

Dalisay shrugs. "She was crying so hard. She could barely talk. I'm not sure."

Evan sighs and rubs his chin and nods. "Does she need a place to stay? I can convert the office. I've got a cot and some blankets."

Dalisay shakes her head. "It's one thing that she's gay, it's another thing entirely if she stays at an unmarried man's house. Alone."

"Fair," Evan says. "The offer still stands anyway."

Dalisay stares at the untouched plate of spaghetti in front of her. "You know how my mom is. She has this vision of the future, a vision that might as well be prophecy, set in stone, and when anything changes, it's hard for her to adjust."

"No, I understand." Does he? He sounds more resigned than anything. She shakes her head, clearing it.

"It's just not fair," she says. She's repeated those same words over and over, like a mantra, but it changes nothing. "Nicole and Claire can still be together, but they can never . . . be *together*. Not like us. Nicole has to keep hiding who she is from the world." A tear tickles her cheek, and she brushes it away.

Evan takes Dalisay's hand and squeezes, comforting her. Dalisay wishes it were only that easy. As a fixer, this is one problem she can't do anything about. Nicole's worst fear has come true, and it is all Dalisay's fault for suggesting it in the first place.

"I don't know what to do," she says. "I told Nicole this was a good idea. I thought, maybe, because it's her, everyone would be happy that she's happy. But . . ." Dalisay tucks in her lips, trying to stop herself from crying. It's starting to hurt from holding her breath, but she's afraid it might turn into a sob.

Evan squeezes her hand again, stands up, and comes around the table. He kneels in front of her. "It's okay," he says. "It's not your fault. You can't control what other people think."

"But I thought I was helping," Dalisay says. "And now I think Nicole hates me." When Nicole came home, she couldn't even look at Dalisay. She might as well have been invisible. "This is all my fault."

"Nicole can't hate you!" Evan kisses the tears that have fallen down her cheeks and brushes what's left away with his thumb. He's so gentle, and soft, and Dalisay secretly wishes he'd stop because otherwise she might really start crying again. He looks at her, steadily, and says, "Your mom is just intolerant. No one can change her mind."

Dalisay flinches at the word "intolerant." He's not entirely wrong, but the way he says it makes Dalisay feel that he thinks lesser of them somehow. Something in her snaps, and she lashes out. "Please, stop judging her."

"I'm not judging!"

Dalisay turns her head, breaking Evan's touch on her skin, and he pulls his hand back.

Evan licks his lips, flustered. "I'm saying I think it's pretty shitty to threaten to ostracize your kid over being gay."

"Family is *everything*, and it doesn't just mean relatives. She's worried that Nicole will become a pariah in the entire *community*. No one will speak to her, no one will accept her. She's trying to protect her, in her own way."

"So it's right that she's acting like this? Being cruel?"

"Of course not! But I can't let you criticize my family when you have no idea what you're talking about. Just because you have American values doesn't mean everyone else automatically does."

Evan looks taken aback. After a beat, he stands up and goes to the sink, his back turned to her. She can see his shoulders tense up as he holds his breath and slowly lets it out. She can tell he's thinking hard about what to say next.

Dalisay shudders, suppressing this gnawing ache growing in her belly, and she can't stop the tears as they flow.

"I don't know how to help," he finally says. "I want to understand, but at the same time, I can't pretend like that's okay. I can't imagine doing that to my own kids."

"You don't get it," she says.

Evan spins around, pleading. "I'm trying! I care about you! I hate seeing you like this."

"It's not just this," she says. "It's like we're on two different frequencies."

"What are you talking about? We've been good, right?"

Dalisay hiccups, wiping tears away with her knuckles. "It just sounds like you're projecting your values onto my family, when that's not fair. You can't expect everyone to be like you."

"I don't care that your family is conservative or whatever. I care about *you*. I hate seeing how it's tearing you up, and I can't just sit back and take it with a straight face."

"If you cared about me, you would understand where I'm coming from, why this is so important to me. Why my family is the most important thing."

"Dalisay." Evan drops his shoulders. "I don't know why we're doing this. We're from different places, yes, but we're more than that."

"You don't know what it's like. You've never uprooted your whole life to live someplace else. I don't think you'll ever understand what it's like being me, being a part of my family."

"I want to!" Evan says, pleading now. "I want us to be a team! I am on your side!"

"How can we be a team when it feels like I'm always having to apologize for my culture? Like the shoe thing at your parents' house!"

Evan drops his arms to his side, defeated. "The shoe thing? That's still bothering you?"

"I felt like such an idiot, that whole time. They thought I was dirty—"

"I'm sorry! I know! They suck! Fuck 'em! But I don't want you to apologize for anything! I'm the last person you have to explain it to. But I am trying *so hard* to understand because this is all coming out now and I don't know why!"

The tears are flowing now. Dalisay wipes her face and chokes on a sob. She hates what's happening. It's like the foundation she's carefully laid for herself is crumbling beneath her.

Evan runs a hand through his hair. "Why are we even fighting?"

At this point, Dalisay doesn't even know. All she knows is that she's hurting. A deep, aching, gnawing pit of loneliness is wrenching its way out of her, whether she wants it to or not.

Evan comes to her again and kneels in front of her. "I'm sorry, okay?" He holds her hands, bowing his head to look into her eyes. "I'm sorry." He reaches up and lifts her chin, dragging his thumb over her lower lip. She melts under his soft gaze, and the tears that lie heavy in the back of her throat recede.

She kisses him. She wants to forget about everything for a few moments, throw herself entirely into him, disappear under his touch, let her mind go quiet for once. She pulls him toward her, fisting his shirt tightly, and he replies in kind with a soft sigh.

He rises, threading one arm behind her and dragging the other up, tangling his fingers in her hair. It sends shivers down her spine as he nips on her lower lip, and he holds her tightly, as if refusing to let her go. Her heart pounds through her whole body, thumping with heat, and she closes her eyes. She winds her hand under his shirt, desperate to touch his bare skin, feel his stomach and his ribs. Everything else melts away, and all that's left is Evan, here and now.

She spreads her legs, framing them on either side of Evan's body, and he pushes her dress up her thighs and squeezes the softest parts of her hips, teasing at her underwear. He stands, half-hunched over her, and she knows they can't do it here.

"Bedroom," she says.

He takes her upstairs, his hand never leaving her waist, his lips seemingly finding new spots on her bare skin as they tumble into the bed together. He whips his shirt off, depositing it on the floor, and Dalisay grabs at his shoulders, feeling his muscles flex as he braces himself over her body.

He pulls back, a breath away, and his eyes meet hers, as if he's trying to read her. "I don't want this to be makeup sex," he says. "I don't believe in that kind of thing."

"What do you believe in?" she asks, levering her hips against his.

He doesn't answer right away. His eyes widen ever so slightly, blazing with desire, and he swoops in to press his lips against her neck. She stretches for him, letting his mouth electrify the soft, delicate skin below her ear and her nipples harden as he slides a hand against her breast.

Finally, inches from her ear, he whispers, "You."

A laugh wrenches itself out of her but even the cheesiest line doesn't turn her off. She kisses him again and pushes him aside. He topples over, falling onto the mattress.

"That bad?" he asks, grinning.

She straddles him, sitting on his hips, crosses her arms, and pulls her dress over her head. No bra today. Evan's eyes blaze, and he reaches up and grabs her chest, rising to sit and meet her. He pinches her hard, brown nipples, then cups a breast to his mouth. She arches, letting her head fall back, the feel of his tongue wiping every thought from her mind.

Tomorrow, she can figure it out. Tomorrow she can make everything right. But now, all she wants is Evan.

"I believe in making you feel good," he says against her chest. His fingers slide down her underwear. "I like making you feel good."

She pulls herself off him and kicks off her underwear. Evan, too, throws his clothes aside, like they're running out of time. She lays on her back, and Evan's hands hold on to her bare skin, grab her hips, and they're so used to each other, moving with the same goal, and still—even now—when his mouth presses between her thighs, it's like new. Except now he knows exactly how to please her, every tiny movement that makes her lose herself. She needs this, needs to feel like nothing else matters but this tiny universe where only they exist. And while his tongue works against her, drawing the orgasm out of her, she would give anything to live in this moment forever.

He watches her as she squirms under his touch and unravels in his arms. She cries out, releasing the tension that's been building inside her. The pleasure rolls over her in wave after wave.

Evan raises an eyebrow as he lifts himself from her, smiling in that satisfied, self-assured way that used to drive her crazy, and crawls to meet her lips.

Still pulsing with the rush of her heart, she pushes him aside, making him laugh, and gets to her knees and straddles him again.

She can't control many things in her life, but she can control this. She lets him get adjusted with his condom, and then she's on top of him, kissing him, losing herself in the feeling of him under her because now it's her turn to make him feel good. "God, Dalisay." His voice is throaty and raw and the muscles in his neck strain under her lips. Goosebumps rise on his skin as she breathes with each thrust, driving him deeper inside her.

He lets out another gasp, then jerks and wraps his arms around her, holding her so tightly against his chest, she knows exactly how it feels to never want to let go.

When they're done, flushed and breathless, Evan kisses the slope of her neck, her jaw, and then her mouth, like he's planting promises.

"You made dinner . . . ," she says, regretfully, settling into his side, his arm tucked around her. "You worked so hard, and all I did was talk about my drama."

"Believe it or not, I want to hear about your drama. I care about you."

In his arms, she feels safe and secure, nothing like she's ever felt with anyone else. This is how it's supposed to be. "You're sure about the pasta?"

"It'll make great leftovers." Evan reaches over to the nightstand and hands her his phone. "I think tonight is a pizza in bed kind of night anyway. Order whatever you want. I'll be right back." He plants a kiss on her lips and then disappears to the bathroom to clean up.

Dalisay settles into Evan's bed and pulls the sheet over her chest and starts scrolling through their favorite pizza place's menu, when Evan says, from the bathroom, "You know, I was thinking . . . What if you didn't have to leave?"

"What do you mean?"

"Would you consider, at some point, moving in with me?"

Dalisay nearly falls out of bed. "Are you serious?"

Evan reappears, smiling, and pulls his T-shirt on, popping out through the neck hole. "Yeah. I mean, you don't have to move here, we could find our own place." He locates his underwear and hops into it. She would have thought it would have been sexy, if not for the fact that her whole body has gone cold.

"Are you crazy?" Her eyes practically bug out of her skull. Evan's body tenses. "I thought . . . Wait, is it too fast?"

"Too fast? Evan, did the five stages of courtship teach you nothing?" Her heart feels like it's about to burst out of her chest.

Evan reaches over and turns on the bedside lamp. The warm light fills the room, and she can see him clearly now as he watches her with open sincerity. "I'm sorry, I thought we were ready."

Dalisay rakes her fingers through her hair and takes a deep breath. She's still naked, and she feels exposed. She locates her shirt and buttons it up, along with her jeans. She didn't mean to jump on him like that, it just came as such a shock. Most people in Manila live with their parents well into adulthood, even when they're engaged. She expected this as much as a kick in the gut. What Evan's talking about is beyond the realm of propriety.

She's not ready, is she? It's not that easy, is it?

Evan licks his lips. "It's really not that big of a deal in America. Couples move in together all the time. It's kind of like a marriage test run. You see how compatible you are cohabitating, see how well you work together assembling IKEA furniture, figuring out each other's quirks, test out if you could actually put up with me every day."

For a brief moment, Dalisay can actually picture it: her and Evan kneeling on the living room rug, assembling a new bookcase from IKEA, Dalisay organizing all of the parts into neat piles while Evan pores over the instruction manual; waking up in his bed, no—*their* bed—and brushing her teeth next to him in the bathroom; reading together on the couch, not worrying about checking the clock to make sure she gets home on time.

But it would fundamentally change her relationship with her family. Would she really be willing to risk all of that?

"It's different for Filipinos. JM and Pinky have been together for five years and they still live with their parents." Dalisay falls back into her pillow, staring up at the ceiling, letting her mind race. This is yet another difference between their two cultures. "Living with a man is almost unthinkable for an unmarried Filipino girl," she says.

The corner of Evan's mouth lifts. "Then I guess we'll have to get married."

Dalisay looks at him and his smile drops like an anvil. "Don't even joke about that." Her voice is sharper than she meant.

Evan rocks back, his shoulder dropping, and his face softens. "I'm not joking."

Dalisay palms the top of her head, heart pounding. *Marriage? But . . . but—is it too soon?* "People shouldn't rush into marriage. Divorce is a terrible thing."

"Divorce?" Evan almost laughs but catches himself. "Trust me, I know . . . but how did we get to divorce?"

Dalisay sits up and takes a breath, running her fingers through her hair again. "I'm just saying, living together is like . . . a promise. A huge one. The biggest promise you can make. It means we're . . . real."

"Aren't we real right now?"

"Yes, but . . ." She's not sure why she's so hung up on it. Wouldn't she want to marry Evan? Isn't that what her subconscious has been preparing her for? Isn't it so easy to imagine herself walking down the aisle and seeing Evan waiting for her at the altar? Her heart yearns for it, even now while he's frustrating her.

But is she sure she's not rushing into this? How can she be absolutely, one hundred precent positive that this is how it's supposed to be?

Maybe it's like Nicole said. Maybe she's scared to jump into the deep end too. Scared that it changes *everything.*

"I figured we could take what we have to the next level," Evan says.

"But if we move in together, and if it doesn't work out . . ." Dalisay can't finish the thought. *If. If. If.* Damn that word. "If" is the one word that seems to define her whole life. She's terrified of every good thing in her life having an expiration date. So then why is she holding back? Even she barely understands. She doesn't *not* want it to work out. She has never been happier, so why does it feel like she's suffocating every time she breathes? Everything is happening so fast, first with Nicole and now this. She can't catch her breath.

Evan takes up his spot on the bed again, reaches over and tucks her hair behind her ear. "Hey," he says, softly. He cups his hand against her face and turns her head to his, making her look at him. She melts into those big brown eyes and feels her body relax. "I love you, Dalisay."

Is that the first time he's said so out loud? Her heart beats like a jackrabbit.

Evan runs his fingers through her hair, looking at her with such tenderness and care. "What's wrong?" he asks.

"My family . . ."

"What about them? It's not like I'm asking them to move in with me too." He says it like he's joking, but a pang of something white hot shoots through her.

"Did you not hear anything I said earlier? Where I come from, couples moving in together before they're married is out of the question!"

Evan's smile drops. "You were so worked up about Nicole, I thought maybe you wanted some independence."

"Well, I don't!" she snaps, more fiercely than she intended, and Evan leans back. It's like she slapped him.

"You really don't want to move in with me?"

"No!"

Evan looks hurt now. "Because you don't want to marry me."

Dalisay's heart beats furiously in her chest. "That's not why!"

"Then what?"

She stares at the ceiling rendered speechless, trying to find a reason that would make sense. Are they too different? Are they too swept up in the physicality of each other? Are they really compatible, or are they trying to shove a square peg into a round hole? No! She loves Evan, really, she does. But moving in is such a huge commitment. She can so easily picture her life with him here, but it just feels wrong. She is devoted to her family, wants to care for her mom. The filial piety is so engrained in her, it's hard to describe, much like how it's hard to describe why she loves her mom so much, despite her attitude toward Nicole. She just does, she just has to.

Words are her whole life, and for once, she can't find the right ones.

When Dalisay doesn't say anything, Evan throws his hands up. "Who cares what other people want, or what your mom wants? What do *you* want, Dalisay?"

Her throat tightens and the words come out hot. "This is what I'm talking about! You don't know my family, you don't know anything about where I come from. I'm not like you, and just because I say I don't want to do something, it's not because I only obey my family's wishes. What I want is for them to be happy."

"That's not true! It's always been about what your family wants, from the start, and you can't even see that your family is mistreating your own sister, just constantly stuck in this"—he clenches his fists in front of him, searching for the words—"backward mindset. You can't let other people control your life!"

Tears prick her eyes, and she holds her breath, smothering the urge to cry.

The color in Evan's face fades, and something crosses his eyes in a split second that makes him drop his shoulders. He turns, walks away, and drags his hand down his face. When he looks at her again, his eyes are red. "I'm sorry," he says. "I didn't mean it that way."

"Right, so everything about me is backward."

He groans. "I meant, we're in the twenty-first century! Why is living together such a big deal? I don't get it!"

"Tradition is important to me! The Five Stages, all of it! Why isn't that enough?"

"Help me, please! I'm trying to understand! Because we've been sleeping together, all this time, and somehow that doesn't count? I know your family wants you to stay 'pure' until marriage. So why do some traditions matter and others don't?"

Having her own hypocrisy thrown in her face hurts more than she imagined. "It's complicated."

Evan's voice is thick. "But moving in together isn't."

Tears swim in Dalisay's eyes, and it's so much worse when she sees them swim in Evan's too.

"My family is protecting me. They're not controlling me."

"Yeah, well, it's really hard to tell the difference."

She chokes on a sob. Anger makes her face hot. "They don't make decisions for me. My mother is not your father," she says.

That hits a nerve. Evan's face scrunches in on itself and he turns away from her, rubbing his hand on his face again. The tension in his shoulders makes his movements stiff. She can tell he's trying not to cry too.

She watches him, holding her breath, and it starts to hurt. She knows it was a low blow, but she had to say it. She doesn't know how to get through to him. And yet, she regrets it immediately.

Evan, meanwhile, takes a deep breath, hand still on his face, before he turns around again. His eyes are glossy, but he's doing his best to keep his tone level, even though she can hear the strain in his. "So, what pizza did you pick?"

"No, we are not pretending like this conversation never happened!"

"Well, I don't know what else to talk about! You don't want to move in with me, you jump immediately to the prospect of divorce—"

"I just want you to listen to me and respect my decision!"

"A decision hinging on your family's approval. Tell me I'm wrong. Please."

The words are out before she can fully process them. "I can't marry you."

The hurt on Evan's face is acute, like a full-stop punctuation mark. "Okay."

"Okay?"

Evan's breath comes out in a shudder and the tears in his eyes threaten to overflow. "I think you've made the decision for the both of us. You said what you want, or what you don't want. That's all there is to it. Besides, I'm not sure I want to marry into a family whose love is conditional anyway. What if our future kid is gay, or trans, and your mom decides to treat them like she did Nicole? And we have to be cool with that? We have to respect that?"

He's right and she knows it, but too many words have been thrown around for any rational thought to enter her brain. "Let me deal with my mother."

"Sure you will."

The disdain in his voice is crystal clear. "Right," Dalisay says, her chin wobbling. Her cheeks itch as the tears fall, but she refuses to wipe them clear. "We're done, Evan."

He doesn't move, he just watches her with his hands on his hips, his face red as he holds his breath. His words come out in a rush. "That's it? We're breaking up?"

Before she leaves, she turns around and looks at him. It hurts to do so.

"I really had you pegged from the start," she said. "You don't know anything about me."

CHAPTER TWENTY-ONE

It's been five months since Evan has seen Dalisay. Five whole-ass lonely, terrible, miserable months.

He replays their breakup over and over in his mind, trying to find any way he might have been able to salvage things, how he might have said something different, something better, chased after her, tried to make it right. But he didn't. He screwed up. There was no talking to her after that. The night they broke up, he tried calling her, but it went straight to voice mail.

He lay awake all night, psyching himself up to speak to her at work the next day, but he found her desk empty, cleared out. When he asked Naomi, she said that Dalisay had asked to work from home, starting immediately. Nowadays, he only sees her in weekly virtual meetings, but she keeps her camera turned off, and he makes every excuse not to go to the meetings anyway.

A Dalisay-shaped hole has been carved into his life.

There was nothing at his apartment she'd left behind, nothing for her to come back for, no reason for them to see each other again. He didn't want to give up on her, not like he gave up with Becca, but he's certain she's blocked his number by now. If Dalisay didn't hate him before, he's pretty sure she hates him now. She doesn't want to talk to him ever again, she's made that quite clear. The most interaction they have is formal, stilted, work-related. No more emoticons, no more texts, simply Overnight emails relevant to articles and deadlines and assignments when their departments collaborate. They're worse than strangers.

Dalisay goes on the Asia tour without him.

These days, Evan's either working, or writing, or reading, and he's been traveling so much he reckons he sees more of the airport than he does his own house. He misses Tallulah. Sometimes he forgets exactly where he is because he's always thinking about where he's going to be next.

When his flight lands in the Leonardo da Vinci airport, it's just another day at work. Even his jet lag seems to be a permanent fixture. These days, he floats through life, the distinct absence of Dalisay an aching pit in his stomach. Some days are better than others, but he can never truly shake the echoes of their fight. He should have been better, and he should move on, but he can't. Sometimes he catches himself almost texting her that he's landed safely or that he's thinking about her before bed. She left a mark on his heart, like a tattoo, and it might take a carving knife to remove it.

There's been no time to date, and Evan hasn't tried. Despite Riggs, JM, and Pinky suggesting that he put himself back out there, he's not interested.

When he gets to the hotel and checks in early, courtesy of Overnight, he drops off his bags and decides to take a walk. By now, he knows Rome so well, his feet automatically carry him to his favorite haunts.

When they first made the bet, Dalisay said she wanted to go to Vatican City, to "see what all the fuss is about." As a Catholic, it was on her bucket list.

And now, as Evan walks with nothing better to do, he finds himself there, like his subconscious took him exactly where he needed to be. Lines of sun-baked tourists are already circling around the brick wall dividing Rome from the city-state.

He knows time will heal all wounds, but he keeps scratching the scab open whenever he's reminded of her. When he smells lavender, when he goes to a bookstore, when he hears someone snort when they laugh. She's not dead, but she haunts him. The ghost of his guilt rattles its chains every chance it gets.

Evan comes to a stop across from the front entrance of Vatican City and watches as people file in, imagining what could have happened if he'd done things differently that night.

He sits down on a nearby park bench, watching from afar, and finally takes a moment to do nothing for once except think.

At D&D the following weekend, he says what's been on his mind for days.

"I want to do the Five Stages again."

Everyone's eyebrows shoot up. It's like he's proclaimed that he's moving to Mars. JM almost drops the beholder figurine on the board.

"You're sure?" Pinky asks, swallowing a swig of beer.

Riggs stares at him, open-mouthed. "Is the jet lag scrambling your brain?"

Evan's never been surer about anything in his life. He clenches his jaw, determined. "I have to show Dalisay that I believe in us," he says. "I can't lose her forever."

"What if she rejects you?" asks Riggs.

Evan shrugs a shoulder. It was the first thing he thought about while he sat there on the park bench in front of the Vatican entrance. He knew it would always be a possibility, but it wouldn't stop him. "Then she doesn't have to take me back. Simple as that. I want to do the stages again for real this time, not because of a bet, not because I think I have anything to prove. I'm doing it because I want to. For her."

Pinky and JM glance at each other but Riggs shakes his head. "Sounds like a bad idea, man. This could blow up in your face," he says.

"I know. But I need to do something. I . . . I love her."

"Oh, Evan . . . ," Pinky says, her eyes shining.

"There's no guarantee or whatever," Evan says, shaking his head, "but I can't give up on us. Will you help me?" he asks, glancing around the table.

Everyone looks at each other, but they only take a second before all of them turn back to Evan.

"Whatever you need," JM says, "we'll be there."

CHAPTER TWENTY-TWO

Dalisay pushes up the hatch and climbs into the attic. She has to stoop to navigate through the low room and fumbles for the light's pull chain. With a yank, the dim bulb illuminates the attic to reveal the mess before her. Despite living in San Francisco for over a year now, the remnants of their move are still evident in the stacks of unopened boxes hastily thrown in the attic with every intention of finding a place for them "later." It's turned into a Sisyphean task that only Dalisay is willing to handle. And later has become now.

She's completely jet-lagged, having returned from the Asia tour yesterday, so she uses the time when the house is still asleep to get work done. Like she told Evan once, when she's jet-lagged, she doesn't quite feel like a person, as if she's still dreaming. Doing things around the house at least gets her feeling more back to normal.

Garage sales are not something people in the Philippines do, and her mom is excited to host her first one. It's Dalisay's job to sort through the boxes and find things that they don't need anymore, riffling through their contents, and organizing them into piles for her mom to review later.

In one box, she finds her dad's old shirts. She gently picks one up and brings it to her face. They still smell like him. Her eyes prick with tears.

When she was on the trip, she made a special detour through Manila, so she could visit his grave. She sat there for an hour, looking at his name, and missing him so terribly, it felt like she might never be whole again. She told him about her life in America, working at Overnight, how she'd thought he would have loved playing board games with her in The Basement. She told him she wants to come back for All Souls' Day next year, and that she hopes he knows that she's okay.

She makes sure not to put his box of belongings in the garage sale pile.

The next box she finds must have been one of the last to get packed up, because random knickknacks and items are nestled in here too, like candlesticks, an old vase, some paper flowers, and one of Daniel's soccer trophies from high school. The closer it got to their move date, the less careful they became about packing in favor of making sure everything made it into the shipping container. Those last few days in Manila were a blur. She barely remembers any of it, but somehow one of her books made it into this box—her old diary. She thought she'd lost it in the move, but she must have thrown it in here during the chaos.

Emotion creeps up her throat as she picks it up and flips through it, scanning the bubble lettering of her youth. Years pass in a second as she thumbs through the pages. Her last entry was the day before her dad died. The rest of the pages are blank. She never wrote in it again.

Curiously, she flips back to the familiar section of the diary where she had the list of traits she wanted in her perfect man. The list is a lot longer than she remembered. It goes for a hundred lines, and Dalisay smiles at her ambition. Nicole was right; Dalisay was never going to find someone who met all that criteria. But the last line is the most important one, the ink darker—the pen having gone over the lines more than once for emphasis—as if her younger self was putting all her anger into the page.

101. Someone who makes me happy.

She remembers now. She added it after things ended with Luke. As if she needed a reminder that Luke had failed on all fronts in that regard.

A laugh catches in her throat and she looks at the words written by a girl who wanted so much from the world but was always too cautious to find it. Being happy is all she really wants, and she was happy with Evan. She really was. Being with him was like she'd finally set foot on solid ground after being at sea for years.

But it was too late to talk to him. By the time she mellowed out, too much time had passed, and she was sure he never wanted to speak with her again. She typed, deleted, and re-typed so many texts that she never ended up sending, she had to block his number so she wouldn't make a fool of herself and call him in a moment of weakness.

She kept looking at their old texts, unable to avoid smiling when she came across his accidental kissy-face emoticon. At the time she'd thought he'd done it on purpose, a ploy to get under her skin. But when he awkwardly tried to backpedal seconds later, it made her laugh so hard, she snorted milk tea up her nose. Maybe it was in that moment that she really had a change of heart about him.

Their last night together, she'd been so caught up in her pain, it was hard for her to think of anything else, even as their fight dissolved everything they'd built. She panicked. And she ran.

She stores her old diary in the safekeeping pile.

Later that morning, still with cobwebs in her hair, Dalisay finds her mother sitting on the deck outside. The sun is rising, casting the backyard in a warm, orange glow while her mom reads a book with her coffee in a thermos on the armrest. Dalisay remembers how her parents used to sit outside every morning before work, drinking their coffee and reading on the balcony in their apartment in Manila. Now the deck chair next to her mom is empty.

Dalisay collapses into it and lets out a sigh.

"Where is everyone?" she asks.

Mom doesn't look up from her book. "Daniel's in the garage, Lola's on her walk, and Nicole is . . ." Her eyes lift slightly from her book. "I believe she's still in her room."

They're still not talking. It's been months, and Nicole and their mom can barely be in the same room as each other. It's a bad habit in the family not to talk about the things that are bothering them, and their mom is the reigning champ. She would rather pretend it never happened than ever admit she did anything wrong.

There's something about the calm of the morning that suddenly makes Dalisay snap. They're not in Manila anymore, her father isn't here anymore, she and Evan aren't . . . *Nothing* is right, not when her sister is spending all her time in her room to avoid their mother, and she's sick of pretending that it is.

Remember where you came from, her father said. *Remember where you're going.*

Nothing has to stay the same.

"I was sleeping with Evan," Dalisay says.

Mom goes stiff and she turns to look at Dalisay, like her head is on a rusty joint. "Excuse me?"

Dalisay knows this is a can she cannot stuff worms back into. Heat spreads on her face, but she's committed. "When Evan and I were dating, we were having sex."

"Dalisay Rose—"

"Are you going to throw me out for losing my virginity before marriage?"

Her mom's eyes are wide as she stares, totally at a loss for words.

"I didn't want to tell you because I knew you would react like this," says Dalisay.

"Have you lost it? What man will want to marry you if you're not a virgin?"

"Guess I don't want to marry someone who cares about that in the first place."

Mom's face is bright red when another voice comes from behind. "I smoke weed." It's Daniel. He's standing in the doorway, leaning on the frame, arms crossed over his chest. The glint of the morning light makes the lenses on his glasses look like they're on fire. "After studying all day, I like to unwind. Shall I pack my bags too?"

Their mom is speechless, mouth agape, as she stares at him.

Daniel locks eyes with Dalisay briefly, and an understanding passes between them. They're a united front. Daniel moves from the threshold and onto the porch, this time leaning on the wooden railing.

She looks like she's going to pass out. In the Philippines, a person can be put in prison for life for having drugs, even something like weed. "Drugs?" Mom says, finally. "In this house?"

"Lots." Daniel pulls out a clear baggie of gummy bears. Edibles. "Welcome to California, Mom."

She looks between the two of them, aghast. "Have I done such a terrible job raising my children? Is this because your father died? Are you acting out?"

Daniel sighs loudly and shakes his head. "We're a little old to be 'acting out,' Mom."

Dalisay says, "The point we're trying to make is all of us have secrets. Nicole wanted to tell you hers because she loves you, and she wanted you to know because all *she* wants is to know you love her too, no matter what."

"I do love Nicole! I just want her to be . . . *safe!*"

Dalisay's heart hurts. It's true, being queer in America is a lot better than in the Philippines, but it's still not as safe as it should be. But that means Nicole needs her family to stick up for her, not reject her.

Mom's eyes shine as Dalisay leans forward, elbows resting on her knees, and says, "We can all help keep her safe. You always say family stays together, that's why Lola moved here with us, right? But you'll lose Nicole if you're so concerned about what other people think."

Her words hang in the air between them for a while, filled only with the sound of birds chirping away in the trees. Even Daniel seems to be holding his breath.

Dalisay has never done anything like this before.

Mom's eyes are hard when she says, "I am so disappointed, in the *both* of you." She snaps her book shut, emotion welling up in her eyes, and she leaves, closing the door behind her.

When she does, neither Daniel nor Dalisay say anything else for a long moment.

Dalisay can't help but feel like she failed. She tried to stand up for Nicole, but now it's only made her mom even angrier. She expects that this will be yet another thing that won't be talked about in the house.

Dalisay doesn't regret doing it. She would do anything for her family, even if it means saying they're wrong. It's not too late to try to change things for the better.

"I know what you were trying to do, noble as it may be," Daniel says, "but I'd really rather that be the last time I have to hear about your sex life." He gags and shivers.

"Evan and I are done, so . . ."

"No, I know. That ship has sailed. I don't think I ever told you I kinda liked him," Daniel says. "Too late now I guess."

"Yeah, Nicole did too. He even offered to let her stay with him after the whole thing with Mom."

Daniel looks impressed. "He seemed like a good guy."

"He *is* a good guy."

She had been so caught up in her emotions at the time, she barely had time to process how nice it was that he offered. She regrets a lot of things about how it ended. There are *a lot* of things she regrets, but finally standing up to her mom isn't one of them.

She holds out her hand toward Daniel. "Wanna share?"

He passes her the bag of gummies, and she takes one. Sometimes it's good to be a little rebellious.

Dalisay slaps the book closed a little too hard. It's one of Lola's, an epic Filipino romance.

She almost doesn't notice she dropped her bookmark as it flutters to the floor. It's the one she uses most often these days, the note Evan left attached to her book-scented candle.

Here's to stories worth telling. —Evan

She picks it up from the floor and traces her finger across the edge of the card. It's soft now, from her touching it so much, but it still smells like that candle.

"Sitting all alone?" Lola asks.

Dalisay looks up to see Lola standing in the hallway, shuffling toward the kitchen and making a beeline toward a plate of *turon*, the family's go-to snack.

"I was just reading," she says as she wipes her cheeks with the back of her wrist and helps Lola with a plate. Lola makes no mention of her tears or the puffiness of her face; instead she hums a little love song that Dalisay doesn't recognize.

"What book?" Lola asks.

"*The Story of Florante and Laura in the Kingdom of Albania.* I hope you don't mind. I found your copy in the attic when I was cleaning it out."

Lola's face crinkles when she smiles. It's so easy to see Papa's face in hers. "Ah! A true classic."

From what she managed to read, Dalisay knows it's one of the most romantic stories she has ever read. Told in song-verse called *awit*, it's about lovers separated during Spanish colonial rule; about injustice; and how love can win the day. If only life were like the stories.

Nicole appears in the kitchen, checking her phone, dressed and ready to go somewhere.

"Where are you heading to?" Dalisay asks.

"Out, with Pinky. And you're coming with us." Nicole reaches over and takes a *turon*, pinching it in her teeth. "Ooh, this is good, Lola."

Lola seems more than pleased with the compliment.

"Where are we going exactly?"

"Mall. You in? Pinky won't take no for an answer."

Dalisay considers it for a moment, then says, "Sure. Why not."

Lola makes Nicole take another *turon* before her sister heads back to her room, saying she forgot something. Of everyone in the house, Lola is the only one who hasn't treated Nicole differently. In her own subtle way, Lola is taking Nicole's coming out a lot better than Dalisay expected—that is to say that Lola has hardly changed at all.

Dalisay wonders if she's made her own assumptions about her grandmother.

"Did you ever have your heart broken, Lola?" she asks.

Lola considers it for a moment and wipes her fingers on a napkin on the table. She pinches a gold necklace and Dalisay realizes she's reciting a passage from *Florante and Laura*.

"'*Is there an ache that might exceed the pain that parting lovers heed? The notion, let alone the deed, could shake a heart of staunchest breed.*'"

She must have the entire *awit* memorized.

But the way she says it makes Dalisay think maybe Lola's been in a similar situation, that she's lost someone dear to her.

"Do not let a broken heart break you," Lola says. She touches Dalisay's cheek just as Nicole reappears.

"Pinky's here!" she calls, already heading to the door with a slight skip in her step.

Time to go. Can't keep Pinky waiting. But Dalisay can't help but wonder what secrets her grandmother may have, what kind of life Lola lived before she had children, a life that Dalisay realizes she knows almost nothing about. Dalisay wants to ask, but like most things, perhaps she needs to be patient and wait until Lola shares it with her. She imagines it's a story worth telling.

Dalisay gives Lola a quick kiss on the cheek before she leaves.

Dalisay can't remember the last time she's been to a mall; it feels like a lifetime ago. In the Philippines, the mall was one of her favorite places to go after school. Her favorite one in Manila was called the Shangri-la Plaza, and it really lived up to the name. It seemingly had everything: all the best American fast-food restaurants; expensive designer stores she could only window shop in; a movie theater where she saw *Pride and Prejudice* for the first time; even a chapel where she half-joked she'd get married to Keanu Reeves one day. It's nostalgic going to a mall now, even if the one here in San Francisco just isn't the same, but Dalisay thinks maybe it's because she's not the same person now as she was when she was in Manila.

The Westfield Mall is similarly structured like the Shangri-la, with five floors pierced through the middle atrium by what Dalisay can only describe as an inverted Christmas tree hanging from a glass dome. The marble floors echo almost every sound back tenfold as Dalisay, Nicole, and Pinky ascend the escalator and Pinky picks a seemingly random direction, and they begin their much-needed girls' day out.

Pinky and Nicole seem determined to step into every store they see, even the ones that sell beauty products that smell like dessert or clothes and jewelry for goth teens. Both Nicole and Pinky giggle like teenagers themselves, trying all the products, and Dalisay can't help but smile.

Nicole points out a mannequin in the Nordstrom window who is wearing a man's suit. "Hey, doesn't that look just like the one Evan wore for Simbang Gabi?" she asks.

"Yeah, I think so," says Dalisay. He looked so handsome. She could tell he was tired, and yet he seemed to wake up when he saw her. He tried so hard during Mass to blend in, and it warms her heart even now thinking about it. He really did try.

At the nail salon, a result of Pinky's loud and repetitive complaints that her nails were abysmal, Nicole picks out a shimmery pink color for Dalisay. "Doesn't it look like capiz shell? So pretty!"

It does. It's a soft, delicate color that definitely looks like their old *parol*, the one Evan broke.

"You should pick that one! It's so you," Pinky says, smiling from the waiting area, and Dalisay agrees.

The color is subtle and catches the light now and again, drawing her eye to her hands. She remembers the way Evan looked so apologetic, sweeping up the pieces, the flush of embarrassment deepening the color in his cheeks. Evan was so determined to make things right.

When they stop by a candle store, drawn to it by an intense aromatic river floating through the air, Pinky holds a candle for Dalisay, thrusting it under her nose. It smells exactly like old books. Dalisay lets out a contented sigh and her shoulders relax.

"I knew you'd like it!" Pinky says, taking a whiff too.

"You should buy it then," says Nicole, cradling a pumpkin spice candle to her own chest.

She had no intention of spending money today, but Dalisay does. It reminds her of old maps, and Evan's lips on her skin, and towers of books threatening to topple over.

Later in the evening, they decide to see a movie at the theater. They've re-released *Moulin Rouge*, starring Ewan McGregor and Nicole Kidman, but Dalisay is just thankful she can be off her feet for a few hours. Even though she's not one for musicals, it's a lot better than Dalisay expected. While it's no *Pride and Prejudice*, Dalisay doesn't try to hide the tears streaming down her face when the lights come back on. It was a sad story, but a good one.

She hangs back, letting Pinky and Nicole take the lead as they head back into the mall, laughing and chatting about the movie. Dalisay can't bring herself to join them.

She misses Evan.

It's been months, and she should have moved on by now, but she can't. She misses the spice of his deodorant, the way he looked at her, kissing him. It's an ache, deep down inside of her, that she can't shake. Everywhere she goes, she's reminded of him. He made her happy, and she blew it.

She almost lets out a cry as someone walks their dachshund past her. She even misses Tallulah!

Nicole must sense that Dalisay is in the thick of it and appears at her side.

"Doing okay?" she asks.

"Don't worry about me," Dalisay says, waving her off. "Must be allergy season or something. What were you saying?"

Pinky says, "We were talking about how Ewan McGregor looks just like someone, but we can't really place him."

"Oh, I know now!" Nicole says with a snap of her fingers. "He looks like Evan!"

Dalisay twists up her face. "Bit of a stretch," she says. "They look nothing alike."

Nicole shrugs and resumes chewing on the straw of her drink from the concession stand. "Maybe so."

"You know what!" Pinky says, brightly. "It might just be that the movie reminded me how cute you two were together. How he was so crazy about you. Enough to start singing for you and all that."

"Right!" Nicole says, bobbing her head. "That must be it."

Dalisay stops walking but Pinky and Nicole go on without her. It's almost too much of a coincidence, isn't it? Almost like it's stage one, the "Teasing of Friends."

Something inside Dalisay stirs, and her heart skips a little in her chest.

It can't be . . . can it?

CHAPTER TWENTY-THREE

Evan marches up to the Ramos house before the morning sun rises. He had to get up an hour early to catch the bus to Dalisay's neighborhood before work because Bettie refused to move this morning, the one time he needed things to work out for him. It's almost as if the universe is actively working against him, telling him that all his efforts are for nothing, but Evan is not one to let the universe or anyone else tell him what to do.

The morning promises that the day will be warm, but a haze of fog lingers over the street and the house is dark. Evan supposes most of the family will be asleep, but he doesn't need to disturb them.

The "Presentation of Gifts" went horribly the last time Evan went through this. This time around, he needs to make the gifts personal.

On the porch, he sets down a folded packet of paper adorned with a simple paper bow. It's a map of Kyoto, one of the places Dalisay says is the most romantic. He remembers. He was listening. Maybe they can still go together someday, just like they'd planned.

He adjusts the bow on the paper and leaves it on the doorstep as he heads to work. Someone will find it in a few hours, including the note he left, quoting Lao Tzu:

THE FIVE STAGES OF COURTING DALISAY RAMOS

A journey of a thousand miles begins with a single step.

The second day, he leaves a Vietnamese-style lantern, like the ones seen in Hoi An. It's made of red paper, hand-painted with delicate jasmine flowers, like the flowers Dalisay wore in her hair during the first day of Simbang Gabi. He still thinks about how beautiful she looked.

The third day, he leaves a framed sketch he drew himself depicting the Parthenon in Rome. When he was there, he thought only of Dalisay. As he leaves her house, he spots Mrs. Ramos watching him from the window. Evan simply waves and continues his trek to work, feeling Mrs. Ramos's eyes following him all the way down the block.

The fourth day, he leaves a framed photo from their day with Lola at the ice-skating rink on Christmas Eve, the one the photographer had taken in front of the tree. The built-in lights on Dalisay's sweater threw off the exposure of the photo, pitching the rest of the background into darkness but making their smiles brighter. It was one of the best days of his life.

Before he can set it down, the door flies open and Mrs. Ramos stands there, staring at him. Her eyes go to the gift in his hands, and he holds it out to her. When she takes it from him, he just smiles and leaves for work.

The fifth and final day, Evan makes leche flan. He found a recipe, bought all the ingredients, and—the whole week leading up to the day—he tested it himself so he could get it just right. It was a lot more technical than he'd expected. He's no baker, but he's proud of his work, despite it looking like it's melting. He nearly dropped it getting off the bus.

On the note, he wrote:

> *I know this won't be as good as your mother's,*
> *but I have to start somewhere.*

He leaves the Tupperware on the doorstep and by the time he turns to look back, it's gone.

Dalisay watches Evan go, holding herself tightly in the living room window, but she leaves before he can look back. She hears the door close, and her mom comes up the stairs, holding the Tupperware. Another gift from Evan. She can't help the thrill that swoops inside of her at the sight of it. All of his gifts have made her swoon.

The map, the lantern, the sketch, the photo . . . It's all perfect. He's actually doing it, the Five Stages. She's not reading into things at all. A ridiculous smile spreads across her face and she doesn't even try to hide it. Pinky and Nicole have to be in on it. If she didn't love them so much, she would pinch them for it, both by way of appreciation and for playing with her emotions.

Her mom hands her the note Evan left, and the family gathers around the kitchen island to look at his attempt at a leche flan.

"It looks like it's melting," says Daniel.

Mom takes a spoonful and tastes it. She nods. "It's not terrible."

That, coming from her mom, is practically singing praises.

Lola barges her way through, peering into the Tupperware. "Hmm. This from the boy?" she asks.

"It is," says Dalisay.

Lola gives her a knowing wink and takes a spoonful. She doesn't say anything, but she hums a love song as she heads back to her room.

"Who made the fucked-up leche flan?" Nicole asks, appearing from the bathroom. Her hair is wet, having just gotten out of the shower.

Their mom doesn't reply. She cuts an untouched slice and puts it into another, smaller Tupperware. "Take this to work tomorrow," she says, handing it to Nicole. "For Claire. Tell her next time she comes over for lunch, I'll make her a real one."

Nicole's eyes are round as she wordlessly takes the Tupperware. It's like she can hardly believe her ears. She and Dalisay lock eyes and Dalisay's heart swells at the hope in her sister's eyes.

Dalisay takes her portion of Evan's leche flan to her room. Working from home has been a blessing, but she does miss working in an office. Sure, being remote means she gets to see her family more, the thing that's always been most important to her, but she misses the buzz of being downtown, of seeing familiar faces . . . One in particular. Heavily, she drops in her chair at her desk and sighs as she looks at the book-scented candle on the corner of her desk. Evan's old note leans against it.

Here's to stories worth telling. —Evan

She's smiling so much, it makes her cheeks hurt, but she takes a bite of the flan. Her mom was wrong—it's perfect. Creamy, sweet, delicious. Maybe it tastes even better because of who made it.

The sun breaks through the window, basking her in morning light. Despite the brightness of the day ahead, she lights the candle and gets to work.

"You really think Mom's coming around?" Nicole asks. She's out of her scrubs and in her bathrobe, having just gotten home from the hospital earlier that night. She sits on Dalisay's bed, her knees tucked up to her chest while Dalisay finishes editing an article.

It's late, and her eyes hurt from looking at a screen all day, but Dalisay finishes typing with a flourish and spins in her chair. "It's a start, right?"

"It has to mean something," Nicole says. Her cheeks are pink, and she presses her face between her knees.

"Have you talked to Claire about it?"

Nicole nods. "She understood what it's like for family to freak out. She told me her parents reacted the same way too . . ." Her gaze goes distant, then she blinks a few times, as if clearing her thoughts. "And Claire loved the flan, obviously, but the fact that Mom wants her to come over for lunch again? Maybe you're right, maybe she's mellowing out."

"Mom loves you," Dalisay says. "I think maybe she was in shock at first. You know how obsessed she is about tradition and grandkids."

Nicole nods slightly. She squeezes her knees tighter to her chest and furrows her brow. "You really think she likes Claire?"

Dalisay nods. "Because you do."

Nicole buries her face in her knees again, but Dalisay can tell she's smiling. Dalisay goes to her side, bouncing on the mattress, and leans into her, wrapping her arms around her shoulders. "Thank you," Nicole whispers.

"For what?" Dalisay asks.

"For talking to Mom for me," Nicole says, peeking over her knees.

"You knew?"

Nicole nods. "Daniel blabbed."

Dalisay smiles. No one can keep any secrets in this family. Nicole wraps her arms around Dalisay too and Dalisay realizes they haven't hugged like this since their dad died. It's like nothing has ever changed. And yet *everything* has changed. But now it's not so scary anymore.

Dalisay breaks the hug, only because she hears something. "What is that?" she asks. It almost sounds like singing, but Dalisay turned off her headphones, so it's not coming from her laptop.

"Is that music?" Nicole asks.

"It's coming from outside," Dalisay says. She leaves her room, Nicole following behind, and the music is getting louder. When Dalisay goes to the living room window overlooking the driveway, she sees four people dancing in the dark, lit only by the light of the garage.

"The Serenade," Dalisay says, grinning.

Evan, JM, Yoon-gi, and . . . Daniel! What? Even he's in on this?

They dance in a line like backup singers as Evan takes center stage. In the lights from the garage, he belts out to "I've Fallen for You," a song by the Filipina singer Toni Gonzaga. Growing up, it was Dalisay's favorite song in the world, slow and soulful. Daniel must have told Evan about it; he had to suffer through her playing it on repeat for weeks straight when he was studying for exams. She can't stop smiling.

They sound pretty good actually.

"They must have practiced a lot," Nicole says. "At least he doesn't have to sing in Tagalog." That makes Dalisay laugh. Nicole had heard about the time when Evan serenaded her at the museum. This time there's no need for boy band dance moves. Evan's voice carries through the window, and he locks eyes with her, making her heart pulse through her whole body.

She can't take it anymore.

At the final chorus, she throws open the window and sings along, throwing her head back and belting to the night sky. He stops dancing to watch her, and she can't believe how handsome he looks. She's missed him so much.

The song ends and Dalisay stands at the window breathless.

"Hey," he says, panting, as the song fades. He beams at her, blushing hard, and Dalisay can't help but laugh. It's just like last time, only so much better.

Nicole appears at Dalisay's side and yells down to them. "What are you doing? It's late! Don't you know people are trying to sleep?" She slams the window shut and Dalisay hides her grin behind her hand. She's overjoyed.

"Should I go down and say hi?" Dalisay asks, breathless.

"No way," says Nicole, guiding her by the wrist back to her room. "Stay right where you are. Keep those doors locked. This is only the third stage, remember?"

Right, Dalisay thinks, *get it together*. It's so hard to stay put; all she wants to do is run down the stairs and throw herself into Evan's arms. At least now she finally knows how it feels to have fallen really, unbelievably in love.

CHAPTER TWENTY-FOUR

Evan braces himself, takes a breath, and knocks on the Ramos's front door.

He's prepared himself for this moment, the worst of the stages—Servitude. Last time, the Ramos's threw everything at him. It felt like a never-ending list of chores and duties. Now, *he's* ready for anything they throw at him. In his backpack, he brought kneepads, gardening gloves, sunscreen, anything he could think of that he might need doing service for the family, even a first aid kit just in case. Whole-ass mode.

Last night, during Facetime with his dad, his father asked Evan what he was packing for.

"I have to be prepared," he said after he explained what the Five Stages are in the Filipino tradition and how he was trying to win Dalisay back. "Stage four is where I go to her family and serve them, showing that I can be responsible and dependable."

"You want to go through all of that again?" his dad asked. "Are you up for that?"

"It is hard work, but Dalisay is worth it." He wasn't going to let his dad talk him out of anything again. "I love her."

His dad took a deep breath and stared off toward the garden from his seat on the patio, soaking up the bright sun.

"Well . . . ," he started to say, then paused before trying again. "Relationships are like a garden. They need to be cultivated, cared for. There will be weeds, that's something you have to come to terms with, but things will grow anyway."

"A garden metaphor? Really?"

His dad chuckled. "I thought you would appreciate the literary nature of it." He took another moment before saying, "Your mother and I, we didn't do any of that. We off-loaded a lot on each other, and it spilled over onto you. For that, I'm sorry."

Evan had never heard his dad apologize before. He didn't know how to reply.

"Learn from my mistakes. Communication is key," his dad continued. "Never leave the unsaid thing for later. Trust your gut and you can't go wrong."

Evan takes that to heart.

At Dalisay's house, Evan knocks again on the door after not hearing anything at first and this time frenzied footsteps hurry down the stairs. The door opens to reveal Melinda.

She carries an infant swaddled in her arms, and deep, dark circles run under her eyes, but her face breaks into a relieved smile when she sees him.

"Oh, thank God," she says. The baby starts fussing and Melinda makes gentle shushing noises.

Evan is taken aback. Somehow, he'd forgotten that she was due to give birth. Where did the time go? "Whoa! A baby! Congratulations!" he says.

Melinda lets out an exasperated sigh and smiles. "Yeah. It's a lot!"

Inside the house, Evan can hear Little Luis's scream, piercing through the air and making Melinda wince. It must be tough raising a rambunctious toddler and baby at the same time. She smiles apologetically, but Evan can tell she's at the end of her rope.

"I'm here to help," Evan says. "Anything you and the family need, I'm more than happy to be of service."

"Perfect," Melinda says. "I've got my hands full with baby Rosie. I need someone to look after Little Luis. I don't care what you do, just get him out of the house."

As if summoned like a demon from hell, Little Luis appears at the head of the stairs holding a plastic baseball bat. He smacks the railings and laughs maniacally, wild-eyed and obviously planning some mass chaos.

"Everyone else is out," Melinda says. "I can't put the baby down, I haven't taken a shower—"

It's clear she could go on forever. Evan stops her before she loses her breath. "It's okay, I can take him off your hands for a few hours."

"All day."

"All day?" Evan asks.

"All day! All day! All day!" Little Luis chants, thrusting his baseball bat over his head like a gladiator pumped with bloodlust.

Evan swallows a lump in his throat. He knows his dad told him to trust his gut, and right now his gut is telling him to be afraid, be *very* afraid. But of course, he can't say no.

Evan smiles at the terrible two-year-old. "We'll make an adventure of it, right, buddy?"

Little Luis seems to know exactly what he's getting into, his lips curling.

Melinda says to Evan, "Good luck!"

Evan takes Little Luis to the San Francisco Zoo. Some of his favorite childhood memories were of his parents bringing him here to see the giraffes and rhinos. It's been years since he's set foot in the zoo, but he's surprised by how little it's changed. Memories come flooding back to him: riding the carousel, taking the Little Puffer train around Bear Country, and getting face to face with a lion behind thick glass. He decides that Little Luis deserves to have those kinds of memories too.

Despite Little Luis's predilection for chaos, the day starts off spectacularly. They walk through the African Savanna while Evan points out the kudus and gorillas, and he likes watching Little Luis's eyes go wide as his brain undoubtably melts at the sight of them. Kids love animals, it's an easy win.

As the day progresses, Little Luis becomes even more manageable than Evan ever hoped. Evan expected Little Luis would get cranky and start throwing a temper tantrum, but instead he's the one who leads Evan by the hand to see the bears and the lions and the anteaters. He sort of reminds Evan of himself when he was that age, full of curiosity and wonder. His interests just needed to be directed in the right place. One day Little Luis might even make for a good travel writer if he really wants to be one.

They eat lunch at the cafe and watch the flamingos stand in the shallow waters of the pond. Little Luis does his best impression of a leaping lemur, much to the amusement of other visitors. When he gets tired, he even accepts Evan's offer to let him ride on his shoulders.

Evan buys Little Luis a lion balloon and Little Luis has a steel-like grip on the string as they continue to walk through the zoo. Evan's only goal today is to tucker this little tot out so that Melinda can finally get some peace and quiet. This is the least he can do to help out the family. In fact, Evan starts to think it's one of the few things he might actually be good at. Little Luis and Evan may have started out rough with introductions, but Evan is truly starting to think he could manage having a kid of his own someday. Hopefully with Dalisay. But he's getting ahead of himself. It's still early. She could always say no at stage five, but . . . He has to believe in something.

At the koala exhibit, Evan's stomach starts to hurt. A quick, sharp churn that sends a shudder through him. But it passes quickly enough, just in time to see Little Luis trip and fall, letting his balloon go.

He cries out, on the verge of a meltdown, but Evan checks him over. He's not hurt.

"You're okay, buddy," Evan says, putting him back on his feet.

Little Luis's eyes are rimmed with tears and his chin wobbles. But after he looks at Evan, finding reassurance in his face that he really is okay, his eyes go skyward.

"Balloon," he whimpers, pointing.

It's stuck on a branch overhead.

The ramification of what just happened sinks in. Like Willem Dafoe in *Platoon*, Little Luis falls to his knees, his arms stretched overhead, as if pleading for the balloon to come back to him.

"We'll get you another one," Evan says.

Little Luis's face screws up, and more tears fill his eyes.

"Uh-oh" is all Evan gets to say before Little Luis has a full-on tantrum in the middle of the sidewalk. Passersby stare, giving them a wide berth, as they watch the toddler scream his head off.

Evan tries to shush him, but he knows people are watching and judging him.

"I'll get you a new one, I promise!" Evan assures over the noise. He winces as his stomach cramps again.

"No!" Little Luis screams, pounding his fists into the pavement. "NO! *NO!* Balloon! Mine!"

Evan looks around for help, but most people give him sympathetic smiles or avoid eye contact. They must think he's an awful parent. His stomach churns once more. Something is definitely happening in there. He might be getting sick. He's not in the mood to deal with this right now. There is only one way to get Little Luis to stop screaming.

Evan looks around, checks for anyone in a khaki vest or wearing a walkie-talkie, then he gets up and starts climbing the fence to the koala enclosure. The balloon is snagged on a branch just close enough where, if Evan can get up there, he can grab it.

While Evan climbs, Little Luis screams and carries on, his voice echoing through the zoo no doubt, and Evan's heart pounds as he climbs even higher on the fence. He knows he'll get in big trouble if he's caught, but he'll get in big trouble if the Ramoses find out he let Little Luis cause mayhem over a stupid balloon.

He gets halfway up the fence when he stretches out, his fingers just barely missing the string. Little Luis keeps screaming,

"Balloon! Balloon!" and passersby watch as Evan tries and fails to grab it.

Sweat breaks out on his forehead as he stretches out farther than ever, his muscles straining, and finally he's got it. He climbs back down from the fence and Little Luis's face brightens. In an instant, he stops screaming, as if Evan flipped a switch, and he goes back to being the happy, carefree toddler skipping away toward the orangutan enclosure.

"Hey! You!" a voice barks, making Evan whip around. It's a security guard, running right for him. Busted.

Evan's moving before he realizes what he's doing. He scoops up Little Luis, who giggles happily, and Evan runs with him, full tilt, as the security guard's boots thunder behind in hot pursuit. Instinct kicks in and Evan feels like prey in the savanna as Little Luis bobs in his arms, laughing his head off. At least one of them is having a good time.

Evan dodges through the crowd, weaving through the masses, trying to get lost in the fray. His stomach churns again, adding more sweat to his forehead, but he can't stop. He can't get caught.

Eventually, he breaks through the crowd and looks behind him. There's no sign of the security guard. He lets out a sigh of relief. He can't believe he just did that. But a part of him is exhilarated by his evasion of zoo security.

He sets Little Luis down on the ground but Little Luis holds up his hands toward him. "Again! Again!"

Evan feels awful. His stomach twists and turns, and saliva gathers at the back of his throat, and not because he's just escaped the long arm of the law. "Next time, buddy," he says, patting Little Luis on the head. Sweat drips down his pits and more settles in the small of his back. "You're going to get me in so much trouble," Evan says to him.

Little Luis grins at Evan and clutches his balloon like it's his most sacred treasure.

Evan presses his fist into his stomach to ease the pain and catches his breath while Little Luis wanders toward the penguin island. Something is really going on in his gut, but he's not sure if it'll pass.

"Evan?" He knows that voice.

Evan turns around and his stomach drops. "Becca!"

His ex-girlfriend hasn't changed a bit. Her blond hair is pulled up into a bun, secured with a headband, and her blue eyes are the same color as the sea just next door. Even in waders and carrying a bucket of dead fish, she looks fantastic.

"Hey!" He tries to sound enthusiastic and friendly, despite the roiling in his gut.

Becca's eyes go to Little Luis, who is threatening to wander off. Evan grabs him by the arm, securing him in place, and Little Luis laughs.

Before she can ask if he's his, Evan says, "I'm babysitting."

Becca holds up her fish bucket. "I'm working."

"I thought you were in Boston."

"I was!" she says. "But a position opened up here to care for the penguins and I missed San Francisco. Are you still at Overnight?"

"I am, yeah," he says, heat rising on his face. "I had no idea you were in town."

"Yeah, well . . . ," she says, trailing off. "I didn't want it to be awkward."

Evan's stomach makes an odd gurgling sound and he muffles it with his fist. They stand in silence for a second, neither of them knowing what to say.

"Are you doing okay?" he asks, bridging the silence.

"Yeah! I'm good. Are you?"

"Totally!" This is about as awkward as it can get. At one point, he thought he was going to marry her, but then she left, and now here she is, standing in front of him again. He's not quite sure what to do.

"Are you seeing anyone or . . . ?" she asks.

"Uh, yeah, actually. She's, uh . . ." He's not sure if he should say more. Will it make her jealous? Is she going to take it personally that he's moved on? But Becca doesn't look disappointed, she actually laughs. "How did you know?" he asks.

"You look happier," she says. "It's all over your face."

"Really?"

"Yeah," she says, smiling slightly. "I'm glad you're doing better."

"You don't think I was happy when I was with you?"

Becca considers it for a moment, squinting in the bright afternoon light and tapping a finger on the bucket handle. "I think when you're with the right person, you just know. There's not much more to it than that. You might not have realized it at the time. But I think we both knew we weren't right for each other," she says.

Deep down, Evan knows she's right. They weren't meant to be, like they were riding on the same highway but in different cars going along until the route diverged, taking her one way and him another.

Suddenly, he realizes that maybe they both ended up where they were supposed to be. And he met Dalisay. Evan really did trust his gut by staying in San Francisco. If he hadn't, he never would have met the girl of his dreams.

Little Luis is starting to get fussy. He wants to see the penguins. He pushes against Evan's hand, straining to go. Evan plants another hand on him, keeping him locked in place. "I hope we can still be friends, though?" he says to Becca.

They may have broken up, but that can't mean they need to treat each other like strangers.

Becca smiles. "Yeah. I think so. I'm single if you know of any leads."

"Yeah," he says, trying to smile back. "I do . . ." He has a few people in mind, but his stomach twists, making him queasy.

"Are you okay? You're looking a little . . . green."

"All good!" Evan lies, trying to ignore the saliva gathering at the back of his throat.

Becca starts walking toward the penguins. "Well, it was good seeing you!"

She leaves and not a moment too soon. Evan's stomach lurches. He knows what's happening, but he can't stop it. He claps his hand over his mouth and rushes to the nearest trash can, puking up his lunch with such intensity most other visitors flee in case whatever it is, is contagious. His hot dog and nacho combo tastes horrible coming back up.

Little Luis laughs as food poisoning makes Evan's life miserable.

Evan stops puking long enough to lift his head and wipe his mouth when he sees a security guard standing in front of him, arms folded, frowning.

"Had enough of climbing fences?" the security guard asks.

Evan smiles, guiltily, but lurches when more puke comes up. Little Luis just laughs and laughs.

Finally home, Evan lets Little Luis run up to the door.

"Momma!" Little Luis cries when it opens. Instead of Melinda, it's Dalisay. She must have seen them from the living room window.

"Come on, little monster. Did you have fun?" she asks as Little Luis darts inside to show off his souvenir to his mom.

Evan is exhausted and sore and a little sunburned and mostly puke free but it's all okay now that Dalisay is here. She smiles at him, an amused look in her eye. "You survived," she says.

Evan holds up his fists in victory.

"He looks like he had a good time," Dalisay says, tipping her head toward Little Luis.

"Then my work here is done, unless . . ."

"No, no more from you today."

Good, he thinks, relieved. He's not sure he has much gas left in him after what he went through. He almost fell asleep on the bus on the way back.

Dalisay gives him a shy smile and tucks her hair behind her ears, her hand fiddling with the doorknob. It's as if she's debating whether to go back inside.

Evan wants to talk to her. He realizes this is the longest they've spoken since they broke up. What comes after stage four: The Sequel? He knows the tradition requires him to keep his distance, to continue to be of service to her family until he proves how useful he can be. But how can he pretend to be a stranger? It's excruciating.

It hurts turning away from her; he knows he has to, but every muscle in his body is screaming at him to turn back around and grab her tightly and hold on to her and tell her how much he's missed her. But he can't. He clenches his teeth, steeling himself against every desire, and walks down the driveway, but Dalisay's voice makes him stop.

"I'm planning to take a walk on the waterfront tomorrow. At the pier," she says. "It's supposed to be a nice day."

He turns to see the look on her face, the openness, the want.

Evan's heart skips a beat. Is she doing what he thinks she's doing? He licks his lips, shifting his weight from hip to hip, and takes a hesitant step forward. Either he can be reading into things or this is the breakthrough he's been waiting for. He watches her for a moment, his whole body vibrating, and she looks back, expectantly, waiting for his answer. Color rises in her cheeks and he knows, if he doesn't shoot his shot now, he might lose her forever.

"Well, since I've been permanently banned from the zoo, I think the pier would be a great place to take a walk tomorrow."

Dalisay barks out a laugh. "You *what*?"

Evan sighs, smiling. "It's a long story . . . Maybe we can talk about it over some ice cream."

Dalisay nips at her lower lip and looks at her feet. When she looks back up at him, her eyes sparkle like the night sky. "Ice cream sounds amazing."

CHAPTER TWENTY-FIVE

Dalisay has to force herself not to look back before closing the door behind her. She knows Evan is watching, and her body is screaming at her to run into his arms and kiss him and apologize for everything that went wrong between them, but for the sake of tradition, she doesn't.

She closes the door quietly, presses her back against it, and slides down to the floor.

Hunched like a little garden gnome statue, Dalisay presses her cheeks into her knees and smiles. Perhaps they—whoever the grand overseers of the Five Stages are—should include a stage four and a half: grin like a giddy idiot.

Her heart pounds so hard, she feels like she's just run a marathon. Talking to Evan again is the one thing she's wished she could do and seeing him again in person, with his black curly hair and his sloping smile and his warm, dark eyes . . .

They've made it this far. What will go wrong?

She practically asked him out, telling him she was going for a walk, hinting that he should join her, a total departure from protocol. Maybe she is becoming more of an American girl after all. She's feeling brazen, the rush of the day going straight to her head like a glass of wine on an empty stomach.

She can hear Little Luis and Melinda deeper in the house. He's enthusiastically telling her about his time at the zoo, something about Evan seeing a penguin lady, and a balloon, and a mean man. The way Little Luis says it, Evan is his hero. It's mostly baby talk, but Dalisay can't wait to hear the details in person.

"Are you feeling all right?" Lola stands at the top of the stairs, watching Dalisay with a curious eye.

Dalisay nods.

Lola beckons her. "Come. No use sitting there like that."

Dalisay rises and readjusts her skirt, taking the stairs one step at a time as Lola shuffles around the kitchen and gestures to the island for Dalisay to sit as she pours her a tall glass of *sago't*.

"The boy has left?" Lola asks. She tips her head, lifting her nose, like a queen might when surveying her domain.

"Yes," Dalisay says. "He's done enough for today."

Lola puckers her lips and sighs. "I see. I guess he can regrout the bathroom another day." Dalisay can see right through Lola. Her grandmother can try to maintain appearances all she wants, but Dalisay knows that Lola likes Evan. She can pretend to be hard and curmudgeonly, but the truth is hard to mask.

Dalisay wraps her hand around the cold glass and takes a sip. The sugar is even sweeter when she thinks about tomorrow.

"You are going for a walk at the pier?" Lola asks. Despite her age, Lola's hearing is as sharp as a fox's.

"Yes," Dalisay says. It's customary for the couple never to be left alone until all Five Stages are complete, but of course, if anyone asks, Dalisay and Evan just happened to run into each other. That's all. "I don't imagine I'll need an escort."

"Yes, indeed I don't think you will. That boy has manners, I will give him that."

"He does . . . ," says Dalisay. "He really is special."

Lola's eyes dance a little and she puts the remaining *sago't* in the fridge. "We can't help who we love," she says. "But the special ones do make it a lot easier, don't they?"

Dalisay smiles at that.

"Are you ready to take him back?" Lola asks.

Dalisay takes a deep breath and another sip of her *sago't*. She thinks she is, but does she deserve it? Does she deserve him? She can't answer, at least not at first, and twists her mouth thoughtfully, tapping on the glass with her finger. "I didn't think it was possible."

"What happened between you two when you first met?" Lola asks. She brings out a cutting board and a chef's knife and begins slicing ginger roots into even sticks.

That is a question no one's asked her yet. Even Nicole didn't press when Dalisay admitted she and Evan were breaking up.

"There were . . ." Dalisay searches for the right word. "A lot of differences. It felt like we were speaking two different languages sometimes."

Lola nods, scooping up the sticks of ginger and putting them into a bowl. Already, Dalisay knows she's going to be making her famous *arroz caldo* soup, a chicken and rice comfort food. She's always made it when someone is feeling sick, or down, or in need of a boost. Dalisay wonders if Lola knows that she needs that extra kick of confidence.

"It's difficult dating someone from another culture." She crushes cloves of garlic with the flat edge of her knife and expertly peels the paper shell in two moves. "I wish there was a simple guide, as simple as the Five Stages, to walk you through it. I loved someone before your grandfather. I gave up too easily," Lola says. "I said things I didn't mean, said things because I was afraid. I walked away and that was it." She pauses mincing the garlic and pinches her fingers around her golden necklace, a pendant of two hands holding one another.

Dalisay squeezes the glass a little tighter. After all that's happened between them, it would have been so easy for Evan to walk away from her forever, never look back and wonder what could have been. He didn't give up on her, and she . . . she might have given up on him a little too readily. Like Lola, Dalisay could have easily lived with her regret, but now she has a chance to start over with Evan.

Lola continues, "I was so ready to find faults in our relationship. It was as though if I could somehow find the things that would break us apart, it would be easier to justify how it would end. I thought I was protecting my heart, but I should have trusted it." She shakes her head slightly and gets back to prepping the ingredients.

Dalisay made that same mistake. But Evan still came back. He broke down her walls, and maybe it's time she used a sledgehammer to help finish the job.

"No one knows when they'll fall in love," Lola continues. "But when it happens, you must take it, grasp it with two hands, and trust it completely. There are no hard-set rules, no maps, no compass. Love is love and that's all it needs to be." Lola's dark eyes crinkle when she smiles. "Are you in love with him?"

Dalisay nods, certain. Her father's words ring true: *Remember where you're going.* And it's finally time she goes for Evan.

Pier 39 is more of an outdoor shopping mall than it is a pier. It almost reminds Dalisay of the markets in Manila, especially with how packed it is. The sun is bright, and the sky is blue, and she nervously smooths out the pleats of her skirt as she walks through the crowd. Ringing bells from the arcade and children's laughter rise up against the honk of a tourist boat ready to depart. Seagulls call overhead and sea lions basking on the rocks below bark as if in response. The smell of fries and burgers overtakes the briny sea air, making her stomach growl. She forgot to eat anything today, spending way too much time deciding what to wear. Her anxiety always gets the better of her. She looks at every face, searching for the one that means the most to her, but so far she hasn't seen Evan.

He's late. Only by a few minutes, but still. He's always punctual, especially with things that matter to him. She should have seen him by now. Anxiety coils in her gut. What if he decided not to come? What if he changed his mind about her? What if he came to his senses and realized she wasn't the one for him? Too many good things have been happening. Oh no, she's catastrophizing again—

Then, she sees him, and she can finally breathe.

He's in line at the ice-cream vendor, smiling and talking to the cashier who hands him two cones, one cookie dough and the other, she notices with a smile, chocolate covered in sprinkles. He remembered her favorite.

Evan steps out of line and turns, only to look up and see her. His smile grows wider.

He dressed for the occasion, wearing an ironed pair of khakis, his usual blunnies, and a white, button-down shirt with the sleeves rolled up his forearms. Her heart thumps and she doesn't realize she's smiling back until she puts her hands to her warm cheeks.

"Wild running into you here," he says when he gets to her side. His eyes are bright as he hands over the sprinkled cone.

"What are the odds?" She takes a bite of ice cream, but she can't take her eyes off Evan.

"To think I would have had to eat all this ice cream by myself. Good thing I ran into you."

Dalisay can't help but laugh as they walk together, side by side, along the pier. They don't say anything, not while eating their ice cream, but Dalisay's mind races. It's been months since they've been together. Looking at Evan, her heart swells. He squints against the sun, his eyes landing on the sightseeing boat on the horizon, and he points out Alcatraz, the famous island prison, in the distance. But Dalisay only has eyes for him.

She manages to get her ice cream down to a manageable level without it dripping down her hand just as they reach the end of the pier and take a break to lean on the railing.

They both lean on the railing, standing in companionable silence. A seagull hops along the rail toward Evan, eyeing his ice-cream cone, and Evan turns away from the bird. "Don't even think about it, mister."

Dalisay doesn't know where to start. It's been so long since they've spoken. How can she possibly start over?

"How's Tallulah?" she finally asks. She wishes she could have had a better opening line, but it's the best she can think of.

Evan waves his elbow in the hungry seagull's direction and says, "She's good! She's happy and healthy. That's all I can ask for."

"Good! That's . . . really good." Dalisay's heart feels tight in her chest. Is she making this awkward? She tries not to blush as she notices she's been tapping out a rhythm on her hips with her free hand this whole time. She sees Evan's eyes dart down to look at her hip, and a smile lifts one corner of his mouth. She forces herself to stop. She knows it's a nervous habit. God, she is so obvious.

"How's Little Luis?" Evan asks after a long moment.

"Happy! He passed out almost instantly after getting home yesterday. You knocked your task out of the park. What happened at the zoo? You said something about you being banned?"

Evan bows his head and laughs. "Ah, yeah. I climbed a fence trying to get Little Luis's balloon after he dropped it."

"What!"

"I didn't want people to think I was being a bad parent! You should have heard the way he was screaming. I had one job!"

Dalisay doubles over laughing. Tears gather at the corners of her eyes, and she wipes them away. She hasn't laughed that hard in a long time and it aches in a good way. She's glad to see Evan's smiling too, despite himself. "You could have just gotten him a new one."

"You know kids and balloons. To him, it was like losing a limb."

"I'm not sure it was worth it," Dalisay says, lips curling in amusement.

"Tell the zoo people that . . . Who even monitors lifetime bans anyway?"

When Dalisay and Evan dissolve into laughter again, imagining Evan's face on a poster with an "x" through it at the zoo entrance, the seagull takes a stab at stealing Evan's ice cream.

"Aha! Nice try, mister," Evan says, holding it out of beak's reach. The seagull flaps its wings, annoyed, and takes off.

Laughing together significantly lifts Dalisay's mood, and any anxiety she might have had melts away. She's happy, and for the first time in a long time, she can finally admit it.

"I liked your gifts," she says.

"You did?"

"Didn't throw a single one out. Except I think Lola used the map of Kyoto as wrapping paper."

Evan barks out a laugh and Dalisay smiles. "How about the leche flan?"

"My mom said it was good." Evan looks pleased at that. "I have to ask—the serenade. How did you rope Daniel into it?"

Evan's cheeks go pink again. "Daniel and I . . . we've actually become friends."

"Really? Since when?"

"A couple weeks ago. He apologized for what he did at the church, tricking me about ringing that bell at Mass and all, and I told him it was no big deal. Water under the bridge. He was the one who helped me practice for the serenade, telling me your favorite song. I admit, I was suspicious at first. I thought it was going to be another practical joke, but he was right, I think. Turned out good in the end."

Dalisay can't believe her brother's been going behind her back to make things right and she didn't even notice. He's clearly improved his poker face.

"Those are my favorite kinds of endings," Dalisay says slowly. "The good ones."

Evan looks back at her, his eyes so hopeful it hurts. "Yeah?"

"Yeah," Dalisay whispers.

"God, I've missed you," he says.

Dalisay's heart nearly stops. Hearing him say it is everything she's wanted. She lets out a small breath. "Me too," she says.

Evan turns to face her squarely, leaning on the railing. "I've been thinking about you. Nonstop. You're the only person I want to be with. I'm sorry. I am so sorry. I never want to make you feel like that again."

"I'm sorry too." She pauses, wanting to say more, but not finding the words.

Evan's eyes dance between hers, hope blooming there. He opens his mouth. "Dalisay, I—*DUCK!*"

Dalisay has just enough time to get down before the seagull dive-bombs for Evan's ice cream. It's a flurry of feathers and wings and Evan stumbles back, losing his footing, and falls to the boardwalk. The seagull screams in victory as it takes off across the water with its prize.

Passersby stare, dumbstruck, at what just unfolded in front of them. Evan sits on the pier, dazed, as if he's not sure that just happened either.

"Oh my God! Are you okay?" Dalisay asks, rushing to Evan. She grabs his hand and hauls him back to his feet.

His curls stand up every which way and he looks shocked. "I can't believe—Did you see that?"

Dalisay starts laughing, and eventually Evan joins in. His hand squeezes around hers. With a jolt, Dalisay realizes they're still holding hands. Reflexively, she lets go and the second she does, she admonishes herself. She wants to hold his hand, she wants *this*, what they have right now. She tucks her hair behind her ear and ducks her head, hiding the blush creeping up her cheeks. Are they official? Is this stage five? Holding hands in public? Are they a couple again? But she wants to be sure, without any doubts, that Evan wants it too.

Evan smooths his hair back down, eyes skyward, and his laugh eases out. When he looks at her, his eyes are clear and steadfast.

"When I was in Rome, I couldn't stop thinking about you," he says. "Everywhere I went, I would have this urge to point things out to you, but you weren't there and that—that was the worst feeling. I don't want to be apart from you. Not for another moment."

A lump forms in Dalisay's throat and she nods. "I'm sorry too. I handled everything so poorly, I—" He's looking at her so earnestly, she drops her gaze to his chin. "When you said you thought about our future kids . . . it made me realize that you were already building a future with us in your mind, that you were serious about us, and I was so afraid of losing it that I panicked. I'm always worried that something horrible will happen that will take everything I care about away. Like what happened with my dad . . . I don't let myself get what I want because I don't want to lose it like I did him. And I ended up hurting you."

Evan reaches out and brushes his thumb against her cheek, and only then does she realize she's crying. His gentleness only makes more tears flow. She missed the way he touched her, and the way he could hold her and remind her everything was going to be okay. Slowly, she lifts her gaze to meet his eyes.

"Can we start over?" he asks.

Looking into those deep, dark eyes, she could fall straight into them. And when she nods, his chest rises and falls, like he's finally able to breathe, and his shoulders drop with relief.

He brings her hand up to his mouth and kisses her knuckles.

"Remember what happened after the last time we first held hands in public?" she asks, her lips curling into an amused and naughty grin, despite her tears.

"They've got some pretty nice public restrooms here," he says with a wink.

She shakes her head and snorts when she laughs too. This time they kiss in the sun.

CHAPTER TWENTY-SIX

Six Months Later . . .

"To the brides!" Dalisay says, finishing her toast as she holds her champagne glass high.

"To the brides!" echo two hundred voices just as the music rises on the speakers in the reception hall. Nicole and Claire can't stop smiling, and they kiss to roars of applause. Dalisay smiles at them, tears in her eyes, as she takes a sip of her drink.

Across the hall, she spots Evan—looking dashing in his suit and tie—clapping from a nearby table. He catches her eye and winks. She winks back at him, heart warm in her chest.

It's been six months of meticulous planning, full of seemingly endless dress fittings, cake tastings, and DJ audition tapes. It felt like they were in an endless wedding prep purgatory and then all at once it was over. Claire and Nicole are finally married, and Dalisay almost wishes they could do the whole thing over again. Almost.

A couple weeks after Dalisay and Evan got back together, Claire proposed to Nicole. After their shift at the hospital, she got down on one knee right in front of the entrance and asked for Nicole's hand. Her sister came home sobbing, and Dalisay almost thought something terrible had happened until Nicole threw out her hand for Dalisay to see the ring on her finger.

Dalisay was the maid of honor, and half of Kaiser Permanente were in attendance. JM and Pinky came too. As the coin bearer, Little Luis carried *las arras*, a box of thirteen coins presented to the couple; however, he thought he was the "coin bear" and growled at people as he went, much to everyone's amusement.

Lola walked Nicole down the aisle. Before taking her seat, she kissed both of Nicole's cheeks and said, "Your papa is very proud of you. He loves you so much. Can you feel it?" There wasn't a dry eye in the room. Their mother, already asking pointedly about grandchildren, couldn't stop crying during their vows. Daniel was the designated tissue dispenser.

The day was a total blur, but Dalisay is glad for the party to get started. It means she can finally relax.

The reception hall is decked out in a Winter Wonderland theme, turning the interior of the hall into a frosted landscape straight out of Narnia. White birch trees line the hall twinkling with thousands of lights, crystal icicles and white roses cascade from the ceiling, and sheer white curtains drape across the walls like billowing snow. Their mother oversaw the decorations and by the way she threw herself into the job, leaving no detail to chance, Dalisay knows that she has given her blessing to the couple.

Dalisay makes her way from the head table and takes an open seat next to Evan as the rest of the guests flood the dance floor.

"Good job," Evan says. "You're a natural public speaker."

Dalisay smiles and gives him a kiss on the cheek. "Thank you. You look very handsome, Mr. Saatchi."

Evan tugs at his collar with a raised eyebrow and his eyes sparkle. "Thank you, Ms. Ramos. This wedding is going off without a hitch."

Almost as if on cue, Little Luis tears across the hall, screaming and laughing as Melinda chases after him. As he's grown these past few months, his powers of chaos have only increased. He dodges and weaves around tables and crawls under them, no doubt thinking this is the greatest game of tag ever. But he screams and kicks when JM scoops him up and hands him over to Melinda just before he can knock over the swan ice sculpture.

Pinky sidles up behind Dalisay and rests her forearms on Dalisay's shoulders. Her cheeks are pink from the champagne already. "Get up, lazies! Let's dance!"

"I think I've had enough dancing in public for one life-time," Evan says, taking another sip of his champagne. Something is up with him, Dalisay doesn't quite know what. He keeps patting the pocket of his jacket and biting his full bottom lip. His leg is bouncing like crazy under the table.

"You go on without us," Dalisay says to Pinky. Pinky's too tipsy to protest and she moonwalks to the dance floor.

Dalisay turns back to Evan. "Are you okay? You look a little pale."

Evan laughs. "I'm fine! Really. Just a big day."

"You can say that again," Dalisay says with a relieved sigh. "I'm ready to fall asleep under the table."

Evan glances at her, and smiles, and then clears his throat. "I'm going to get some cake. Do you want any?"

"Yes, please! And some more champagne, please!"

Evan nods and snakes his way through the crowd toward the dessert table.

As the music kicks up, Dalisay slides her heels off and leaves them under the table. Her feet ache from being in them all day, and now it feels like her toes can finally breathe. Everyone seems to be having a good time as the DJ blasts the latest Blackpink single, and she is more than happy to sit back and watch everyone else dance.

Dalisay feels Nicole slide into Evan's empty chair. She kicks her bare foot up onto another empty chair, looking as if she's lounging at home even in her beaded wedding gown. "Is Evan having a nice time?" she asks.

"I think so." She watches him as he smiles and chats with her extended family, balancing desserts in one hand and holding a bottle of champagne in the other. She looks at Nicole again, seeing a small smile on her face as she looks at Evan too.

"Hey," Dalisay says, making Nicole look at her. "I'm really happy for you. I love you a lot."

Nicole wraps her arm around Dalisay's shoulders and brings her in to a hug. They hold each other for a long moment before Nicole pulls back. "I love you more. And I know you're gonna be really happy too."

Dalisay laughs and is about to ask her why but one of their cousins whisks Nicole away to join them on the dance floor just as Evan returns to his chair. He sets the cake slices down, sliding a plate of cookies and sliced fruit in front of her too, and she smiles. He knew she would want some, even though she didn't ask.

But, out of nowhere, Little Luis escapes containment and comes careening into Evan, wielding a fake icicle like a sword. "Whoa, buddy!" he says, laughing, and grabs Little Luis under the armpits. Little Luis screams, foiled once again, and Daniel swoops in.

"You are grounded, mister!" Daniel says, snatching the decoration out of his hands and throwing Little Luis over his shoulder like a sack of struggling potatoes. "Sorry, man," he says to Evan as Little Luis giggles and snorts and Daniel carries him away.

"No worries!"

Dalisay shakes her head, laughing, but her eyes land on something on the floor. It must have fallen out of Evan's pocket when Little Luis bumped into him. She picks up a small velvet box and she freezes when she realizes what it is.

"Evan."

He freezes too, staring at the ring box in her hand, and then he pats his jacket pocket. Whatever he's searching for isn't there.

"Is this . . . ?" She can't get the words out.

Bashfully, Evan nods and sits down. "It's . . . for you."

"Evan," Dalisay gasps, but she can't finish. She has a million things she wants to say, but her mouth refuses to work.

"Open it," he says.

With shaking hands, she does. Inside the box is a diamond ring. It sparkles in the strobe lights. She puts her hand to her mouth. It's beautiful.

"It was Nicole's idea," Evan says. "I wanted to do *pamam—*"

"*Pamamanhikan*," they say together. Dalisay is breathless. He's done his research. It's the traditional way of asking for her parents' permission to propose.

"Of course you know," Evan says, blushing. He gestures to the room. "Nicole said I should do it today, here, but I didn't know when it would be a good time . . ."

At a loss for words, Dalisay shakes her head. She can't believe this is happening. It feels like a dream, and she never wants to wake up. Evan's smile fades a little.

"I get it," Evan says, misunderstanding. "It's too fast. I understand. You don't have to say anything."

He holds out his hand to take the box, but Dalisay holds the box closer to her chest. "You bought this for me? Like, for *me*?"

"Yeah," he says, eyes soft. "I want to spend the rest of my life with you. I want to travel the world with you. I want to do everything with you. Not another day apart."

Dalisay stares at him, her heart practically breaking out of her rib cage. *Yes*, she thinks. *Yes! Yes!* But she waits a beat to take all of this in, to remember it forever. The way Evan leans toward her, eyes full, yearning. He holds his breath, as if readying himself for what comes next. She knows he's never been more confident in saying anything else before. For once, she's not scared of the future. Tradition was thrown out the window a while ago.

Maybe they can make their own traditions, new ones, together.

"Evan," she says again, breathless. "Ask me for my hand."

"You don't want to wait for—?"

"Ask *me*," she says, smiling.

Evan's eyes search hers, and she sees it all coming together for him as his face brightens and he takes her hand. She can feel him trembling, and it makes her giggle. He can be so cute when he's nervous.

Evan swallows, making his Adam's apple jump, and he looks like he's about to melt when he looks at her.

Ask me. Ask, she thinks. She wants to answer with her whole chest because she's never been surer about anything in her life. She's holding on to the ring box so tightly, her fingers have gone numb. Nothing else matters in the entire world except for the two of them now. The rest of the party hasn't realized what's happening.

"Dalisay Ramos," Evan says. Slowly, he makes her stand up as he gets down on one knee, his hand warm in hers.

Oh my God, this is real, Dalisay thinks. She's shaking so badly, he's the one keeping her upright.

Nicole gets everyone's attention by tapping her fork on her glass and gesturing toward the couple. The music fades, and their mother gasps.

But Dalisay has no brain power left to register any of it. All she can see, all she can hear, is Evan. He smiles at her, his eyes already wet with tears.

"Will you make me the happiest man on earth, and marry me?"

For once, Dalisay can't conjure the word. All this time, she's imagined what this moment would be like, and now, as it's actually happening, she's so happy she can't say anything. She can only nod and throw herself into his arms.

Distantly, she can hear people clapping and cheering, encouraging them, but it doesn't register in her mind. All she can do is bury her face in Evan's shoulder and cry with joy.

Evan holds her tightly, rising to his feet, and spins her around, lifting her off the ground. She's dizzy and doesn't care. After a moment, he sets her down and cups the back of her head with his hand. He's so warm, and everything is so perfect. Nothing could have prepared her for this moment.

"Um. Is that a yes? I hope that's a yes," he says.

"Oh!" she says, pulling back. Dalisay kisses him, holding the sides of his head, and pulls back again. Tears blur her vision, but she can see Evan's smile through it all. Finally, her mouth works. "Yes! Whole-ass yes! Yes!"

Evan laughs and the other wedding guests burst into applause again but neither Evan nor Dalisay can hear it. It's like the whole world has faded into the background, and the only one who matters is in their arms.

They kiss again, and neither of them can stop smiling.

* * *

Acknowledgments

Maraming Salamat to everyone at Union Square including my amazing editor Laura Schreiber, my longtime friend and publisher Emily Meehan, and all the team at Union Square, including the fab PR and Marketing team of Jenny Lu and Daniel Denning. Thank you always to my agents Richard Abate and Hannah Carande at 3 Arts and my film mama Ellen Goldsmith-Vein and everyone at Gotham. Thank you to my mom and pop who inspired the idea of the five stages and to all my fans, friends, and family, especially Mike and Mattie, everything is for you two, always.

About the Author

Melissa de la Cruz is the #1 *New York Times*, #1 *Publishers Weekly*, and #1 IndieBound bestselling author of *Isle of the Lost* and *Return to the Isle of the Lost*, as well as many critically acclaimed and award-winning novels for readers of all ages. Her books have also topped the *USA TODAY*, *Wall Street Journal*, and *Los Angeles Times* bestseller lists and have been published in more than twenty countries. Today she lives in Los Angeles with her family.